THE TALKER

THE TALKER

short stories

Mary Sojourner

TORREY HOUSE PRESS

SALT LAKE CITY • TORREY

This is a work of fiction. All names, characters, places, and incidents are either the products of the author's imagination or are used fictitiously. No reference to any real person is intended or should be inferred.

First Torrey House Press Edition, March 2017
Copyright © 2017 by Mary Sojourner

Published by Torrey House Press
Salt Lake City, Utah
www.torreyhouse.org

International Standard Book Number: 978-1-937226-69-5
E-book ISBN: 978-1-937226-70-1
Library of Congress Control Number: 2016936763
Author photo by Chris Gunn
Cover art by Christina Norlin
Book design by Alisha Anderson

For Mike W.—
road pal for twenty years and counting.

Pin your ear to the wisdom post
Pin your eye to the line
Never let the weeds get higher
Than the garden
Always keep a sapphire in your mind
Always keep a diamond in your mind

TOM WAITS

"Get Behind the Mule"

TABLE OF CONTENTS

THE TALKER

GREAT BLUE

It all started with black olives, the bogus kind, the ones that look like patent leather and taste worse. They were the first thing we agreed on, this new male possibility and me. We agreed that we hated them and we wondered why, in a desert city where streets were lined with shining olive tree after tree and sidewalks were greasy with the crushed fruit, you could rarely find the real thing, the wrinkled ones that taste of garlic and pepper, and the craft of the one who picked and put them up.

The bogus babies were everywhere, in pizzas, in salads and even on the freebie bonne bouches we served at Coyote, the nouveau Southwestern restaurant the new man and I worked at. Coyote was predictably turquoise and beige and red rock pastels. A long-tailed neon coyote howled over the bar, snout pointed up, moon left to the imagination of those who might have one. Which, as the new man Ben saw it, our customers did not.

"Rich punks, Mollie," Ben said to me on his fifth day with us. "I hate 'em and I hate myself for hating 'em." He had a Masters in Biomedical Engineering and a brain courtesy bad genetics aided by anything you could chug or smoke. At Coyote he washed dishes and I, his equal in genes and bad choices, arranged carved vegetables on the saguaro-shaped dishes the waiters hustled out to the R.P.s—and we gossiped.

Ben was a gossip champ. He had wit and malice honed wicked as the edge on the sous-chefette's pet knife. Felice was five feet nothing, about thirty inches around her most abundant parts and she loved Roy Orbison immoderately, rest his soul. We were treated all hours to Mr. O's sweet 'n sour reminders of all the grave-yard loving we'd ever done. Most times, somebody was huddled off in a corner sobbing into their apron. Felice would turn up the volume and check out my creations.

Ben's fifth night with us, I'd finished setting up a plate of jicama, poblano peppers and pickled carrots carved into suns, moons and lizards.

"Mollie," Felice said, "those are regular little art darlings. You're wasted here."

Ben snickered.

Felice glared at him. "You're always wasted."

"Not too wasted," he drawled, "to remind you again to get rid of the fake olives. Talk to Stu. He'll listen to you." Stu was the maitre d, who in fact didn't listen to anybody. "Tell him I'll pick and put up our house brand. They grow everywhere. They won't cost us a penny." His eyes went snakey, his voice alluring. "Come on, Felice, I've got a truck. I like to steal. Mollie can help, right?"

I nodded. I hadn't had a date in a while. And the guy needed a pom pom girl.

"Yeah," he said, "the Midnight Gypsy Olive Company. My truck, my buddy here and my old man's recipe. A sure winner."

Felice patted him on the butt and told him the boss was rich but dense and wouldn't go for it. "Besides," she said, "if you want to run goodies so bad, why don't you just truck on down to your old pals in Meheeco and bring us back a little surprise. I'll front the money."

"No way," he mumbled. And that was that.

I couldn't figure out why Ben was so obsessed with those olives. He wasn't some organic hippie fossil and he didn't seem the type to drop a thirteen-dollar jar of sun-dried tomatoes in his shopping cart. He was an ordinary looking guy about forty, tall, sweet-skinny and ginger-haired, presentable enough to get by anywhere. Only if you looked close or knew the routine could you tell that his sharp jeans and shirts came from Catholic Charities, his spit-shined cowboy boots from Goodwill.

I was starting to love the way he talked—and I really loved the way he listened. We both loved books. I'd watch him on his break, sitting in the shadow of the fake adobe wall, smoking a joint and reading. That was when he looked most happy. Otherwise, his happiness seemed stretched thin. Sometimes when he got really loaded, he'd stand over the sink, moving slow, talking about rats and lethal dosage. He'd swear they do shock monkeys, they do squirt hairspray in those poor rabbits' eyes.

By that point, it was usually past closing. I'd turn from cleaning and he'd be head down on his arms on the baker's table. I'd finish up, turn out the lights and throw his jacket over his shoulders. By morning, when I came to set up, he'd be gone.

Around Lent, the customers thinned out. Ben guessed that with religion being back in style, they were doing penance for the tubs of ganache they inhaled the rest of the year. "Shit," he said, "why bitch about R.P.s? If they'll eat those plastic olives, they'll swallow anything." He was three bowls to the wind, up to his elbows in greasy suds, his fine broad shoulders moving with the work and driving me crazy. He had on his favorite Goodwill shirt. It was polyester, with blue-green flowers on lime paisley and about a hundred pearly-bronze snaps to set off its Western cut. The sweetest part was that somebody had made it for somebody else who'd loved it so much that the collar and cuffs were frayed clear through.

"Now, rich punks," I said, "would never appreciate that shirt. Just you and me and Tessa and Duane. We're the only ones who love that shirt."

"That Tessa," he said, "putting all that work into this shirt, after graveyard shift at the diner and getting the kids off to school— and Duane not even her real hubby."

He'd begun the Tessa/Duane story almost as soon as he and I started talking. He'd bring them into our hours together - Tessa, Duane, the kids and Tessa's clueless hubby—into the quiet kitchen in clean up time, when the cooks had repaired to the bar and the beautiful boy waiters were out by the dry river bank doing a little blow and finishing off the gorgeous wines the R.P.s left behind. I caught on quick and brought the two phantom adulterers into almost every conversation—into our gossip, our longings, our shyness and the earnest chaos of our lives.

We knew the names of Tessa's three kids and how the littlest, Scheyenne, had nearly caught Tessa and Duane going at it one August afternoon. We judged the real hubby as mean and dumb and cowardly. We knew that Duane had an ex-wife who'd taken his kid, the house, the 1989 Mustang, two-thirds of his pay and everything else but his good heart and slow hand. I told Ben a few things he didn't know: how Tessa hated her stretch marks, how sometimes she'd do that binge and throw up routine, how she worried about Duane's tendency to polish off a six-pack most every night. Ben said Duane liked women with a little flesh on them and saw stretch marks as medals of honor. As for the booze, Duane was definitely on top of it.

The night everything changed for me and Ben, he was asleep at the baker's table. I finished wiping down the prep area and went to drop his jacket over his shoulders. He reached up, tugged me down and kissed me stoned and sweet. His mouth tasted of Beaujolais and dope, and his curls felt exactly as I'd known they would, soft as a kid's, clean and feathery under my fingers. We were hanging on to each other with a fierce saved-from-drowning hug when Felice and Stu barged in through the back door.

"Holy moley," she said, "who died?"

"Wait," Stu said. He was elegant and black and he despised most humans, of all races and sexual persuasions alike.

"They're sharing," he said, "deeply, personally, warmly." He touched the tops of our heads. "Bless you," he said. "Be blissful, at least for a week, y'all."

"Be nice," Felice said. She lifted a bottle of Moet out of the cooler.

"Unh, unh, unh," Stu said. "You're a very naughty girl this evening and I don't mind if I do."

Felice uncorked the Moet so smoothly you would have thought it was Chablis. Ben had buried his face in my collarbone. He didn't move. I wondered for a long second if he *had* died. His hair smelled like rain, which didn't make any sense, but made me like him even more—which worried me almost as much as the fact that I wanted to shield him from the dazzling duo. And everything else. I wanted to kiss, talk, breath and love the sadness out of his seaweed eyes.

"You are fucked up, kids," Stu said cheerfully.

"You're in wuv," Felice said. She raised the Moet in a toast. I wanted to smack her, but I didn't want to let go of Ben. He was breathing so gently and evenly against my shoulder that I guessed he had passed out.

"No," I said, "it's family troubles. His cousin Tessa up in Chandler, you know." I felt a soft snort against my shoulder. "Bad marriage. You guys know how that can be." I lowered my eyes.

"When will you lambies ever learn?" Stu said to the ceiling.

"Come on, preacher," Felice said. "We're outta here." She piled some hot peppers on a plate and headed for the door.

Stu paused. "You can share with Uncle Stu," he said.

I shook my head. "Some things," I said, "are just family." He handed me the Moet and watched me take a good chug.

"Easy does it," he said, lifted the bottle from my hand and was gone.

I drove us to my place, guided Ben into my room, dumped the books and magazines off the bed and unsnapped the hundred snaps on the green shirt. He glided his wise mouth down my body and I rose up like a wave. I coiled up and over more times than I can bear to remember now. I took him with me, and Tessa and Duane and all the world's renegade sweethearts and cast us up on some warm shoreline, where the two of us wiped ourselves dry with the beautiful shirt and fell asleep.

Morning was weird. First, there is always the hangover; second, we had to face what we'd done and with whom; third, we had to say how many before, how AC/DC, how drugged out and deadly; fourth, I could not remember his last name.

"I never told you," he said. "Look, it's all going to be up-hill from here. You make some coffee, look out a window, cry a little and come back. I'll be here." I did what he'd suggested, then put plates out and burned a couple of English muffins. We ate them with a jar of peach jam he foraged out of the back of the cupboard. He took my hand and led me back to bed and soon I wasn't sad anymore.

We had it easy for a while. Easy is a dangerous way to think. We let Tessa and Duane tell our stories and get us over the rough spots. Tessa's husband went on the road for a week and Duane cut back to three beers a day. Tessa wondered how the future might be. Duane admitted he was scared about what would happen when he was too old to do the work he did. They had their first fight, an incandescent flare-up about something they wouldn't remember later. One midnight, they decided to go out and steal olives from the trees around the parking lot of one of the country's biggest and meanest banks.

So did we. Ben wore his new bandito shirt that I'd found in a little second-hand store on Speedway. The shirt was black with moon-silver snaps, and scarlet roses satin-stitched on the pockets. Even though it sparkled under the parking lot security lamps and we made a stunning amount of noise for two quiet people, nobody saw us. Ben figured we came home with enough olives to restore Coyote's reputation for six months.

Next morning, when Felice came into the kitchen, Ben said, "We've got us a passel of olives, boss."

She shook her head. "You win. I'll try them. If I like them I'll sell Stu on the idea and he'll intimidate the big dogs into featuring them."

You couldn't put up olives in a motel room, so Ben moved in with me. He hung his shirts in my closet and laughed at my suggestion that he bunk in the living room. "Why would I want to sleep alone?" he asked. "I've done it for twenty years, including the fifteen I was married."

"Guys," I said. "Space."

"I'm not that kind of guy. I need space, I'll let you know."

We bought hot pepper flakes and garlic and borrowed a few real hot peppers from our neighbor's garden. Ben hunted through his suitcase for his old man's recipe. It wasn't there. That evening after work, we sat on Coyote's parking lot wall while Ben fired up a bowl and held forth. "Those olives are going to put Coyote on the map. We'll take a little road trip up to Flagstaff and get my stuff out of storage. The recipe's got to be there. *Bon Appétit* feature story, here we come. Besides, sweetpea, we need a break from this."

He waved around at "this," which was air so hot it seemed white, like a blowtorch blast in your throat. Next day we asked Felice for a three-day mid-week weekend and she agreed. She was agreeing to anything. There was a fling going on with the boss. He was abruptly generous. At closing, we'd find white lines of gratitude on the mirrored top of the employee bathroom sink.

"I do not know what's going on," Stu said. "It's absolutely a fantasy d'amour around here." Even he was flinging, the flingee being a scarily handsome bus boy named Squeeze, who wore a tiny silver lizard in his ear and was steadily cheerful—without chemicals. "It's a mystery," Stu said. "At first I thought he was doing that dreary one day at a time thing, but he's not. He's just an angel." He closed his eyes and sighed.

"Good thing," I said, "him being angelic. Seeing how you hate mortals."

"A brief reprieve, I'm sure," Stu said and kissed me on the cheek. He set his hands on his hips. "Now listen, girlfriend. It's all a little too rosy here. You two be careful on your little vacation."

He unlooped the silk cord and crystal from around his neck and draped it around mine. "I don't believe in these New Agey things," he said, "but these are strange times. We mortals need all the help we can get."

Ben and I left before Tuesday dawn in his primer-patched old Bronco and headed up Route 87. "Here's to the road," Ben said. "Here's to freedom." He pulled me over next to him and we cut northeast. We wound along a dirt road high above a river, came around a curve and there was a lake shimmering in late morning light. It seemed a mirage, nothing but gunmetal water and hard desert rising on all sides.

"It's a fake," Ben said, his breath cool against my cheek. "Dammed." I looked out over the brilliant water in the rose-gold desert and thought of my childhood home. Up north and east, there were huge lakes, mad rivers, flat gray water and glittering green water and water like obsidian, black water that tore ass around boulders, rippled against banks of wet ferns. I told Ben all of that and he kissed me.

"Where I come from," he said, "the water's salt, the marshes are salt, the air is salt." He shook his head. "The women, too. Salty." He leaned forward and looked up through the cracked windshield. I moved away. I was still spooky about a man thinking I was crowding him.

"Oriole," he said and pulled off on the shoulder. "Hooded, I think." He opened the glove compartment and pulled out binoculars. I watched while he slid out of his seat and hunkered down next to the truck. The back of his shirt was patched with sweat and he was barely breathing. "Get out," he said. "Crouch next to me." He handed over the binoculars. "It's not hooded. It's a rare one. For here."

The dust we'd kicked up glittered in the sun. The bird shimmered. It was soft orange, black-capped and winged and had perched on a red-flowered weed as though posing for a poster. Tessa looked at the bird. She looked at Duane's sweat-drenched hair, how he held his body absolutely still. She saw that he was in the grip of something urgent as lust and private as prayer. She saw that for the first time since their first kiss, she was invisible to him.

Distant thunder whomped to our right. The sky was clean, morning sun shuddering off the truck hood. Gray and brown birds fluttered up through the skeletal bushes, feathers bobbing on top of their heads, goofy as one of Felice's retro hats. "That's quail," Ben said, "that sound. Mollie, we are in paradise." Ben climbed back in and we rattled down a dirt road toward the lakeshore.

"You like birds?" I said.

"I do," he said, "immoderately."

"You never told me that." I could hear a possessive little whine in my voice.

He laughed. "You don't know everything about me."

I didn't say anything. I couldn't figure out what was going on with me. I felt like a spoiled bitch, one of those chicks who has to own everything about her man. I wondered if it was the raw September heat and the way everything around us looked not just dead, but reduced to bone.

The truck's interior was an oven and when I started to latch my seat belt, the buckle burned my hand. Each bounce of the truck slammed me against the door. The lake sparkled viciously ahead, looking alien in all the cholla and prickly pear and spindly palo verde. I thought of rhinestones and how their cheap glitter set my teeth on edge. Tessa thought it was just beautiful. You could tell the kids would be out of Duane's old Blazer before it came to a full stop. They'd run straight into the sparkling water, sneakers, shorts and all.

Ben parked near the shoreline. I stepped out into the relentless light. I could feel the sand burning through the bottoms of my flip flops. "Hey," Ben said as though it had just come to him. "We've got food. We've got water. Let's stay a while." He didn't look to see if I agreed. "I read there's Great Blue here," he said. "All year round. Maybe we'll stay till evening and drive up to Flag in the cool. They'll come to feed at twilight. You'll love them. You'll see." He threw out his arms and took a deep breath. "Smell that, Mollie. Water and desert. I love it. It's the smell of the impossible."

I took a sniff. The place smelled all too possible, like a low rent dumpster in mid-August—stale beer, piss, rotting worms, plastic diapers and Arby's wrappers everywhere. There was the mean glitter of broken glass all over the sand and rocks. There was not one second of silence. When the ski-doos cut out, the motorboats cut in. Everybody on the shoreline had a boom-box. Everybody was competing to be the winner in quickest death by noise. Only Tessa had the good manners to wear earbuds. She listened to Rosanne Cash, a soft smile on her face.

"Ben," I said, "what's a Great Blue?"

"Heron," he said and walked toward the water. I followed. My head throbbed. Itchy bumps were rising up behind my elbows and knees. I tried to summon Tessa, couldn't seem to find her. Maybe she'd disappeared into the crowd at the snack shack or onto one of the huge rafts—or into the back of the Blazer with Duane, where they'd put on the air-conditioning and were lying next to each other, keeping an eye on the kids playing.

Ben waded out into the murky water. "Tadpoles!" he said. His voice was gleeful. I followed him and stood at the water's edge. "Come on out," he said. "You gotta see this." I walked out next to him. He bent and cupped his hands. The tadpole settled down against a strand of lakeweed.

"Ha!" I said. "He's not there. You can't see him."

Ben lunged and came toward me, his hands cupped in front of him. "Oh yeah," he said. "Me? The tadpole champion of Patchogue, New York?" The tadpole jittered in the tiny puddle in his palms. Tessa shivered. She thought of her hubby, how he'd catch her in his big hands, how he'd grin down at her, triumphant.

"Put it down," I said. "Imagine if two big hands scooped you up and held you where you couldn't breath."

Ben looked at me. "Hey, weren't you ever a kid?"

"Not so you'd notice," I said and proceeded into the pity party I'd started with the first damn oriole, a pity party I stayed in all that endless hot stinking afternoon. By the time the power boats started to thin out, I was sitting in the water, willing to risk cholera just to feel a little bit cool. Ben had wandered off, stooping to poke at crud on the shoreline, raising the binoculars to his eyes to scan the lumpy brown hills. I was just starting to get comfortable in the cooling air when he hunkered down beside me.

"I'm sorry," he said. "I'm not sure what for, but I'm sorry. We'll grab a motel up in Payson for tonight, maybe run over to the little casino. I'll make it up to you." He nuzzled my damp hairline and set his wet hand between my shoulder blades. I felt ashamed. I heard his breath catch and he stood up. "Look," he said. "Great Blues. Two of them."

As I raised my head, two gleaming shadows flew low over the water and fluttered down to a dead cottonwood down the shoreline. Ben handed me the binoculars. "Go ahead, honey," he said. "Look. Please look."

I held the glasses to my eyes. The birds were like nothing I'd ever seen. I couldn't compare them to anything, the way we humans do. They weren't angels. They weren't a dream. They were more than all of those. They dropped to the water in slow motion and began to hunt, their silvery-gray and blue feathers catching last light.

"Are they real?" My voice was soft and high as a little girl's. Ben held my shoulders lightly in his fingertips.

"They are." We watched them for a long, silent and perfect time. The light faded and the Great Blues went on about their business, stretching out their long necks, stepping through the water slowly and carefully.

I convert fast and when I do, I'm hooked. Gin, good olives, love and birds: they're all the same. I like them, I want more. The next day we bought me binoculars in Flag, picked up Ben's meager possessions and drove the short way back to Tucson. I saw ravens up in the mountain pines. I saw crows and learned the difference. Ben saw a red-tailed hawk on a telephone pole and I missed it. There were no more Great Blues. That suited me fine. I was happy with the pictures in my mind, how the light had silvered on their feathers, how they had moved so slowly, how the brown hills had gone black, the saguaro rising up like guardians.

We reached home early evening and sat out on the front stoop poking through Ben's stuff. The recipe was in a cloth-covered diary that said, "My Year." I could hardly read the cobwebby writing, but Ben said it was enough to bring it all back.

"I watched my dad every fall," he said. "This was my great-gran's recipe book. My dad never taught me anything but to say, 'Look out,' or "Move, kid.' Or 'Hand me that,' but he let me watch. I can see his hands now, how he cleaned the peppers, his sure touch with the knife, how he mixed the spices with his bare hands."

I began to cry. Ben touched my throat. Right where that tight sore spot is. He took my arms in his hands. He stirred my hair with his fingers. I could smell the heat and sorrow rise up from me, and the sweet oil he'd rubbed into my skin the night before and the rosemary soap I'd washed my hands with that morning. Tessa raised her wet face and kissed Duane. She tasted him. She licked the salt from his cheeks and told him someday she would be free. He held her tight and promised her olives for their first supper in their own home, olives put up in oil from the first pressing. He asked her to love him for his whole self, not just because he was a little wild, not just because he was forbidden, not just because he was part-time and beautiful and broken.

Ben made the olives and took them to Felice. She was mad for them. Stu finagled Ben a raise and he started to save money. He paid all the rent for us. He bought a new shirt, a brand new shirt from a shop on Fourth Avenue. He started making trips to Nogales and parts south and he brought me presents. There was a peyote cactus in a donkey planter and a clay grandma skeleton in a black dress and shawl. She held a spray of cloth flowers in her arms. When I picked her up, her head bobbed back and forth.

"She's your duenna," Ben said. "You know what that means. She keeps you safe. And she keeps you honest."

I held her gently. She nodded yes. I didn't bother to think what kept Ben honest. We had gotten so good. We could tell the truth. We could get through what sometimes follows after truth is told. We kept saying how good it was, as though our words were a charm.

"This is so good," he might say, "sitting here before the day gets hot, just drinking coffee, listening to those doves, just the two of us, quiet like this."

"It is, Ben," I'd say. I loved saying his name. "It's gorgeous."

There we'd be, just those few words between us, maybe his hand on my wrist, my ankle crossed over his. Tessa and Duane had drifted away as friends do, or maybe as helpers must. Ben and I both knew they were gone and we believed they had given us their blessing.

How it happens with people like Ben and me, how the changes can be almost invisible, how the dream can stop as if you were awakened by an unknown sound—I knew all of that. Still, the end snuck up on me. Ben upped the Nogales trips to once a week. He started to lose weight. I noticed he was leaving the binoculars behind and the presents were becoming more expensive—vanilla beans in good rum packed in a hand-blown glass jar, a dress embroidered shoulders to hem with real silver thread, pre-Columbian statues that scared me. I wasn't too surprised when he quit Coyote nor when the boss invited us for dinner. I was surprised that we went.

There were Ben and me, Felice and the boss, Stu and Squeeze at a big glass table set up next to the lit-up pool. The boss' cook had created a feast: barbecued quail, blue corn tamales, pomegranates, their juice glowing on our lips and hands, on the front of my Mexican dress. I remember looking down at the blotch a long time, the stain so dark on the fine pale cotton, on the delicate silver birds. I think Ben leaned over and kissed me there, but I'm not sure. Everything got busy and loud, people going here, going there, Felice swinging her pale legs in the pool, Stu up to his neck in front of her, Squeeze rubbing my shoulders. Ben went off somewhere and returned, his face gray, his eyes like mica.

The boss play a tape of Navajo flute music over and over. If you'd looked over the fence at us, over the green leafy posts and red blossoms trembling in the light, you would have seen a magical picture. You would have heard the music trembling too, the way a howl can in the summer air.

When I wanted Tessa with us, when I wanted good old solid Duane watching our backs, I couldn't find them. I was alone with it: with how Ben's face began to scare me, skin stretched tight over the bones, the way the green shirt he'd started wearing to bed, cuffs buttoned, hung on him like a robe, how I was seeing so little of him, of my phantom lover, that I was glad to see him at all. I knew what it was. I knew that he was being eaten alive and he had offered himself up for the feast.

I called to Tessa and Duane in the long hours I spent alone in the cool dark of early morning, the duenna nodding at me, a Virgen de Guadalupe candle burning next to her, its warm light flickering on the bone-white face. I hadn't prayed in years. I wasn't sure I knew how.

"Mother," I whispered, "whoever the patron saints of sad lovers are, please let me see Tessa and Duane again. I need their heat, their laughter and the scent of oil on their twined bodies." I'd try to see their faces in the candle shadows, how their eyes were no less shining and soft than Tessa's kids'. I'd try to catch what they might be saying—all that hope and reassurance and promises kept. I couldn't do it.

I couldn't do anything. People like me and Ben, like Felice and Stu, we don't even dare dream that you can cure somebody else. We know the truth, maybe because we can smell hopelessness right away or because we can taste surrender and surely because we've stewed up messes ourselves. We know. And I knew that Ben was gone—even as he lay next to me, even as he moved in me, first tentative, then frantic, then gone from me into a cold desperation that ground his sharp hip bones against mine and left me dry and aching.

The duenna watched over our last night together. The Virgen candle had burned down to a moon-white puddle. Ben stood in front of me in the blue light of the huge TV, his most recent gift. He was so handsome it cut my heart. He couldn't look at me.

"Mollie," he said. "Can you do me a favor? Can I borrow a couple hundred bucks? I ran out, must have miscalculated something. I'll pay you back in the morning."

"No more," I said. "And I want you to leave. Please. Now."

Ben picked up the duenna. I took it from his shaking hand.

"Honest," I said. "I want you to go away."

He began to move toward our bedroom. As he stepped full in the television's glow, I saw the shining curve of the Great Blues. I saw the stillness, the careful way Ben set his feet. I saw the concentration and in him, it was terrible.

Ben took a half hour to pack his things. I heard him moving in our bedroom, then the kitchen, then his steps fading away on the front walk. I couldn't move from the couch. I knew if I did, I would go to him, put my arms around him and beg him to stay.

I sat quietly for a few minutes, then went into the bedroom. He'd left almost all his clothes, except for the green shirt and the black bandito shirt. His binoculars were gone from the dresser, his duffle bag from the closet. I walked out and closed the door. The black shirt, clean and ironed, was on the kitchen table along with a jar of olives. I pulled on the shirt and wished he'd left it smelling of him. I opened the jar, took out an olive and bit into it.

It was sweet. I remembered him reading the recipe. I could

see his face, the way his lips moved and I remembered how I'd taken in the sight the way you take in a song you think you may never hear again. Then the pepper hit and my throat warmed. There was the taste of garlic and my tears and the spices he'd mixed with his naked hands.

I chewed every bit of fruit off the stone and put it to dry on the window sill between the cactus and the little Nogales duenna. The truck roared to a start. I wrapped my arms around myself and waited till Ben had driven away. Then I took a white candle out of the cupboard and set it in front of the Virgen.

I lit it. The candle flame shimmered on the Virgen's downcast eyes and on her hands held out for mercy. "If I knew how to pray," I said, "I would ask you only for a way to make it through what comes next. Only that."

FAT JACKS

Even with the divorce and all, even with his kid Jacob living on the other side of town most of the time, even with losing his latest job and not finding the new one for five months, Davy was starting to have a few decent moments. Being a night shift Security Engineer wasn't all that bad. The building was peaceful, the other engineer quiet and friendly. Sophieann didn't come on till eight, so for three hours he had the place to himself. All he had to do was cruise the building, key in the couple dozen checkpoints and then sit in the tiny office keeping an eye on a computer screen.

Sometimes in the little room with its cool metallic air, the blue-green light of the computer screen, the corners of the room murky and silent, he would pretend he was in a submarine. He would imagine that luminous creatures drifted through the gloom outside and that the red and green and blue lights were signals of their presence. He would hope that they were friendly and not at all hungry. He would tell himself that Safe and Serene Security Systems was a doorway you might see on a re-run of The Twilight Zone, something you might stumble through in a dream.

Spring evenings, he would take his dinner break outside on the marbleized steps. The desert twilight would go pearly. He would stare off into the vastness of the Rio Rialto Office Park, aware that the birds had stopped their sunset noises. No planes would fly overhead and the whine of I-10 would fade clean away. An impossible silence would fall over the city's edge.

Davy would open his cold yogurt soup or sesame spinach wrap or Canton chili noodles. He was taking a course in vegetarian gourmet cuisine, as his ex-wife's shrink had suggested. "Something new," the shrink and Lisa had said. "A way to take care of yourself.

A way to move on."

He would take a bite of his dinner and look out past the black wrought iron fence, across an acre of parking lot. Slowly the mass of the abandoned building to the south would begin to shimmer. For less than a minute, the sleek black stone would reflect the twilight. He could imagine he was looking into a great, curved and empty mussel shell. The deep silence would seem not only possible, but necessary, and the building's transformation reasonable and essential.

It was just that sort of thinking that had lost him his real job as a computer salesman. It was just that sort of thinking that had sent Lisa out the door. And it was just that sort of thinking, she loved to point out, that was causing her to tell her lawyer and the shrink that she didn't want Davy seeing her kid more than twice a month.

"Mystery building," she said. "Mystery brain's more like it. Meaning, Davy, that your brain is a mystery to me and I could care less to solve it. Jacob needs grounding now."

Davy cared very much to solve the mystery of the building. It was the Inc. That was all that was left of the glittering stone letters on the long side that faced the Interstate. He wondered what they'd taken away. They'd left no clue. They'd removed the letters with the same attention to detail they'd brought to the parking lot, the grounds, the stone and glass of the building and how the desert light fell on it and lured the eye.

One skinny dead tree rose in front of the big smoked-glass doors. They'd set a floodlamp at the base of the tree, planted some lush ground-cover and set sprinklers there. At dusk, breezes stirred the dust and the little tree became a ghost in the cloudy light.

Sometimes Davy walked along the Inc. fence, past the little tree and giant doors, then back to the trimmed Bermuda grass of Safe and Serene. There the fence stretched away to the west. Sighting down the black iron stakes, he watched I-10 shimmer. At sunset, the drivers on the Interstate might think they were looking at a wall of fire. If he could hold onto this job, he might be driving into work some December evening, look over and surprise himself. He might feel the sweet spooky lurch of "Where am I? What's happening? This might be awful, but it could be new!" It was something to work for.

Lisa hadn't liked his weird goals. She was about Safety. He was about Surprise. The two of them were Maturity vs. Fun, Planning vs. Spontaneity, What Works vs. Weird. He had seen the words in capital letters when they fought, like chapters in one of the how-to books Lisa tried to get him to read. Of course, it hadn't been that way at first. Of course, they'd promised each other that wouldn't happen. Of course, it had. And that was a mystery he couldn't have cared more to solve. Even if he had a clue.

Nobody seemed to know what mystery or what business-as-usual the Inc. had held, if it had ever held anything or anybody. There was a service entrance to the east, big enough for five eighteen-wheelers to dock. There was a garage for at least another dozen trucks. The parking lot was bigger than all of Villa Encanta, the trailer park Davy lived in. It was always then, right when he was considering the comparative size of the Inc. parking lot and Villa Encanta, that he would feel his gut knot. He would realize he was hanging on the iron fence so tight the metal edges bit into his hand. He knew unfairness and bitter consequence and how the universe was clenched around him, sharp and fixed in concrete as the iron stakes.

He'd been awarded the travel trailer, half the CDs and old tapes, all the National Geographic collection and two plates, bowls, cups, forks, spoons and knives. All that really mattered was that he'd been granted Jacob, every other weekend for forty-eight hours. They would see how things went before Lisa and her lawyer decided about Easter and Xmas and other national holidays. It would depend on whether or not Davy was finally ready to face reality. They would see how the job went. Maybe a few classes at a community college to show he was thinking about the future. The gourmet vegetarian course didn't count.

Lisa had driven over the morning after they signed the papers. They'd made love for the first time in a year. She'd gone fierce and soft the way he loved, waited till he finished, jumped up and disappeared into the john. She came out glum and naked. While he watched her from the bed, she opened a beer and chugged it down.

"Don't eat me with your eyes that way," she said. "You make me feel weird."

She pulled on her clothes. When she went out the screen door and as usual, didn't bother to latch it, Davy had figured that was all she wrote. But just as he started to throw back the damp sheet, he'd seen the door open and her hands setting their senile cat, Ray Cooper, on the carpet. By the time Ray C. got his bearings, Lisa's pick-up was crunching out over the gravel drive.

Davy discussed all this with Sophieann, Security Engineer 1, in those peaceful hours between eight and midnight. "Jacob awarded to me part time?" he said. "Like I was getting some kind of half-ass prize?" They talked about everything, what men want, what women want, marriage and why bother, Sophieann's arrangement with her boyfriend, Larry the Fake Chicano, and her pure terror at the thought of Larry's possible departure.

"We don't have anything solid," she said, "not even a magazine subscription—or a cat."

"It doesn't matter," Davy said. "Lisa and I started out with all of it, a kid in the oven, one of those Hollywood production weddings, Ray C., who wasn't senile at the time, and a joint National Geographic subscription. It made no difference."

"Why's the cat named Ray C.?" Sophie said. "Not to change the subject."

"Ray Cooper," Davy said, "is the best drummer in the British Isles. Lisa and I used to care about stuff like that."

Sophieann sighed. "Seems like Larry and I don't agree on much. But he's got some definitely interesting ideas about things."

Davy waited. He'd had his fill of Larry's interesting ideas. There'd been the run-of-the-mill ones like a Jewish left-wing conspiracy being responsible for Larry not being able to find a job. There'd been the entrepreneurial ones like Davy investing in Larry's chasing UFO sightings in Nevada. Larry would need a truck, a big one, and video equipment and lots of gas money.

Sophieann stared into the computer screen. Her face was eerie and beautiful in the flickering light, her dark hair picking up little festive Christmassy glints. Davy thought of a tropical fish in one of those black light tanks. He liked that he could see her beauty and know that they were strictly on the friendship track. They'd discussed that right off and said how their hearts were tied up at the moment and probably would be for a long time.

"Larry says it's Mafia in that empty building," she said.

"No way," Davy said. "Not in Phoenix."

"Excuse me," Sophieann said, "1976? That reporter that got blown up with a car bomb? Larry says The Boys are everywhere. Bullhead City, Lake Havasu, we're just a hop, skip and a jump. Larry knows."

"Whaaat," Davy said. "What does he know. He plays a little poker, he loses a few bucks over in Laughlin. That makes him Senor Juice?"

"Hey," Sophieann said, "people talk at those tables, they say things, Larry listens. And watch that racist Senor stuff, gringo!"

"Gringo yourself," Davy said. He was getting sick of chicano Larry and his inside track on things. The guy's mom's mom's mom had come up from Sonora and his dad had been a trucker passing through on his way back home to Iowa. Larry was the kind of dude who stuck a big magnetic Guadalupe on the dashboard of his truck and hung a pair of electric blue fuzzy dice around its neck. He talked constantly about going back to his family in Sonora. And he wore a trucker hat that read Don't touch my chingaderas. Davy figured the hat was to cover up the fact that Larry's hairline was the only part of him heading south.

"Peace," Sophieann said. "But you watch. Next thing you know there'll be all these snake-eyed guys in great suits around, you get my meaning? You know, where afterwards you're not sure you really saw them?"

"Sophieann," Davy said, "you're straight from Ponca City, Oklahoma. You're twenty-six. You go to business college days. When did you ever see a Mafia to know one?"

"Movies," she said. "Not just Al Pacino flicks or The Sopranos. Real documentaries. I feel quite informed on this. You wait and see."

"What documentaries?"

"On PBS. That building is a tax write-off. They build it, it stands empty, they lose money, they write it off. That was in The Family: Behind the Scenes. That was PBS, Davy. They don't lie."

"The Mafia doesn't pay taxes," he said. "But I sure will. Lisa's going to make sure of that."

"Ah," Sophieann said, "now it's getting interesting. Hold that thought. I gotta key in."

"Jesus, Sophie," Davy said. "Where'd you learn that? Lisa's shrink always says, 'Hold that thought.' But it's always only me that's holding my thoughts."

"Everybody says it," she said. "Just hold it. We'll tear those biotches apart when I get back."

Bitch hung in the air like a bad smell. A red light flickered on the monitor board where a green light was supposed to be. Davy hit a key and things went back to normal. Bitch. It amazed him that it was one thing if he thought it about Lisa and another if somebody used the word about her. It roused him to a dumb chivalry. It made him want to say, "You don't understand, you didn't know her the way I did." Sometimes he thought he'd seen her with the same goofy magic with which he saw the Inc. In a certain light, at certain times, with his mystery brain.

He never got used to the hour before Lisa dropped Jacob off. It was partly four cups of coffee, partly that no matter what he did with the trailer, it was too small, too bare and too grown-up. They were fixing up a room, he and Jacob, cruising garage sales, checking the toy bins at Goodwill, beginning to cover the walls with

Jacob's drawings, making space for Jacob's birds. The birds were another story. They were doves. Lots of them. And they were totally invisible to the ordinary, meaning non-Jacob, eye.

Davy set a box of frozen Danish on the shelf. Ray C. scouted it from the floor, but he was cross-eyed and always missed his jump by humiliating inches, so he just sat there, giving Davy long, tragic, visually-impaired looks. That was another draw-back to the trailer. Ray C. was having a last surge of senile and improbable lust. Davy figured the phenomenon was like the old guys he saw around Phoenix, the sagging fellows in their pastel pants and white shoes, their tautly held-together, somewhat younger wives on their arms. He felt that same sorrow and affection for Ray C. that he felt for those old guys. No way he'd kick him out.

Jacob liked to have a second breakfast. They ate whatever he wanted, which was always a raspberry Danish, glass of milk and bag of nacho chips. Davy checked the cupboard. He had enough nacho chips for all of Larry's mythical Sonoran relatives. He poured himself another cup of coffee and waited for Lisa's truck to roll in over the gravel.

Two mourning doves on the telephone wires were setting up their liquid ruckus. They made him think of love, of how silky Lisa's skin could be. Consequently, they made him mad. Besides being consistently late bringing Jacob over, she'd somehow become maddeningly desirable to Davy. Once he'd known it was over, he'd gone from limp disinterest to a steady readiness that tormented him day and night. He called it "The Phantom."

The Phantom wanted Lisa. It wanted only Lisa. It had demonstrated this on the one mutually unfortunate date Davy had attempted. Her name had been Claire. She'd been nine years younger and she had never encountered an unwilling member before. She'd been the one that cried and Davy'd been the one to console. He hoped it wasn't going to become a theme. Only The Phantom knew.

He opened the chips and ate one. You could taste the chemicals. The cooking course had taught him that. He closed the bag. The clock jumped one minute. Lisa was an hour late. The doves had shut up and gone wherever doves go in the brutal heat of a Phoenix noon. He called. The answering machine told him she was out, but she did want to know who called and have a nice day and, uh, if it was Brad, would he please meet her at the pool at three. Davy set the receiver gently down. Lisa hated people who hung up without talking. He called back five times and hung up five times. He knew how to change her message from remote. He didn't do that. He wanted her to hate him and want him. He didn't want her to think he didn't have any class.

He heard Jacob before he saw him.

"Davy, Davy, we're here!"

Davy opened the door. Lisa's truck was already gone. Jacob stumbled toward him. He wore his little turtle backpack so his hands were free to safely carry the doves' cardboard box up the steps. The old fake Indian blanket was draped across the top of the box. That was the signal that the doves were in there. Later Jacob and Davy would take them to the side fence for the first time and let them go. You could only do that at sunset. You could only do that when it was almost too dark to see.

"Davy," Jacob said, "I got tons of them this time. Mom said it was okay to let them loose here."

Jacob didn't call Davy "Dad" anymore. Lisa had been working on him. Maybe there was a move in the future, one of those legal kidnappings guys get to live through. Maybe there was even a new candidate for "Dad." Somebody safe, somebody mature, somebody named Stephen or Charles or Brad.

Davy took the box. It weighed almost nothing. But that was how doves were, Jacob said. You couldn't hardly feel them because they were almost always flying around in there. And they were gray and that was a light color.

"Davy," Jacob said, "I'm pretty hungry. I could eat some breakfast now. I caught almost all these doves this morning before Mom even waked up." He pulled himself up into a chair. "You can put the doves next to me," he said. "I like to hear them while I eat. They're not plain ordinary doves, you know. They're rock doves!"

Davy set the box on the end of the table. Jacob picked up the blanket's corner and scattered something inside. "It's their seeds," he said. "Springtime, you got to give them more than just left-over nacho crumbs." He tugged the blanket firmly over the box. Ray Cooper cruised hopefully around his chair.

"No way, Ray," Jacob said. He moved the doves closer and dropped a nacho chip on the floor. "Besides, these birds taste like clouds."

Next day Sophieann came in late. She sat next to Davey and kept her shades on. "How'd it go with Jacob?"

"Same old, same old," Davy said. "Unbearably good. And this time, we let the doves go. Lisa hasn't let him bring them over till now."

"Sweet," Sophieann said. She sounded tired and a little sad. "What was it like? Letting them take off?"

"Jacob waits till the sun's down, till there's practically no light left in the sky. He says they like gray light. He lifts up the blanket and he talks to them in dove talk. He coos. He really sounds like doves. Then I have to close my eyes because it scares them if a human being is watching. I hear him pull the blanket off the box. He says, 'You go home now.' Then he starts to giggle. I have to wait till he says 'Okay,' then I can open my eyes."

"I have to ask," Sophieann said. "I just have to. Did you see any doves?"

Davy paused and tried to look cosmic. "I did."

"What? What did they look like?"

"They looked like doves. They were on the telephone wire, in that scraggly palm. There were even a few sitting on my neighbor's roof."

"Get out." Sophieann punched him in the arm. "What happened then?"

"We went in and played checkers. He beat me. I wasn't even letting him win."

"That makes two of us," Sopphieann said and took off her shades. "Put on the desk lamp."

Her right eye was swollen shut. The skin around it was purple and green. She glared at Davy, then looked down. "Scumbag," she said. "Sold my CD player. Lost every penny. He doesn't even have to drive to a casino anymore. There's a card club in the strip mall. The big man lost three hundred and change and came home and decided I was the reason for his bad luck. I am not a chee-ca-na. I am not one of his people." She winced. "So I said, 'Okay man, I'll talk Spanish.' And I said, 'Chinga tu pinche madre' and he slammed me good."

"Oh shit," Davy said. "Real dumb, but real classy."

Sophieann grinned. "Ouch," she said. "Whoa, my face hurts. He's gone. All the way. Took him five minutes to pack. I was grateful we didn't have a joint magazine subscription—or el gato."

"Sophieann," Davy said. He started to say more, but she set her hand on his arm, put her shades back on and stood.

"I'm going to key in," she said. "When I come back, I want to talk about it. And I want to talk about some other things too. Like why don't you fight dirty to get Jacob. And why do you let him call you Davy? Your name is Dad, your name is David Jacob Martin. Like mine is Sophieann Elizabeth Jones, not puta or mama or you dumb broad. It's time we didn't forget that!" She bowed. Davy applauded.

"How about if I go out for donuts while you're gone?" Davy said. Sophieann dropped five bucks on the keyboard. "You fly," she said, "I'll buy."

If you got the cream-filled or frosted donuts at Nuts for Donuts, they had a special, fourteen for the price of twelve, so Davy went a little overboard. He ate three chocolate creams on the way back to work. What Sophieann had said about getting Jacob and about being called Dad had left a hollow in his gut. The donuts descended, settled in and did the job. By the time he pulled into employee parking, he was out of his mind on sugar. He sat a minute to slow things down.

He looked out into the cool Milky Way of his headlights. He could see every blade of grass, sandstone pebble and chalky splash of bird-shit. He could see the fence spikes and their shadow on the Inc.'s parking lot. He had a half-dozen deep thoughts so fast he missed them. He was only a little surprised when three jackrabbits hopped cautiously into the light. They were huge. When they turned their faces to the light and froze, he saw their yellow eyes, slanted and mysterious, like the old magician's in one of Jacob's picture books.

Davy turned off the headlights. Everything went black, then gray, then lit by a brilliant full moon. The Inc. fence was a perfect series of brushstrokes against the pale grass. The jacks hunkered down and ate. Their backs, their ears, their bent powerful haunches were silvered, moonlight rippling along their fur like water.

Davy wondered if Sophieann was back in the room. Was she hungry? Worried? He didn't want to scare her, but he didn't want to be anywhere but where he was.

"Dad," he whispered, "a.k.a. David Jacob Martin. He decides to stay where he is. He could open the door. He could get out with the donuts. But David Jacob Martin will not scare those jacks away. He won't. He doesn't move."

A week later, Sophieann came for dinner. She wasn't that crazy about gourmet vegetarian which, along with frozen raspberry Danish, nacho chips and milk in a glass with a warrior reptile printed on its side was David's menu, so she brought a steak and they grilled it on the hibachi on his little patio. David made a salad with romaine, good olive oil, lemon juice and chunks of blue cheese. They sat in the gathering dusk to eat.

Sophieann said, "I saw you that donut night sitting out in the car. It was kind of weird."

David put a steak sliver in his mouth and sighed happily. "No more vegetarian," he said. "So, how was it weird?"

"When I came out, you were sitting there totally still like you were stoned or something. Those bunnies didn't move. Finally, you waved out your window and hollered, 'You go home now.' And they didn't budge." She picked a lemon seed out of her salad. "Of course, I wondered if they could. Those are some fat jacks. Those are some serious chubbettes."

"Chubbos," David said. "Give the dudes among them some respect."

She laughed. While he grilled the steak, he told her about the Davy business finally getting to him, about being thirty-five and looking twenty, about the vegetarian cooking actually being a big deal because till Lisa left, he'd never put together a full meal in his life. Lisa hadn't let him. He guessed that women's lib had passed him by, and Lisa only got the ladies' magazine parts, the parts where you dressed up and went to work and the kid was in day care and you came home and did everything your mom had done even better than she had and got pissed off at the unfairness of it all.

"So, David, what are you thinking you'll do about Jacob?" Sophieann said.

"I don't know," David said.

"You could maybe learn what to do? From some other guys with the same problem?" Sophieann had a funny gleam in her eye. It worried him. Lisa had gleamed like that the first time she came back from the therapist.

"Meaning?"

"Meaning I started going to this group over at a wellness center—all women. We talk about our lives. There are guy groups too."

"I'm not into that godstuff," David said. "Don't you have to have a higher power or something like that?"

"Nope, this is different, but excuse me, I do have a higher power."

"You told me you were a born-again nothing. Who's your higher power?"

"Madonna," she said. "She's old school, but if I was in trouble, I'd want her watching my back."

"Wait a minute," David said. "You can't have a pop star for a higher power."

"You have rabbits. Jacob has doves. Case closed."

"Man," David said. "Maybe I ought to get a higher power. Lisa's turned up the heat."

"Time to fight dirty," Sophieann said.

"Just hear me out," David said. "There's nothing definite yet, but Lisa wants to discuss something with me at the therapist's. Jacob's all of a sudden talking about those California doves. He's pretty sure they're all different colors. They live right by the ocean, right near Grandma Raines. And he thinks those California doves might even know how to speak human.

"Lisa called and said, 'We have to talk, but I can't for a few days.' Man, I hate it when somebody says 'we have to talk,' and supposedly can't make time for it right away."

Sophieann looked up. There were the black shapes of birds along the telephone wires. They were silent and still.

"Oh, dude," Sophieann said. "I wish I had an answer. Maybe all we've got for sure is those birds up there right now, the fat jacks, all your sea monsters floating around Safe and Serene, Jacob being such an amazing kid, you, me, Ray Cooper here. None of us hating each other. All of us just trying to get by."

"I'm not sure about Big Ray C.," David said and put him in her lap. "He's just trying to stay alive." Sophieann scratched Ray behind the ears.

They sat together, the three of them scarcely moving, one of them purring, with the birds quiet above them, till the silver thumbprint of moon had dropped out of sight.

It was all very simple. Jacob would be with his mother for

the school year and alternating major holidays, Davy would get him for the summer. They'd work out something fair for child support since Lisa earned more than Davy. It was really a good sign that Davy was holding on to his job.

Jacob was adjusting nicely to the idea of the move. In his crayon pictures, he'd started to color the doves purple and blue and red. Sometimes they had little balloons coming out of their mouths, saying "Her comes Jacob. Sunflower sedes are gud. We're going to go hom to the oshin." The only thing that seemed a little strange to Lisa and the shrink was that Jacob kept putting a big black office building in the picture. Sometimes he even wrote its name in the title: Mistere Bilding or Rock Doves, Inc.

"Did you take him there?" Lisa asked. The shrink leaned forward, eyes alert, a patient smile on her lips.

"A few times," David said. "I thought he should see where his father worked. I mean, near there. You know."

The shrink nodded. "These days when so much is in upheaval, it's good for children to know that what Mom does is important to her and what Dad does is important to him." She nodded again. Lisa stared at her. The shrink tapped Lisa's hand. "There's no sense in running those old family patterns, is there? Remember? What we talked about? All those one-parent families when you and Davy…"

"David," he said.

"…when you and David were kids. All those supposedly intact families, with no real dad at all, all those dads gone off to some mystery job and not fully present at home."

David wanted to agree with her. But, way inside he heard Sophieann. She'd said, "My dad, that poor sonofabitch—by the time he made it through the kitchen door, it was long after dinner. It was all he could do to keep his head out of his plate. The wells were running out and he was double-timing to try to get ahead a little."

David stood. The shrink glanced at her watch. "Ten more minutes, David."

"I'm done," he said. "I don't like what's been decided. In fact, I think it sucks. But the judge has already made the decision. I don't have much choice."

Lisa stared at him. He saw that she was tired and possibly scared. She glanced down at her hands.

"I'm sorry," she said. "Davy, it's just that…"

"You might be sorry," he said. "I'll give you that and if you are, stop calling me Davy. My name is David and tell Jacob it's time to call me Dad. Grant us that little bit."

David didn't wait for a reply. He left the room. He drove a long way before he let himself pull the car into a far corner of the Basha's parking lot. He waited till he was sure he was alone and no one could see him. Then at last he cried.

Lisa brought Jacob to the door. He carried the box in himself and set it on the kitchen table. The Indian blanket was stapled on three sides, taped shut on the fourth.

"He wanted to be sure they didn't escape," she said, "so he could let them loose to live near you." She looked at the refrigerator and studied Jacob's drawings. "Mystery building," she said. "Oh Davy, do you think it's inherited?"

"I hope so," he said. She turned to go and stopped.

"David is what I meant to say," she said. "I'll try to remember. I told him you'd explain it to him. About your name. About Dad." She kissed Jacob on the cheek and patted his butt. She reached out to shake David's hand.

"Wait," he said. "Why this change? What made the difference? Something about me? You got your way?"

"Oh David," she said. "Who knows? Who fucking knows."

The next time David and Jacob sat outside in the aqua twilight, with the smell of the neighbor's tamales floating in the air, the sound of hip-hop thumping in off the street, Jacob held the box in his lap and said, "Dad, you can keep your eyes open. You can watch the doves take off. You will love it. It will be so good you will laugh yourself sick."

He peeled back the tape and peeked inside. David moved a little closer.

"Goodbye," Jacob said. "Goodbye Pikachu and Long Feather and Freddy Krueger. It's time to fly." He held up the box.

"Pull off the blanket, Dad," he said. David tugged. The blanket slid to the ground. There was rustling, there was the faintest whisper of feathers moving, of wings ruffling in the air. Jacob giggled.

"There they go, Dad," he said. "They're going home."

Saturday night, David and Jacob drove over to keep Sophieann company at work. He'd packed a spinach and feta cheese salad, nacho chips, steak fajitas and a raspberry-chocolate torte. He wore his new Security Engineer 2 shirt, the one with David embroidered on the pocket.

Sophieann let Jacob wear her special Safe and Serene hat. They watched the computer lights flicker. They heard the sea monsters drifting and bumping outside. David told Jacob the monsters' names. One was Pikachu and one was Long Fins. He wasn't sure about Freddy Krueger. He didn't think there was anything in the ocean that dumb and mean. He told them about the immense weight of black glittering water pressing in on the tiny room and how they were safe, the way the walls held strong, the pressure stayed steady and they had all the air they needed. Jacob told them about Pikachu and Long Feather, how they could fly in water and might be flying toward them right that minute, maybe even bringing them sunflower seeds. The Freddy Krueger dove had flown south.

"Probably has family in Sonora," Sophieann said.

"You guys stand up side by side." She flicked on her flashlight and held it under their chins. "You two are soul brothers," she said. "You got those big mystery brains."

"No," Jacob said, "he's my dad. I'm his kid. That's how

it's always been. That's how it'll always be. He told me that. So did my mom."

They finished off every crumb of the raspberry-chocolate torte. David kept feeling tears salty in the back of his throat. He and Sophieann cleared things away. Jacob disappeared. They found him curled up in the brown velvet Reception Seating Module nearly asleep. David sat down and pulled Jacob into his lap. "Could you stay awake a few minutes more?" Jacob nodded. "I want to show you something. It's really good." David cradled Jacob in his arms and stood. Sophieann opened the door and did the fancy dance you had to do to keep the alarm from going off.

Jacob laughed. "That's so we can breathe water," he said. David stepped into the alien glow of the security lamp and walked on out into the darkness near the fence. He hunkered down, Jacob a feather in his arms. Jacob looked out across the Inc.'s lawn.

"Bunnies," he said. "Big fat bunnies. Zillions of them." He slipped out of David's arms and crouched next to him. "They look like ghosts," he said.

"Listen," David said.

Jacob leaned forward. "I can hear them, Dad," he whispered. "They're chowing down." The biggest jack glanced at them. His jaw went still.

"Where do they live?" Jacob said.

"Guess," David said.

Jacob looked up toward the Inc's flood-lamp beaming out into the dark. The spindly tree seemed a glowing crack in the black face of the building. A little jack sat up, her long paws dangling in front of her. They heard her sniff the air. She twisted and dropped to her haunches.

"She's going," Jacob said. "You go home now," he whispered. The jack hopped a few steps and paused. "Go home now," Jacob said and giggled. The jack startled and began to go. She was a shadow in the dark, a leaping in the light. When she came to the ground-cover just outside the Inc., she stopped and sat. Jacob waved once. The jack disappeared into the shadows. Jacob snuggled into David's chest. "She was all shining," he said. "Like magic. Dad, I've got a question."

"Shoot," David said.

"Do they have magic bunnies in California?"

"Maybe not magic," David said carefully, "but these jacks will always be here." Jacob burrowed in closer, his breath warm against David's throat. "Good."

KASHMIR

First my dad died. Then Mom found out he'd borrowed from the life insurance right down to the dust on the last nickel. Then she said, "Jenn, I hope you'll get a part-time job. Otherwise I don't know how we'll make it." I'm sixteen so there's not a whole bunch of jobs out there—especially in Yucca Valley where lots of people sleep in their cars. But my best friend Liana's mom works as an aide at Hopecare, a local nursing home. She talked with the head nurse. They said they needed somebody three to seven to help out with meals and visit the residents. And could I start right away? Almost the next thing I knew I was being given a blue and white striped Hope Helper's apron, handed a vase of silk flowers and a card and told to head down the hall to Room 136 to get it ready for the new resident.

I read the card as I walked down the hall. *Welcome to your new home. We hope you'll like it as much as we do.* Nobody had signed it and I wondered if the new patient would wonder if anybody here actually liked it at Hopecare. I set the flowers and the card on the dresser, tugged the bedspread tight over the blankets and sheets and sat in the La-Z-Boy chair next to the window. I could look out on the Vons parking lot behind Hopecare. I watched a couple shaved-head kids playing Bash a Shopping Cart. I remembered when Liana and I had done that. We got caught and had to clean up the parking lot for a month. When the store manager told my dad, my dad had tried to look like he was mad. Later, I heard him talking with my mom and the two of them were laughing their asses off.

I wondered if I would ever be able to look at anything in our town and not think about my dad. He'd been gone three months. There was no warning. One morning my mom woke up next to him in bed and his skin was cold. She shook him and when she knew it was hopeless, she called 911. She woke up me and my brother and sister and sat us down on the bed in my brother's room. "Something really sad has happened," she said. I knew right away. "Your father died sometime in the night." She waited and gave us time to let the words go all the way into our brains. Chris broke first. He threw himself into her arms. Stacy grabbed my hand. I'm the oldest of all of us, so I just looked into Mom's eyes. She nodded. I knew in that instant my childhood was over.

I watched the kids in the parking lot be kids and cried a while. I was wiping my nose with a corner of my apron when there was a tap at the door. "Incoming," a wheezy voice said. I looked up and saw a little old guy with a long gray braid being wheeled into the room. He had on a faded black leather vest with patches on it. He wore a silver hoop in his right ear and a string of turquoise beads around his neck. "Hey, little sister," he said, "where'd you get those flowers? Are they for me?"

"Isn't that nice, Mr. Guidry," the aide said. "You've got a welcoming committee." The guy snorted. The aide parked the wheelchair next to me. "I'll just leave you two alone so you can get to know each other," she said, set a duffle bag on the bed, fluffed up the pillows and left.

The old guy shook his head. "Ah jeez," he said, "what a bummer. Not you, missy. Just what the hell am I supposed to do now." He picked up the card. "My new home? I liked the old one just fine."

"That vest is so cool," I said because I couldn't think of what else to say.

The guy looked down. "I earned every one of them patches," he said. "I was a real biker, not one of those yuppies you see riding around on fancy-ass—'scuse me—Harleys. I rode with the Half Moon Hellers. You ever heard of them?"

"Nope," I said. "But my dad was going to get a bike." I

heard myself and wanted to take back the words. The guy shook his head. "'Going to' and 'got' are two different things. You tell him that. He buys himself a bike, he'll wonder why he waited so long."

"Okay," I said. No way was I going to spill my guts to a grouch.

"Excuse me," he said. "I forgot my manners." He reached out his hand. He had a big old skull ring on his thumb and a silver snake around his little finger. "Let me introduce myself. I'm Red Billy. Red Billy Guidry."

I shook his hand. "I'm Jenn Martin. I just started work here."

"Well then, that makes us both newbies, right?"

I laughed. "Yep. Red Billy—that's a great name. If you don't mind my asking, where'd you get it?"

Red Billy undid the braid and shook his hair loose. "See all this hair. It used to be red, not carrot red—goldy red like Robert Plant. You know who he is?"

"Led Zep," I said. "My boyfriend Travis says they're gods. I'm more into stuff like *My Chemical Romance*."

Red Billy faked taking a hit off a joint. "Tell me about it."

"Oh jeez," I said. "You better be careful."

"What are they going to do?" He laughed. "Bust me and send me to jail? That'd have to be better than here."

Just then the aide looked in. "Hey, Jenn, Karen wants to orientate you. She's at the nursing station."

"You go on, missy," Red Billy said. "I gotta get me and all my possessions settled in." He nodded at the duffle bag. "Should take me about five minutes."

I got off work at seven and called Liana on my way home. "I have to talk," I said. "The weirdest thing happened at my job." She and Trav drove over and we headed up Old Woman Springs Road to get high. I love where I live. It's big old desert and you can do what you want and nobody ever finds you. Travis parked and we climbed down into a little wash that snakes past the landfill.

Somebody had hollowed out a little cave in the side of the wash and set a piece of old carpet on the sand. We crawled in and hunkered down. Liana pulled out her pipe. "So, Jenn," Travis said, "how's the new job?"

"Pretty cool," I said. "First off, all I have to do is take supper trays in to people and talk with them for a few minutes. Some of them are pretty weird, but nobody's mean. I don't really have a boss. It's mostly aides on in the evening and all they want to do is get their jobs done and hang out at the nurses' station and bitch."

"Awesome," Travis said. Liana handed me the lit pipe and I sucked in a good hit. You can't smoke but one hit of this dope. It would rip out your brain. Travis' brother has a little greenhouse in his back bedroom and grows some deadly weed. We're too young for medical marijuana so it's a good thing Trav and his brother are pals.

I passed the pipe on. "But, what's the most amazing thing of all is that there's an old hippie just got brought in to live there. His name's Red Billy. Guess why, Trav."

"He's a socialist? Fuck that." Travis' dad hates the president and anybody else he thinks isn't a patriot. He's always going on about libtards and socialists and reds and how if they want his gun, etc. etc. Sometimes Travis hates socialists and sometimes he hates his dad.

"Duh," I said. "No way. He's got this long gray braid down his back. So when he told me his name was Red Billy, I was like, 'Huh?' and he said that his hair used to be all goldy red like Robert Plant and then he asked me if I knew who Robert Plant was and I was like, 'Of course,' and then—"

"Whoa," Liana said, "you're getting all a thousand miles an hour like you do. Slow down. I do not know why I smoke with you. You might as well as be a tweaker."

I giggled. Trav giggled. Liana glared at us. "Come on, Jenn, take a deep breath. So the guy is called Red Billy because he once had red hair which he doesn't anymore because he's old but he likes Led Zep?"

"Excuse me," I said. "Now who's tweakin'?"

Liana whacked my arm. "Okay, smart-ass, but you gotta watch out for one thing."

"What?"

"What if he's one of those dirty old men?" she said.

For a second I felt a little sick. Then I thought about how Red Billy hadn't checked out my boobs, which I have some pretty terrific ones, and how his eyes were so gentle and I felt better. "No way, Liana," I said. "No freakin' way."

We decided to climb out of the wash and lie down and watch the stars. There was an old fallen-down Joshua tree that had a branch sticking up that looked like a big gray Buddha. We threw our coats on the sand near it and lay down next to each other. For all the time we lay there looking up into the shiny black sky, the stars wheeling over us, orange flares bursting up from the Marine Base near TwentyNine Palms, I didn't think about my dad once—until I realized I hadn't been thinking about him.

Red Billy wasn't in his room when I went to work the next day. I checked at the nurses' station. "He's in Activities Therapy," one of the nurses said. "But, they need you in the kitchen. The prep gal didn't show up and somebody needs to get the trays ready for dinner."

It took me a while to get the trays set up with napkins and silverware. The whole time, the cook, a scrawny Mexican with only one front tooth, muttered to himself in Spanish. I knew a little Spanish, so I figured out he was calling the missing prep gal's mother a whore and a miscarriage. I finished up and went looking for Red Billy. He sat at a long table with five old ladies playing bingo. As soon as he saw me, he waved me over. "I need to go to that appointment with the social worker right now?" he said.

"Yeah, I'm supposed to bring you to the office to sign papers." The activities therapist fake smiled and called out, "G23." She checked off Red Billy's attendance slip. "You run along with your little friend, Mr. Guidry. You were supposed to be here till five, you know, but I'll excuse this once."

I wheeled Billy into the hall. "You're slick," he said. "I thought I'd died and gone to hell and was there for eternity. And the old gal next to me kept farting like a dray horse."

I didn't know what a dray horse was, but I laughed. "Where do you want to go?"

"How about the so-called patio?" he said. "I need a smoke."

I wheeled him to one of the tables on the little concrete slab. A torn chicken wire fence closed in the patio. Somebody had once woven red and green plastic tape through it. "This is right cheery," Billy said. He pulled out his makings and rolled us both a cigarette.

There was nobody in the Vons parking lot except a gang of scraggly black birds. "I love those guys," Billy said. "They're cowbirds. I almost called myself Cowbird. Want to know why?"

"Sure," I said.

"Well, first off," he said, "they love the road. Second, they always get by. Third, they leave their eggs in other birds' nests to raise."

We were quiet for a while. One of the cowbirds figured out how to tug on the edge of a garbage bag in the Vons dumpster and the birds chowed down madly.

"So," I said, "do you have kids?"

Billy winked. "None to speak of." He must have seen something in my face because he said, "Hang on. I didn't really mean that. I've got a couple sons and daughter. They're all grown now. My exes pretty much raised them. I don't know where the boys are, but me and my daughter talk now and then. I used to send her postcards from wherever I was, but she couldn't write back because I was always moving." He looked away. "Dang, look at those birds. It's party hardy time."

Right then, I almost told him about my dad, but he shook his head and said, "Man, I miss the bad old days." So all I said was,

"So you were a real biker?"

"As real as you can get," he said. "There was one time back in the early Seventies, me and my buddies decided to take off from Barstow and head for Chicago with no money and full tanks of gas and see what happened. Bluehorse, this squinchy little Indian with one eye who ran with us came up with the idea. He was always trying to sell us Jesus and he figured if we made it to Chicago, it was proof Jesus was real."

"What happened?"

"What do you think?"

In fact, what he'd said about Bluehorse had made me think about my dad dying and the stupid Jesus shit people said to me at the funeral. "I think you all became atheists."

"Whoa, missy," Billy said, "you're too young to be so cynical. What happened was we made it to Kingman, Arizona. We was running on fumes. One of the brothers was a big tall handsome guy with steel blue eyes. He called himself Odin. He went into an old trading post and when he came out, he had a sassy lady in tow. She tossed him the keys to her trailer which was behind the post and said, 'There's beer and hamburger meat in the fridge. I get off work in an hour. You boys fire up the grill and I'll meet you there.'"

"No way," I said.

"For sure," Billy said. "It was different in those days. The lady and us partied till morning. She gave us fifty dollars for gas and we headed for Flagstaff. A couple Navajo guys saw Bluehorse, yelled, 'Hey, bro,' and pointed us to the Sunshine Rescue Mission. We ate and got preached at. Bluehorse fell in love with a cute little volunteer with a Jesus is My Co-Pilot t-shirt. A hippie kid gave us a couple joints and twenty bucks and we were back on the road again.

"See, back then the real people recognized each other. We knew we were strays. Then, that frickin' coke came into the scene and it was all high commerce."

"Did you make it to Chicago?" I said.

"We did. It was road people watching our backs all the

way. When we got to Shakeytown, Odin and a couple of us sold a few ounces we had stashed for emergencies and we rode the long way back, through all this tall grass prairie that was one of the most beautiful sights I've ever seen. Sunset would turn that grass to pure copper."

"Did it make you believe in Jesus?" I said.

"Shoot, I already did. I've always figured he was a road stray. His stories just got cleaned up when somebody figured out how to make money off of him." Billy reached into his jeans pocket and pulled out a little package of crackers. "Toss those over the fence for me, will you? We cowbirds got to take care of each other."

I threw the crackers as far as I could. The Activities Director stepped out onto the patio. "Miss, miss," she said. "Don't do that. You'll just attract rats." She took hold of the back of Billy's wheelchair. "Time for dinner," she said. "You and your friend can talk more tomorrow."

Billy looked straight ahead, deadpan. "Thanks for the talk, missy. I hope to see you tomorrow."

"You bet," I said.

"That's enough chat, people," the Activities Director said. "Mr. Guidry, you don't want your din din to get cold."

I was walking home from work when a text from Liana came in. Talk soon. I called her. She picked up on the first ring. "Jenn, we need to talk. As soon as possible."

"I've gotta go home. It's my turn to cook dinner," I said. "Meet me at the house."

Stace and Chris were playing on their phones when I came in. "Mom called," Chris said. "You're supposed to figure out which of the vegetables have been in the fridge the longest and cook them."

Stace giggled. "Ketchup. Right? That's been in the longest plus it's a vegetable. Right, Chris?"

He nodded.

"So, we can have hamburgers because ketchup goes with hamburgers and that's a balanced meal," Stace said. "That's fair, Jenn."

Just then, Liana came through the back door. She has family privileges and doesn't have to knock. Same with Travis. "You want me to help?" Liana said. "What are you making?"

"I can help," Stace said. "I can get the ketchup out."

"Get, Stace," I said. "You too, Chris. And no spying. Go outside and ride your bikes. You know the rules."

Stacy slouched out the back door. Chris slammed his phone down on the table. "You are so not the boss of me," he said.

I put the phone in my pocket. "I so am."

He slouched out the back door. "I hate it here."

I checked the veggie drawer. The green beans were limp and the cauliflower had a few little dark spots on it. I tossed the bag of beans to Liana and unwrapped the cauliflower. "So what's the big deal?" I said. "Did you get pregnant or something?"

Liana set the beans on the counter and flipped me off. "No, Jenn. It's not anything like that. I want to meet Red Billy. Soon. I want to check him out and make sure he's not some old pervo."

"He's not. Why do you keep bugging me about this?"

"I don't know. It just freaks me out. It's not like anything weird ever happened to me or anything. It's just that old guys are so weird. You know like those geezer hipsters that hang out at the hippie café and try to flirt with the waitresses. They are so pathetic. Plus they are really ugly."

"Yeah," I said, "but Billy's not like that. He's got like a calm in him and he's old, but he's not ugly. I'd love for you to meet him. Trav too. Why don't you guys come visit tomorrow? There's hardly ever any visitors, so the staff won't give a care."

Trav and Liana picked me up after school. Trav had bought himself a classic Morongo Basin beater, a 1999 Malibu that was so rusted out you could see air through the fenders. He figured some greenhorn easterner had driven it west till it gave out and died. Cars don't rust out here. The tires melt. You can see old wrecks looking like they had melted down into the sand everywhere outside of Twentynine Palms and J Tree.

"I brought a little treat for this guy and us," Trav said. "Check out the glove compartment." It was easy to do that because the door was hanging by one hinge. Liana poked around and came up with a plastic bag with three fat brownies in it. I sniffed them.

"I don't know, Trav," I said. "There's this nosy activities Nazi lady who checks up on Billy every five minutes."

Trav pulled his dad's Make War, Not Love hat further down over his eyes. "You let me worry about that. It's all gonna be good."

"Okay," I said, though I remembered the way the last three times Trav's all-gonna-be-good had played out. The best had resulted in me and Liana grounded for a week with no texting privileges. "Billy's room is 136."

I pointed Trav and Liana toward Billy's room and checked in with the aides to see if there was anything urgent on my to do list. There were three newbies coming in and three silk flower deliveries. As I walked toward the first room, I heard giggles coming from behind Red Billy's closed door.

I cop-knocked. The giggles stopped. "Just a sec," Billy said. I waited and Liana opened the door.

"These are good people," Billy said.

"We are," Liana said. "Okay, you win Jenn, so is he."

"Told you so," I said. "I've got to go, you guys. I'll check in later."

I finished up the newbie room preps and was headed back to Billy's room when the Activities Nazi called to me. "Jenn, Ms. Lane said you could help me out for a few hours. I'll need Rooms 201 through 220 and 106 to 118 brought down for bingo. And I'd like you to call the numbers. Mrs. Cray isn't feeling well and I don't really trust anybody else to do it."

I didn't say what I was thinking, which was, "Most of them could call the numbers. You treat these people like they're little kids." I just said, "136 has company, but I'll check on everybody else and see who wants to come."

The Activities Nazi smiled her dead frog smile. "Well, I'm afraid most of them will have to come whether they want to or not. It's these activities that keep their brains working."

I wondered what kept her heart working. I was learning so much about psychology working at Hopecare, more than I could ever have learned in college or anywhere. I nodded. "I'll bring everybody I can."

By the time I'd rounded up the twelve folks who wanted to take a chance on winning a pen or an extra dessert or an old Reader's Digest and we'd endured an hour of B-6 and O-12, six of the residents were asleep and I wanted nothing more than a smoke. I wheeled and walked everybody back. Mrs. Wilkins was the last one. She's not really Mrs. anymore since her husband died, which is how she came to the home. She always dresses up for meals and activities. And her hair is in a modern cut. I helped her into the chair by the window. She looked up. Her eyes were wet.

"Mrs. Wilkins?" I said. "What's wrong? Can I help?"

I'm not really supposed to get too involved with the residents. My supervisor says that most of them have detached from the real world and too much closeness upsets them. It's probably really risky for me to hang out with Billy, so I always have a cover story.

Mrs. Wilkins took a note out of her dress pocket. "I don't think you can," she said, "but I need to tell somebody." She handed me the note. "Jennifer, please read it."

"My dear Maddy Wilkins," the note said. "I so enjoy those times when we eat dinner together and talk. With your permission, I shall endeavor to make those times happen more often. Sincerely—

I do not write that lightly—Roger Abbott."

I handed the note back to her. She held it carefully. "You see, don't you?" she said.

"I'm not sure."

"I have to decline his offer. Someone is bound to notice and there will be a great fuss made about Roger Abbott and myself. We will be that cute little old couple." She began to tear the note up.

"Wait," I said.

"No, child, it's best this way. I couldn't bear to be made into a ridiculous joke about two old people finding affection. I couldn't bear to be made to wear a crown when we are forced to go to the weekly dances. Can't you just hear that dreadful activities woman, 'And lets have a round of applause for the Homecare King and Queen of the Week.'"

She tore the note into tiny pieces and handed them to me. "Keep them safe," she said. "It will be our little secret."

"I promise," I said.

"I'll rest for a while now," Mrs. Wilkins said. "Thank you."

I walked down the hall and knocked on Billy's door. It took him a couple minutes to open it. Liana and Trav were gone and Billy was grinning even more than good dope can make happen.

"Jenn," he said. "You and your friends just made my day. That Travis kid had me listen to a bunch of tunes. He said they were old school but they sure sounded modern to me. That band, Rage Against the Machine? I couldn't understand a word they sang, but they sounded for real. I'm not too sure about My Chemical Romance, but Jenn, it doesn't really matter. You three give me hope for the future."

"Awesome," I said. "I need to talk to you for a minute."

"Anytime," he said.

I held out the note scraps. "This has to be a secret, right?"

"Sworn," Billy said.

I told him what the note said and what Mrs. Wilkins had

said. He bowed his head. "This fuckin' place." He handed me back the scraps.

"I'm going to keep them safe," I said.

"Of course you are," he said. "You get it, right? There is nothing cute about two people falling in love—not if they're two years old or a hundred and two. We're like animals in a zoo to these people. For chrissakes, all we are is them forty or fifty years down the road. I sure hope that instant karma stuff is real."

I knew that very minute what I needed to do next. Billy and I talked till I heard Ms. Lane calling me from the front desk. "I gotta go," I said.

"That's okay," he said. "You and your gang might not be here tonight," he said, "but I've sure got some righteous memories of today to keep me company."

I walked home that evening. The mad heat of the day had faded into a few sweet warm breezes. I could hear the thump thump of hip hop in some white boy homey's car. There was a sliver of moon overhead, a few clouds drifting over it and in those twenty minutes I loved where I live more than I ever had.

I imagined what I was going to do and the way Billy would smile when he figured out what was happening. It was when he'd said "old school" that I'd remembered that my dad had once had an old-fashioned Walkman, headphones, and a couple boxes of old tapes. I wasn't sure what was on the tapes, but I had a hunch.

The kids and I started making tacos for dinner. I was slicing lettuce when my mom came in the back door. I waited till we were at the table eating to ask her about the tapes.

"I'm not sure," she said. "Start in the garage. That old backpack might be the place. It's up on top of the trunks. Take all of it if you want. I'd eventually have to do something with it." She turned away. I started to say something, but I knew she didn't like to have us kids see her upset.

It was twilight by the time I walked into the garage. The trunks were stacked in a corner with the backpack on top. I climbed on the stepladder and hauled it down. It was lighter than I expected.

I took it outside to the backyard picnic table. My heart started beating fast. It was the closest I'd felt to my dad since he'd died. "Dad," I said, "I know that if you'd had time you would have left this to me. You're going to love what comes next."

I opened the backpack. The Walkman was on top, wrapped in a black paisley bandana. I carefully lifted it out, dug down and found a bunch of bootleg tapes: The Clash, Sex Pistols, Ian Dury, The Animals, The Who, Led Zep and somebody named Roky Erickson. I'd never heard of the guy, but later when I was in my room and had put in fresh batteries and listened to his song, "If You Have Ghosts," I thought how perfect it was for my dad now. But, right that moment, in the garage oven, with sunset burning in the dust that had drifted up, all I cared about was what was on the Zep tape.

I hadn't hardly cried about my dad. But when I read his faded writing on the tape and saw "Kashmir," I just doubled up over the backpack and cried till my chest ached. "Zep lives, Dad," I said.

I took the pack to my room, put in a candle and my lighter, stashed the pack under my bed and tried to sleep. I wanted to sneak out, run over to the home and tap on Billy's window. Every now and then, I reached down and checked to make sure the pack was still under the bed. Who knows what I thought would happen to it? I hadn't believed in the under-the-bed monster for a long time. It took me a while to figure out that I felt just like a little kid—the kind of kid who knew the bed monster was waiting for her to go to sleep—and that kid, i.e. me, was waiting for Xmas Eve.

I must have fallen asleep because next thing I knew Stacy pounded on my door and yelled, "Pancakes." Mom doesn't have to work on Saturdays, so she always makes pancakes for us. I didn't bother to shower, just pulled on my jeans and my dad's Pink Floyd t-shirt and went into the kitchen.

"You're not working today?" Mom said. She slid a stack of corn cakes on my plate. "I could use you to watch the kids while I get the shopping done."

"I'm not working," I said. "But I need to go over to see one of the residents for a little while."

"We'll figure it out," she said. "Eat your pancakes before they get cold." She dropped about a ton of butter on my cakes. I normally love pancakes more than any other food item, but I was so excited about my project that I could only eat about half the stack.

"Are you okay?" Mom said.

"I'm great. I'll explain later. Gotta run."

Richie, the cute aide, waved at me when I came in. "You are looking delicious," he said. "I thought you were off today."

"I'm a VV," I said. The Activities Nazi had made up the corny name: VV for Visiting Volunteer.

"Man, that chick is lame," Richie said. "She got on my ass a few days ago 'cause Mr. Wobbles didn't want to go to bingo."

"We're not supposed to call him Mr. Wobbles," I said, but I was cracking up. Mr. Wobbles was actually a really cool not-very-old guy who loved watching horse racing on the tube and had Parkinson's.

"Goody two-shoes," Richie said. "You high or something?"

The only reason we could get away with our conversation was because Hopecare was always short-staffed on Saturdays. The big bosses knew visitors never came—if at all—till Sunday. So the big bosses cut corners where they could.

"I wish," I said.

Somebody buzzed the nursing station. Richie sighed, hauled himself out of his chair and headed for the elevator.

Billy wasn't in his room. I checked the Activities Room.

Three ladies played bingo while a fourth ran her finger back and forth across her card. Mrs. Wilkins sat back from the bingo table, reading. She looked up and smiled. The Activities Nazi was calling out the numbers. "Are you looking for Mr. Guidry?"

"Yeah."

"He's on the patio—smoking again. It would be appropriate if you could talk him into coming in for a game or two."

"Actually, I'm not on duty today," I said.

"Have you registered as a VV?" the AN said. "O-29. G-5."

"There's nobody at the front desk," I said. "I'll do it when I leave."

Billy sat next to the fence, tossing crumbs to the cowbirds. "Care for a brownie?" he said. "I'm feeding my friends, but hell, they're feeling good already."

I took a big bite out of the brownie. "Mmmm," I said, "cashews."

"Good and good for you," Billy said. "What's going on, my little sister?"

"I've got something for you," I said. "But I want to give it to you in private."

Billy undid the wheelchair brakes and rolled toward me. "Give me a push. I seem to be a little hazy on directions right now."

I wheeled him into his room and pulled the blinds. He shoved the last of the brownies under the bed.

"Okay," I said. "Close your eyes."

"Done," he said. "Shooooeeee, I got all these neon squiggles line-dancing in my eyes."

I set the candle on the dresser, lit it and put the Walkman headphones over his ears.

"Get ready." I hit Play and set the Walkman on the arm of his chair.

Billy didn't move for a little while. Then, he bowed his head and whispered, "And my eyes fill with sand, as I scan this wasted land trying to find, trying to find where I've been."

He slipped off the headphones and looked up. Tears

shone in the candlelight. I reached out and took his hands in mine. "Goddamn it," he said. "*Kashmir*. Damn you girl. You couldn't have brought me a better present. You brought me a time machine."

"It was my dad's," I said.

"Was?"

I nodded. "He died. A little bit ago."

Red Billy turned his hands so he was holding mine. I was trying hard not to cry, but finally the lump in my throat got so big, I just gave up. Billy gently ran his thumb over the back of my hand. It had been such a long time since anybody had touched me like that, simple, nothing expected. I cried till I got the hiccups. Billy and I laughed.

"You can stop the tape now," Billy said. "And if you wouldn't mind, I'd kinda like to be alone for a while." He let go of my hands and grinned. "We wouldn't want the Activities Nazi walking in on us, what with me being such a manly stud and all."

I kissed him on the forehead. "About the present?" he said. "It isn't just Led Zep."

"I know," I said and walked to the door. He threw me a peace sign. I caught it.

"I'll see you tomorrow," I said.

SIGN

My mom calls right before Xmas. "Your Dad's on the dining room table," she says brightly. It's nearly dawn, the Arizona mountain sky ice-gray. I stand in my freezing cabin staring down at the cold wood stove. "She's nuts again," I think, "or he's resurrected through pure Kraut stubbornness."

The last time I saw my folks was over a year ago. She was whacked-out from a reaction to her doc's prescribing mistake. My dad was three-quarters dead and not admitting it. Six months later, he went all the way.

"Mom," I say firmly, "what are you telling me?"

"Don't use that mental health professional tone with me," she says. "I'm fine." We both know I have cause for alarm. From the time I was five till I was forty-six, she was steam-rollered by bi-polar psychosis. When she was seventy, she had two Near Death Experiences in a row and was no longer bi-polar. Our family never does things in moderation.

"My dead dad's on the dining room table," I say. "That doesn't sound quite right to me."

"In a gray box," she says. "He's heavier than I thought he would be."

"Oh shit."

"Honey," she says, "that's exactly what I said."

We start to laugh. She catches herself. "Do you believe it's been seven months?" she says. "Shouldn't I be crying?"

"No. Not if you're not." I set newspaper on last night's coals and blow on the embers. The paper catches, perfect blue flames. First tiny miracle of the day, if you don't count my dead dad on the dining room table.

"What the hell are you doing?" Mom asks. She discovered cussing as an anti-depressant just after the second NDE.

"Making my fire," I say. "It's not even dawn here."

"Oh, my little Calamity Jane," she says sweetly. "Out there on the frontier."

"That attitude," I say, "is what turns grown daughters into pioneers twenty-two-hundred miles from their beloved mothers."

She sucks in her breath. It's not shock or outrage, just the umpteenth cigarette of her day. I see her tough little face, her dark glasses perched on her nose at nine a.m. Having her as a mother is like having been born to Lenny Bruce.

"So," I say, "are you going to come see me? You going to drag his ash out here?"

"That's awful," she says gleefully and, as always, sidesteps the invitation. "But I love you. I'll save some ashes. Let me know if you want any."

We say miss you and good-bye. I add a chunk of juniper to the fire and as I feel the first steady pulse of heat, I wonder if I am ever going to cry.

By April, Mom finally gets Dad where she wants him. "He's out in the tomatoes. He'd like that. He always had to be useful."

"Sounds eee-vironmental. He would have hated that." There had been endless dinner table conversations in years past about goddamn tree-huggers. I tuck the phone between my chin and shoulder so I can do the dishes. We're in for a good solid hour—and as Dad taught me, Idle hands are the devil's playmates. "I've got some tomatoes starting," I say. "The ones last year cost me about eight bucks a tomato after I bought all the fancy stuff I had to have to grow vegetables here."

"I miss your father," she says. "Easter was tough."

I say nothing, let the silence be a little solace. She shifts to how she still can't stand Coltrane and she heard a great Dinah Washington hour on NPR. She tells me she's worried about my brother. I'm her first call of the week and in her second, she'll tell my brother she's worried about me. I don't reassure her. She likes it better that way. Mom devotes the next forty-five minutes to telling me how my bro's consulting job is not a real job and how his second wife is not his real wife. She tells me she's sending me homemade peanut butter eggs left from Easter.

"Well, sweetie," she says, "Will Moyle's jazz hour is on in ten minutes. I need to go. I love you to pieces."

"Me too," I say, "not Will Moyle, but love. You know. Whatever."

"My daughter, the writer," she says, hangs up and calls me back a few seconds later. "I forgot to tell you," she says. "I'm putting some of your dad's ashes in with the Easter eggs."

"Hoo boy," I say.

"Love you," she says and hangs up.

I make one of my infinite cups of coffee and stand at the big southern window. Dad is in the tomatoes in Upstate New York. Mine are tiny sprouts on this sun-drenched sill. I moved twenty-two-hundred miles southwest to a place with exactly the same growing season as home. I poke the potting soil around the tomatoes' roots.

"You'd be proud of me, Dad," I say. "My tomatoes are in, you're dead a year and I haven't shed a tear." I pull my rocker out to the back deck. Spring is fat and sassy in the air. I look up at the high desert blue blazing above me. "You should've come out, Dad," I say and I think of the last time I saw him.

I had picked up the phone on All Souls' Day. My mom's voice was weird. I hadn't heard that undercurrent of fear since before she had died on the operating table and come back—down the brilliant green tunnel, her long-dead mother and beloved older sister waving, a beautiful golden mist beckoning—"Imagine the greatest love you ever felt and multiply it by infinity."—then a voice saying, "Not yet, Lillie." And Mom was back, occupying a body stitched and mending, a spirit finally whole.

"Well, honey," she said this time, "sit tight. I've got some hard news."

"I'm sitting."

"They tell us your dad has leukemia."

"Whoa." The Rock. Mr. It's In Your Imagination. Mr. Mind Over Matter with matter going crazy in his blood.

We decided I'd head home. There would be a Thanksgiving clan gathering, my brother and his wife, my kids, my kid's kid and Mom and Dad. Huge meal, three desserts, my brother making me laugh so hard I have to leave the table, my mom and I soul-sisters after all the years and my dad, alchemized by the chaos in his blood into the warm respectful guy I'd always known he could be.

For the time it took to call Amtrak, buy tickets and move through the days till the bright mountain morning I climbed on the train, I felt optimistic. I would go back. There would be love. The silence between my dad and me would be broken.

As though no more than a day had passed, it was a lilac dusk in early December, the Southwest Chief taking me home from Thanksgiving, Chicago glittering behind us. I sat in the lounge car listening to an old tape on my headphones and staring out at the tracks. Salt-N-Pepa were reminding me that "Ain't Nuthin' But a She Thing," and then there was Bruce Springsteen with a freight train running through the middle of his head. I felt really guilty because I was hugely happy, possibly not able to get happier and then Buddy Guy's "Messin' with the Kid" came on and I was happier.

We rolled into a little Illinois town. The broken buildings were rose-gray and shadowed, snow glittering on the frames of their splintered windows. There was the No Holds Bar and a big gorgeous woman with snow on her shoulders, waving at the train. A man lumbered up beside her, one of those big guys who when they hitch up their pants, which they do a lot because their ursine butts are narrow and their bellies big, take hold of the waist of their pants with their finger tips and keep their great paws bunched. The man wore a purple sweater and the pants he hitched up were blue and floppy.

I imagined the two of them in bed. I imagined they would be generous and greedy, lick honey off each other and growl. Like me and my guy Bear, who I suddenly missed fiercely. I wondered if I should be thinking about my dying dad and was glad I wasn't.

I took off my headphones and turned away from the window. A slick-haired scrawny guy and a skinny girl were in the next seat over. The guy jittered and when he laughed, you'd think you wouldn't want to rile him. The girl was a skinny blond who was maybe twelve trying to be sexy. He told her that his favorite author was Poe. She'd never heard of him.

"Nevermore," the guy said.

"Oh yeah," she said, "our teacher read us that. Cool. Totally."

She flipped her silvery hair away from her face. The guy rested his arm along the top of her seat. She squirmed a little, caught me looking and moved away from the guy's arm. I smiled. She looked down and let her hair fall so I couldn't see her face.

I was fifty-six and in that instant, it could have been yesterday that I was locked in Woolworth's Five and Dime ladies room, frantically scrubbing off lipstick, wiping away mascara, yanking my hair into a bun and taking off the wide elastic belt that pulled my waist in so my thirteen-year-old breasts actually looked like breasts. It was 1953. I'd gone downtown alone, tight skirt, ballet slippers, blouse unbuttoned to the third button, hair hanging loose and shining, that belt giving me tits and hips and something that had caused a man, a grown-up man maybe nineteen or twenty, to ask me if I wanted a Coke.

I remembered stammering, turning so fast I knocked over an eye-shadow display and escaping to the ladies room. I remembered the terrifying sense of power, and the spooky joy. I told my mom about it, but not my dad. The one dating tip he ever gave me was that no guy would want to sleep with a woman who had shaving stubble on her legs.

When I looked up from the memory, the pre-teen queen was gone. Poe had trapped somebody else. We were losing light, the bars and crumbling buildings and people heading home from work fading into shadows. I saw a yellow-lit window and had all the usual sweet achy thoughts travelers have about home—not the old one I had just left, the iced-out city, the sullen Great Lake, but the real one that lay a day and a half, cobalt mountain ranges and huge pure sky ahead.

I put my feet up on the window rail. I was alone—and glad of it. It's hard for me to not talk to people and I suspected I might start talking about just one thing, the one thing I didn't know how to talk about.

Since I had gotten the "Sit down, honey" phone call from my mom, I'd read too much self-help advice. All that *there are phases of dying, let the feelings come, death is another beautiful passage in life*, which might have been helpful if I'd had any feelings or if I believed that there was anything beautiful about any of it. It was my mom who had glided down that dazzling green tunnel, not me.

I was getting sick of the great American way of everything being a VALUABLE GROWTH EXPERIENCE. If one more person told me I needed to learn to let go, I would puke. What I was wondering, watching yellow windows flash by that could be in kitchens or used car dealerships or clinics was: How the hell do you let go of something you barely had?

I kept thinking of the pre-teen queen and remembering an unsettling ten minutes I once spent with my dad. I was fifteen. I was baby-sitting my brother, sneaking cigarettes on the front porch, playing music my parents hated, sipping peppermint schnapps and watering the bottle, when suddenly Dad pulled into the driveway. I shut off the record player, turned on the TV and shoved half a pack of gum in my mouth.

My dad barely looked at me. He went straight to his desk and fumbled around in a drawer.

"What are you looking for?" I asked.

He held something out to me. It was a joke miniature jock-strap and while I watched, he took two pecans from the nut bowl on the coffee table and dropped them into the pouch. If those had been the days of "Beam me up, Scotty," I would have gone.

I looked at him, then away. "It's a grown-up joke," he said and giggled. I knew then without a doubt, that my father had two pecans of his own and what went with them. I felt ten billion miles of space move in between us. He looked at me. The only real light in the room was the black and white TV. For an instant, in the thin blue glow, I couldn't see the features of his face.

"Oh," I said.

He dropped the thing in his pocket. "Guess you're growing up. But don't stay up too late." And he was gone out the door.

I wandered back to my seat. I figured I'd read till I was sleepy enough to pass out, which if you're riding coach and you can't drink anymore, is what you have to do in order to sleep at all. Couch seats were designed by an engineering De Sade. At first you think they're great, then after a hundred miles, you begin to realize that there is no way to get comfortable, especially if your seat-mate is a stranger and about six foot three. Which, it turned out, he was.

"Hi," he said, "I'm Jerry DuBeau. I asked the conductor to put me here."

He was skinny, late-fifties, sparse mustache, thinning ginger hair. He wore a double-knit sportcoat, black Goodwill sneakers and a ball cap that told me to Expect a Miracle. He settled an old duffle in the rack and sat down.

I considered pretending I hadn't heard him, but I've got this open face that everybody can read, so I said, "Why?" He sure didn't turn my crank and I had Bear, difficult but large and rewarding in at least one level in my life, so I didn't really care how Jerry DuBeau answered. He leaned down and picked up my pack.

"This," he said. He touched a Viet Nam vet pin that Bear had given me. "I'm a Viet Nam era vet myself. I wasn't there, but I know a lot of those guys."

"My sweetheart Bear was there in '69-70," I said. "I Corps. Special Forces medic. I think we never welcomed those guys back, not really. That's why the pin. Bear thinks I make too big a deal out of it."

There I went. I never know how starved for talk I am till some innocent listener appears. "Where you from?" I asked.

"Prescott," he said. "I live in a group home near the VA hospital. I've got that PTSD. Germany, 1972. Ammo went off by accident near me. I lost my hearing for a while, then something happened like a long black-out maybe. Doc thinks I might be schizophrenic more or less. He gives me medicine. I have to live pretty calm."

I felt the old ten billion miles of space move in between me and Jerry DuBeau. I had spent most of my young womanhood, after a few illegal chemicals, debating with myself whether I needed to be put away. Graduate school was the worst. In my Abnormal Psych class, which I had taken so I could understand my mom, I had every certifiable syndrome in the DSM. Major psychosis wasn't catching, but why take a chance.

I made myself sit tight. "I know that VA place," I said. "I was going to teach writing for the Nam vets. The social worker forgot our appointment to discuss it five times and I gave up."

Jerry nodded. "They've got too much to do," he said quietly. "It can get pretty confusing for the staff."

"So where you live is part of the hospital?"

"Yeah, I'm lucky. Because of my disability, I get fourteen hundred dollars a month, so I don't have to work and I live for free. I volunteer some, just talk with the guys, maybe just listen."

"Bear and me," I said, "we talked about adopting one of those vets, taking him out for drives, camping, maybe get on a river, but it never happened. Bear is not the most outgoing guy."

"He might not want to be reminded of things," Jerry said. "Those guys saw too much. What's so amazing to me is that some of them say it was the best time they ever had. Boy, oh boy."

I'd heard Bear say exactly that, but then again, he'd say in the same breath that he has his arms, legs, brain and his Big Boy, so it turned out Numbah One for him. I didn't tell Jerry DuBeau that. I was starting to feel antsy. We were roughly two hundred miles outside of Chicago and I didn't know if I wanted an 1800-mile friendship with anybody, much less somebody who might be meter on, taxi stalled—no matter how nice he was.

I took a book out of my pack. "Well," I said, "good meeting you. I'm going to read for a while. Maybe we can talk more later."

"Sure," he said. "I'm going back to the lounge, hunt up some conversation. I just wanted to say Hi."

"I'm Beth," I said. "Gant. Catch you later."

He fumbled in his bag, pulled out a wallet and left. I realized I'd been semi-holding my breath. I always breathe easier after I say good-bye. Welcome to the Woman of the Nineties. Yeah, that's me, don't need anybody, when all I'd wanted for Thanksgiving was this: my dad would say, "Honey, I know I'm going to die and I want us to sit down right now and have a good long talk about how we love each other and really say 'good-bye.'" I would have hated it and loved it even more.

I had a hunch that one of my last memories of my dad would be him standing at the foot of my slightly demented mom's hospital bed. He looked like a grumpy skeleton. He'd lost most of his hair to chemo and he was turning the ashy gray cancer patients do. His first words to me were, "Tell you mother to snap out of this nonsense. She'll listen to you. You're both nuts."

"I love you, Dad," I had said. I wanted to grab his shoulder, shake the gray sack of bones he was becoming and say, "You're dying. You know that. So do I. Please. Please. Can we just talk a little like human beings?" All I did was reach out. He held me a second in an A-frame hug.

"Oh shit, Dad," I said.

"Well," he said, "gotta beat the traffic." He was out the door. I watched him shuffle down the hall, bow-legged and all business. I suspected even then, that my last sight of my dad would be him and the seat of his baggy gray pants disappearing down the gray hallway, silent movie, fade to gray.

I'd gone back in the room and grinned at my mom.

"Hey you," I said, "snap out of this nonsense."

She'd laughed. "He won't admit it was the friggin' stomach medicine the friggin' doctor gave me. Your father actually told me that I did it on purpose to get all the attention now that it's his turn to be the patient."

I sat on the bed and took her hand. "The Holy Father Church," I said. "If they get you before the age of seven, they've got you all your life—blame, blame, blame, mea fuckin' culpa."

"Amen," she said, "and of course the priest was too busy to come see your dad right after we got the bad news about his leukemia. They sent some auxiliary ladies in nice hats who told him they would offer up Novenas."

My youngest kid, Max, came in and the three of us held each other, Max's long skinny self bending over me, me holding my mom in my arms.

"Oh shit," my mom said, "this is a shitting mess. At least I've got you."

I turned on the overhead light and looked out the window. The reflection of my face seemed to float between me and the spangled dark. I fluffed out my hair and pretended I was twenty. And remembered the time my dad almost ran away to be a hippie.

It had been 1961. My hair was crazy wild and my dad was putting me on the train to San Francisco. He told me he wished he could go too. He said if he was ten years younger, he'd try that pot himself. "Don't worry about your mother," he said and as I stepped onto the train, he tucked a bill in my hand. "Be mellow," he said. "That's how you say it, right?"

I was in Buffalo by the time I stopped crying, unclenched my hand and looked. The bill was a fifty. That was a fortune in those days.

"Beth." Jerry stood politely in the aisle. I rubbed my eyes, faking sleepy. I didn't want to talk. He held out one of those doll-sized Amtrak blankets. "I thought you might be cold," he said. "I'm going to play poker."

I took the blanket and snuggled down. I felt safe for the first time in years. I was warm. Some state was zooming by in the dark. I didn't have to pretend I was a grown-up. I didn't have to worry about whether Bear wanted me, didn't want me, would wake up hung-over and horny, or hung-over and untouchable.

"Thanks, Jerry," I whispered and next thing I knew it was morning, Jerry snored next to me and I was still wrapped in the blanket, achy in every joint, but warm. I eased myself out. Jerry flopped over into my space. I covered him with the blanket and headed toward the lounge car.

My mom might have had a preview of paradise, but I know what heaven is. You sit with your feet up on the window sill of a train heading out of a silver Kansas morning, toward Colorado, then down into New Mexico noon where there will be charred volcanic boulders, a little canyon holding a silken thread of black water, pale olive chamisa and the tracks of whatever comes down through the chamisa to the river to drink. You can hardly wait for that beauty and you know it's coming and you tell yourself to slow down.

I had two cups of Amtrak coffee lined up on the window sill next to my feet. I sipped on another and I didn't need Buddy Guy, Bear or my dad's blessing to feel hugely happy. Later, I would go to the club car and tell the chipper bartender to nuke me a ham and cheese on rye. He'd tell me he was going to put mayo on it, pickle relish and for his special touch de jour, a few shots of Tabasco. He'd hand me the sandwich and it would be the most delicious breakfast I'd ever eaten a little west of La Junta, Colorado.

I'd had a couple hours of bliss and flat-line horizon when Jerry and the fierce blue-black of the Rockies came into view. He stood by my seat. "Like company?"

I nodded and pointed toward the far mountains.

"I love this part," he said. "When I see those mountains I know I'll make it home." He looked at my empty plate. "Ham and cheese du jour?"

"Mais oui," I said.

"That guy is great. He's invented lots of microwave gourmet treats, nuked chocolate chip cookies and English muffins with hot dog designs of daisies, faces, suns. He says they're mystical."

I decided I'd stay on the train, reach LA, get on the Coast Starlight and keep going, running the sweet edges of the land, up across the northern waters where the oceans slam black boulders, down to the green blurred southern boundaries, not afraid of anything, drinking coffee, watching the sun drop and rise, drop and rise, seeing the moon a slice of mango in a Louisiana pre-dawn, sitting sleepless by my window while the full moon's straight-shot silver burned off whatever swamp or housing project appeared for an instant and was gone. I'd eat hot dog runes and believe them. Bear would miss me. My mom would stay snapped out of it. They'd discover a cure for leukemia and when I finally stepped off the train, my dad would be there and he'd say, "Where the hell have you been? I was scared to death."

"Beth?" Jerry said. "You hungry? Brunch is on me."

"Just coffee," I said.

He came back with two Tuna Surprises. "The guy crunches up potato chips, puts them inside with chopped onion and nukes it," Jerry said. "I had him make me two. If he's going to go to all that trouble, he might as well make a good tip. I always tip twenty-five percent. My ex-wife was a waitress."

"You were married," I said.

"Yep. Six years. Then I stopped drinking and the gremlins came. The docs put me on this medication and some things sort of changed." He blushed.

I looked out the window and kept quiet. My mom had once told me that though she and my dad still loved each other, they slept in separate beds. "Things have changed, Beth," she said. "Who knows why—maybe the blood pressure pills, maybe just him getting old." I had not said anything. It was yet another fact I didn't want to know about my dad's pecans.

"Kids?" I asked.

"No," Jerry said. "I didn't want to take the chance."

Made sense to me. Schizophrenia, some smirking psych prof had lectured us, runs in the genes, so if you have schizzy clients you'd encourage them to stay in their jeans.

"Yeah," I said. "That's tricky stuff."

"You better believe it," he said. "It sets you off from everybody."

"To be honest," I said, "if you hadn't told me, I wouldn't have known you were schizophrenic. You seem perfectly normal. Whatever that is."

"Oh, not my schizophrenia," he said. "I'm talking about the deafness."

"Whose deafness?"

"My mom's and dad's. They were both deaf."

"Wait," I said. "Your mom and dad were both deaf and you weren't and they raised you, and then you temporarily lost your hearing in the army?"

"I think that's what they call that karma," he said thoughtfully.

We sat in easy silence till Trinidad, Colorado, which Jerry informed me was the sex-change capitol of the world. "We had a few of those guys in the army in Germany," he said. "This big old world of ours has surprises everywhere." The train stopped. Nobody dazzling got on. Jerry and I were sorely disappointed.

I told Jerry about my dad's big announcement a few years ago. "We were at a big family picnic. I was trying to get over my most recent romantic disaster. 'Beth,' my dad said firmly, 'your mother and I have discussed this. We want you to know that if you get involved with a woman, it's okay with us.'

'Dad,' I said, 'what brought this on?' He patted my hand. 'You don't have good luck with men.'"

"Oh my gosh," Jerry said, "what did you do?"

"I said, 'As much as I like women, Dad, there's no way I'd inflict myself on one of them.'"

Jerry laughed. "Are your folks alive?" I said.

"Rest their souls," he said, "they died a few years ago within a week of each other. I was glad. It would have been terrible for the one left behind."

"What was it like being raised by deaf folks?"

"I didn't know any different. They didn't either, really. We were on a farm way off from town, truck garden, chickens, cows, no other kids around. When they sent me off to first grade because the County said I had to go, all I could do was sign language and read. I went to first grade reading fifth grade level and hardly talking." He shook his head.

"What happened?"

"The school decided I was retarded and sent me home. My folks didn't understand, but they didn't want to make trouble, so they just kept me out a year and taught me themselves. Then there was a new teacher and she figured it out."

"And?"

"I learned to talk. It still doesn't come that natural." He looked wistfully down at his hands and moved his fingers. "These are my real voice."

"I only know the Love You sign," I said.

"It's a good one."

"Were you close to your folks?"

"I sure was." His face was pure joy.

I looked away toward the western mountains, away from the next question I knew would come.

"Your people? Are they still alive?"

"Kind of," I said. "I mean...I was just there. My mom nearly died from the wrong kind of medicine. My dad has leukemia. So. So."

"Oh my goodness," Jerry said, "I am truly sorry. That's awful. Cancer is awful."

I kept turned toward the mountains. I didn't want him to see my face. I was smiling and I didn't want to explain it. I loved what he'd said. "That's awful. Cancer is awful." No great learning experience there, no big fat spiritual opportunity.

He touched my shoulder. "Are you okay?" he said.

"No. Not really. But thank you for what you said. Thank you for not saying something hopeful."

"Why would I? Nothing's hopeful when there's a tragedy."

"No," I said, "nothing."

We went to the dining car for dinner. It's a crap shoot who you sit with. Jerry and I were in the middle of a "what you do to get by" conversation when a young LA-ish couple sat down with us. The guy was young and cute and white boy hip-hopped half to death. He snagged a gold chain under his shirt and pulled it out. A dazzling triangle in a circle hung there. "You guys friends of Bill W?" he asked.

Jerry and I shook our heads. "Just thought maybe," the guy said. "I'm Dino and this is Starr." Starr snuggled into him and told us that they had been married one week exactly and she was NA. Jerry looked puzzled.

"NA is Narcotics Anonymous," I said. I thought about how some of the Southern Californians who were colonizing Flagstaff would pour out their tragic stories without even knowing the locals' names.

"Okay," Jerry said, "I didn't do that but I don't drink anymore. Lots of the VA vets go to those meetings. They seem to really help."

"Yeah," Dino said. "But sometimes I wanna give up, you know?"

He turned to me. I'm a big woman and have been told I

have warm eyes. Consequently, men often mistakenly say to me, "You're not like other women. I can talk to you."

Dino compounded his error. He started in about how he just couldn't seem to get it right, the obsession wasn't removed, he missed the intensity. I bet Dino'd been using the cute and clueless game his whole life.

"Stop," I said.

He looked away. "So when's the last time you went to a meeting?" I said.

"Uh," he said.

"Talked to your sponsor?"

He looked woeful. "I can't really talk to guys."

"Awww," I said. "Well then how the hell do you expect to stay sober. If you can't stand the heat, get out of the kitchen."

I stopped. I could hear my dad. If you can't stand the heat, get out of the kitchen. No apologies, no excuses. I don't have to say I love you, kids, when I don't, you'll know it.

"I'm sorry," I said.

"No," Dino said, "I was whining. You're right."

Jerry looked over at us. "It's really hard to stop drinking," he said. "I know."

Dino took a deep breath. "Thanks, man."

I left before dessert. Starr hugged me. Dino shook my hand.

I huddled in my seat. I wanted Bear, drunk or sober, holding me till dawn. More than that, I wanted to call my dad, tell him something, maybe that I understood a little, maybe that I was turning into him. I thought about Jerry and his folks, about their sign language, and I knew for sure that I wouldn't make that call because my dad and I no longer had any common language, except for *If you can't stand the heat, get out of the kitchen.*

We were half an hour out of Flag when Jerry settled down next to me.

"Nice kids," he said.

"Me and my big mouth," I said. "Jesus, I sounded just-like my dad."

"No, you did the best you could. He was whining."

"I know better," I said.

We were quiet. Jerry hauled down his duffle bag and poked around in it. "What do you do for a living?" he asked.

"I write," I said. "And teach."

"What do you write?"

"Stories, books, newspaper columns."

"Books," he said. "What are they about?"

"The first one was about a modern woman dreaming the life of a twelfth-century woman."

Jerry stopped fiddling with the bag. "Do you know about dreams?"

"A little," I said. "Mostly my own. Why?"

"I have a dream," Jerry said, "that my guardian angel comes to me. She sits at the foot of my bed. I ask her about my mom and dad, but when I talk she doesn't seem to be able to hear me."

I looked out the window. The San Francisco Peaks rose dark against the stars. The lights of Flagstaff began to glitter, red, green and celestial against those midnight mountains. I saw the big Purina building come into view, the Museum Club, the Kachina Motel. We were almost home.

"Jerry," I said, "what if the angel is deaf? What if you tried to talk to her in sign?"

His eyes went as bright as the downtown lights suddenly outside our window. I saw Joe's. Bear was probably headed out the door, on his way to pick me up.

"Thank you, Beth," Jerry said. "I will try that. I surely will."

"It might not work," I said. I could hear my dad. You and your advice, Beth. What makes you the big expert?

"So what?" Jerry said. "I can try." He opened his wallet and handed me a twenty dollar bill. "Please send me that book."

"No," I said. "I'll give you one. To a friend, okay?"

"Uh uh," he said. "You have a gift. You shouldn't give it

away." I took the money.

The train stopped. I saw Bear grinning up at the window, weaving a little from side to side. Looked like it'd be a horny and hung-over dawn.

Jerry and I climbed off the train. I introduced him to Bear. They said howdy, shuffled their feet, did a little vet talk. Then Jerry turned to me.

"I'll try it," he said. "The signing with the angel. I'll let you know."

Bear looked back at Joe's. "Couple more brews, woman?" he said. I nodded.

"Here's my address," Jerry said. "I'll let you folks get on with your night." He headed for the pay phone, then stopped and yelled, "Hey."

He signed the only sign I know. I signed right back.

My coffee is cold. I go into the cabin and refill my cup. That train ride seems too long ago. My dad is dead, Bear predictably gone on to the next woman, a hardness around my heart I don't want. I turn from the shadows. The tomato sprouts in the window pots are luminous against the black dirt. I water them, sniff the sharp green scent.

I walk out into soft April air to the mail box. There's a letter with the Prescott VA Hospital return address: *Dear Beth, I'm reading your book. Just imagine traveling in your dreams to the past! The angel hasn't come by yet, but when she does, I'll try signing. Thank you for everything. Your Amtrak friend, Jerry Dubeau*

I carry the letter into the cabin and sit by the baby tomatoes to read it again. I think about waiting for a visitor. I think about what it might mean to sign and hope the visitor understands.

"Dad," I say. "Remember my friend Michael R., the one good guy. Remember he wanted to be buried under a pine tree so he could become a tree. Mom's got your ashes in the tomatoes. She's sending me a little of what's left of you. I'll put you in my garden.

And when I transplant my tomatoes, I'll start talking to you.

"I'm going to tell you that every time I asked you to come out to visit and you said 'There's nothing but goddamn rocks out there,' I wanted to say, 'I'm out here, Dad.'

"I'll tell you that Mom said that when you got my last letter, where I thanked you for everything you'd given me, you said, 'Oh you know Beth, she just runs on and on.' I'll tell you I can't believe a father would say that about his daughter's gratitude.

"I'll tell you that I can't believe you told me not to come home in the last few weeks you were alive because I'd make a scene crying. And I can't believe I didn't disobey you.

"I'm going to tell you that sometimes I hate you and sometimes I love you and sometimes, I am you. And this time, Dad, you're going to be a tomato and you're going to have to listen."

UP NEAR PASCO

My aunt calls from Burns. "Jinella, I got some sad news. Your cousin Kyrin laid himself down on the railroad tracks up near Pasco and got hit. Far as the cops could tell, he had his music plugged in his ears, you know how you kids do, and his arms were crossed over his chest." She goes quiet. Some of the women in our family are strong like that.

I make myself stay calm. "Oh Auntie," I say. "That poor boy."

"Maybe you and Lonnie could come over," my aunt says. "Me and grandma want to give Kyrin a feast. Your uncle's talking about a sweat."

"I could come up, Auntie," I say.

"Lonnie take off on you?"

I don't say anything. My aunt doesn't ask more.

"I'll talk to my professors," I say. "When's the feast?"

"Next Friday. You got a ride?"

"I'll take the bus."

"Your brother's coming in from Seattle. He'll pick you up at the station."

Most of all, my cousin was different. Different, really different—not like the gangstahs and goths on the rez—but deep down different. If he heard me say "deep down different," he would have gotten a bracelet made that had the letters WWDDDD on it—like those Jesus bracelets, but stronger: What Would Deep Down Different Do? What DDD did was kill himself. So now he is Deep Down Dead and I almost want to go join him except all the stuff he taught me about living real is keeping me alive.

His name was Kyrin. It's sort of a joke even though a lot of the kids on the rez have gangstah names. His isn't gangstah, I mean he wasn't. My aunt named Kyrin from this soy sauce that was on the table in the Golden Fork Chinese Buffet in town. She and her boyfriend had gone there to celebrate finding out she was pregnant.

Me and Kyrin used to go to the Golden Fork a lot when we could get a ride into town. He was so skinny from his family nature and tweak, but he could put away darn near the whole buffet serving dish of sesame chicken.

Fuck.

He was so proud of me when I got into college here. I know it's just a podunk community college, but to him it was like I had my foot on the ladder that was going to just keep going up and up. He wanted so much. For himself. For his brothers and sisters. For his cousins, especially me. He decided to take the short cut. No ladder for him. Kyrin was on the nose of a bottle rocket.

Friday my best friend Sissie drops me at the bus station. I grab a couple candy bars and a pop from the vending machines. I keep thinking about Kyrin. He wasn't full-blood Wasco like me and my aunt. His dad was from up Yakima way. Maybe Kyrin was trying to get back there when he laid down on the tracks outside Pasco.

We hadn't known exactly where he was for a long time. I'd get postcards from different places—Seattle, Portland, even Los Angeles. They weren't picture postcards. He'd send post office postcards with squiggly drawings on them of robot birds and laser guns with about a million parts; sometimes faces on them or talons or maybe a beautiful Indian chick except where her heart was supposed to be there were gears.

I don't want to think about Kyrin gone, plus my grandma says it's dangerous to think about death, but I sit on the bench in the big bright waiting room and all I can think is: What did it feel like? Was he tweaking? Did he have his tunes on so loud he couldn't hear the train coming? Was he wearing enough to keep him warm?

The bus pulls in on time. It's almost empty except for some loud old white guys. I find a window seat on the south side and sit down with my pop and candy bars. The bus driver makes a bad joke about luxury travel and we're on our way out of Bend.

I always love it when the bus cruises down the long slope after the Badlands turn-off and all of a sudden, it's desert. Not desert like in Arizona. There aren't any of those big cactus that look like Gumbys waving. Our desert is miles and miles of flat sand and volcano rock. There is sage everywhere. Sometimes when you're out there after a rain the air is so wet and green you think the sage is breathing like a human.

Kyrin used to ride his buddy's dirt bike out there, south a ways from Millican, a ghost gas station we just passed heading east. I wonder if I'll ever be able to ride by here without picturing my cousin tear-assing up Reservoir Road, no helmet, no knee or elbow pads, just his black hair flying and a wild look on his face.

I close my eyes. When I open them again, we're miles down the highway. The loud guys have figured out how to play poker on the back seat. They look like the losers who are always at the blackjack tables in our casino. My sister works there and she says she thinks most of them sleep in their cars in the parking lot. She says they must live on snack bar burgers, cigarettes and casino coffee. "If you could call that living."

One of the poker players looks like he meant to get on the bus to Vegas and made a serious mistake. He's tall and skinny and his hair looks like a little Dutch boy's. He has on three gold chains and a red silky shirt that's open down to almost his belly. There's a big medal hanging from one of the chains that says Winner on it in rhinestones. The dealer looks like a weasel, if a weasel wore a t-shirt that said Bad to the Bone.

I don't want them to catch me watching, plus it's an ugly sight, so I lean back in my seat, open a Snickers and watch the desert stream by. Even though it's the saddest reason, I'm happy to have a weekend off from town. It's okay there. The other girls in my pre-nursing program at the college are nice enough, but Bend is really weird. It used to be a dinky falling-down town. Then, all of a sudden all these rich white people started buying the little old logging company houses and painting them colors like pink and orange.

It's even weirder in Sisters which is a few miles to the west. One of my roommates went over there and told me and Sissie we had to check it out. She said there weren't just regular rich people from Portland and California there, but rich hippies. Sissie borrowed her sister's car and we went over to see what all the fuss was about.

We sat outside a little café, people watching and drinking coffee that cost four dollars a cup. We saw a white guy with long silvery hair who rode a Harley that I know cost as much as my mom's trailer; and there were ladies with feather earrings and fancy beaded bags hanging from leather cords around their necks. One of them actually came up to me and said, "Are you Native American?"

Are you a white bitch? I was thinking, but I just nodded. She put her hands in front of her skinny chest and bowed. "Namaste," she said. "I honor your peoples' ways."

She hovered there till Sissie—who is not shy—said, "Excuse us, but we need to be by ourselves. We're planning a ceremony to celebrate N'ugartkim. It's private." The lady bowed again and walked away. Her type walk funny, like they don't have any bones in their bodies. I don't speak Wasco so I said, "Sissie, what's noogartkeem?"

"I made it up," she said. "I don't know any Wasco."

The sugar from the two candy bars plus the desert blurring outside the bus window makes me sleepy. I check my cell. I still hope there'll be a message from Lonnie, which, of course there is not. Per usual. I think about texting my mom, but she's probably per usual too. I turn my phone off, fold my jacket behind my head and settle in for a nap.

I'm jolted straight out of a dream in which Kyrin is standing up on his buddy's dirt bike which he is riding at about a hundred miles an hour past the big park in Bend. He is screaming about how they killed the geese there. He rides into the park, onto the pond, and the bike keeps going.

"Ladies and gentlemen," the driver is saying, "we've clipped a deer. I need to get off the highway and call the Burns terminal."

He parks on the gravel shouler. The poker players bend down between the seats to pick up the fallen cards. I start to feel like I can't breathe. It happens to me sometimes. My mom once told me that I have nerves like my dad. "That's what made him take off like he did. One day he's listening to Willie Nelson over and over. Next day he's gone." A few months later, she left a note on the kitchen table: "Sorry, kids. I love you, but I gotta go. Here's busfare to your aunty's."

I look out my window toward the buttes to calm myself. I name the colors—dark blue, brown, pale where the sun is hitting them. I tell myself a story about a girl stuck on a bus who gets off and goes to see a hurt deer. I clench my hands and dig my fingernails in. It doesn't help. I wish I had a paper bag so I could breathe into it like the nurse at the school clinic taught me, but my throat is so tight I doubt even that would work.

I close my eyes and I see the deer. She is still alive. I know it. I make myself get up and walk to the back of the bus. The poker guys look up at me. "Excuse me," I say, "I gotta check out something." I'm scared they'll hassle me, but the short guy just deals and says, "Ante up."

I kneel on the back seat and look out. The deer lies on the white line, her legs folded under her. She stares straight ahead. There's no blood. Every time a car or truck goes by, she shivers. I want to go to sleep and wake up in my aunt's house.

I turn and look at the poker players. "Do any of you have a gun?" I say. The tall Vegas guy shakes his head. I go back to my seat. "The deer is alive," I say in a loud voice. "Does anybody have a gun?" Nobody answers. That thought comes into my head: What would Kyrin do?

The driver turns around. "We've got to sit here a while. One of the front wheels is bent. They're sending help from Burns."

I go up to him. "What about the deer? She's alive."

"I saw, honey," he says. "I don't have a gun. But the sheriff's on her way. She'll be able to take care of it."

I go back to my seat and watch the light on the mountains. I'm breathing okay, but I can't stand thinking how scared the deer must be. What does she think the cars are? Does she hurt? Does she wonder why she can't move?

The sun is starting to go down. Nobody comes to help the bus or the deer. I sit with that stupid sentence on loop delay in my head: What would Kyrin do? What would Kyrin do?

Shut up, I say in my mind. He'd get high. That's what he'd do. He'd do some goddamn tweak and go to his happy place. He'd lie down on the white line with some gangstah shit thumping in his ears. Forget you, Kyrin.

We must have gone into one of those science fiction wormholes. The sun's copper now, almost all the way down. The buttes are glowing, like they're lit from inside. The sheriff still hasn't showed up. The repair truck from Burns isn't here. At least the traffic has thinned out. At least the deer doesn't have to shiver so much. I look out at the sagebrush. It's gone silvery.

I turn on my cell. I want there to be a message from Lonnie. There's nothing. I call my aunt and tell her I'm stuck on the bus out by Riley. "Jinella," she says, "are you okay? You sound funny."

"Auntie," I say, "I'm kind of freaking out. We hit a deer. She's on the white line. She's still alive. I don't know what to do."

There's a long silence. I hear the TV in the background and the racket of my little cousins playing. "Anybody on that bus got a gun?" my aunt says.

"No. But the sheriff's on the way."

"Good. She'll know what to do. You just sit tight, Jinella. Call me when you're almost to town. And you pray. Pray for that deer, girl."

"I will, auntie. I'll call you as soon as I'm almost there."

We say goodbye. What comes next isn't anything I plan. I go up to the driver and ask him if I can get off the bus and stretch my legs. "Sure," he says, "just be careful."

I step onto the sand and walk away from the bus. There are no headlights in either direction. The deer is a pale shape on the black highway. I move slowly up to her. She doesn't turn her head. I set my palm on her neck. She shivers a little, then lowers her head. I pet her. Only a few times. "I'm sorry," I say. "You will be able to go away from this place soon. I won't forget you."

I don't want to make her more scared so I walk back to the bus. The red and blue lights of the sheriff's car sparkle to the east. I get back on the bus. "The repair truck is right behind the sheriff," the driver says. "We'll be on our way in no time."

It's full-on dark in Burns. My brother pulls up. "Hey, little sister, jump in. I want to grab a coffee at Mac's and catch you up on a few things you need to know before we go to Auntie's."

I haul myself up into the seat. "You ought to have a escalator for this thing." He travels first class. Shiny black Ford Lariat, the inside near bigger than my dorm room. Though I know how he pays for it, which none of us relations talk about, I still am proud that the truck is in our family.

We drive the few blocks to Mac's. Eddie doesn't ever walk if he doesn't have to. "Did enough of that in boot camp," he always says.

I'm scared to find out what he wants to talk about. I hate it when people say, "We gotta talk" and then you have to wait to find out why. Mac's is quiet. Eddie buys us coffee and we sit by the big window that looks out on the highway. I look at the white line and I remember the deer shuddering. I wonder if this highway will always be a sorrowful place to me now.

Eddie dumps three spoons of sugar into his coffee and half the cream pitcher. He holds up his hand. "Yeah, yeah, I know. Diabetes. But, hey, YOLO."

"I'm not your mom," I say.

"Good thing," he says, "but you got that listen-up-son expression."

I narrow my eyes and give him the Jackson women look.

"See?" he says. "I give up."

"So?"

"So," he says, "Auntie got word out and said no hoods at the feast."

"Nobody says 'hoods' anymore."

"Yeah well, you get her meaning."

I wonder why he's telling me this. I'm not about gang-stahs, never have been. I'm not exactly a goody two-shoes, but it always seemed to me that the kids with the hoodies pulled down damn near over their eyes on hundred degree days were just pitiful. Country kids playing big city.

"I passed by a few of the guys today," Eddie says. "Wing, J5 and Cupid the Duck. They waved me over. Wing said that Kyrin was their brother and no way were they going to miss the feast. They said they were going to show Auntie what they were made of."

He shakes his head.

"Oh lordie," I say. "That could mean anything."

"So sister, help me keep an eye on them."

It's all the way dark by the time we pull up to my aunt's house. Every light is on, including the Christmas lights strung clear round the double-wide. My aunt never takes them down. "That way your step-uncle can find his way home when he's had too much fun."

"I feel a little weird," I say to my brother.

He laughs. "That's cause you are a little weird. Come on, grab your bag. I can already smell fry bread."

Eddie jumps out of the truck and heads for the house. I sit a minute. I pretend to check my phone in case anybody's watching and wondering what is going on with that girl? What is going on is I am trying to pull myself together. I feel the deer under my hand. It seems totally weird that Kyrin got himself hit on the tracks and the little deer got hit right on the white line. They both got hit. Except Kyrin did it on purpose. Plus he didn't have to lie there scared to death.

If my mom knew what I'm thinking right now, she'd either get out her bible or burn some sage. "Clean those bad thoughts out," she'd say. "They can bring more bad stuff."

I text her just to say "Hi, I'm here." She couldn't come over because she said she had to work. I know that's an excuse. She's never really approved of my aunt, not since she stole my mom's boyfriend in sixth grade.

I turn off the phone, get my bag out of the back and walk toward the house. My aunt's there in the doorway before I have time to knock. "Jinella," she yells, "you get in here." She holds out her arms.

I'm almost to the steps when I see a red sparkle on the edge of the big old truck tire my aunt grows poppies in. I bend to check it out, but it's gone. I wonder if somebody tossed out a cigarette. "Jinella," my aunt says, "will you please get the lead out?"

It's about a hundred and ten in the double-wide. There's cigarette smoke for a foot below the ceiling. Everywhere I look there's family, everybody talking, everybody digging into their food. I go to my grandma and greet her. She's the only one left of that generation. "Good evening, Grandmother," I say. She looks up at me with her sharp black eyes. "Guess you still know how to mind your manners, college girl," she says. "That's good."

My younger cousin Shana bounces off the sofa and grabs

my arm. "C'mon, you can put your stuff in my room. Plus I have to tell you something—a secret."

I can't figure out why I feel completely safe for the first time since I left home for school and why I also want to turn and run back out into the cool night. I follow Shana to her room. She's painted the walls black. There are posters everywhere—thrash bands, Free Leonard Peltier, Rihanna, an eagle with a quote below it by some guy named Black Elk.

She closes the door behind us. I wait. You don't push the women in our family. "Sit down," she says and pats a pile of coats. I pull off my jacket and sit next to her.

"I know what happened," she says. "I knew he was going to do it. I couldn't stop him."

She takes a deep breath. "He texted me a bunch. There was some white chick named Sarah. He met her in one of those narcotics meetings in LA, you know where they pray and stuff. He was off the tweak. Her too. They were going to work awhile and get enough cash to come up here."

Shana digs in her pocket and pulls out her phone. "I've got it all here. I saved every single message."

I can't figure out how she can be so calm. Kyrin was not just her brother. He was her best friend. She passes me the ashtray on the bedstand. "I don't smoke," I say. She knows that.

"Duh," she says and picks up a roach buried in the ashes. "I've been smoking weed since we got the news. Cupid gave me a big old bud. Chocolate Thai."

I shake my head. "I'm okay."

"It's the only way I can deal with this," she says. "Him dead, me knowing in a way what he was going to do—and I didn't try to stop the fool." She shakes her head and looks away from me. "Plus I cannot tell anybody. Not no one. I was scared to text you for fear somebody would read it."

I think she's paranoid, but I don't say anything.

"What happened is the Sarah chick found herself some

Mexican gangbanger dealer and left," Shana says. "No explanation. No note. No nothing. Just gone."

"That's why he did it?"

"I guess. The last message I had from him was: Gotta go. No worries. Love always. K."

Shana crumbles the J into the ashtray. "This shit isn't working so good anymore."

We sit for a while and don't talk. Finally, Shana puts her head on my shoulder and says, "Okay, I can go back out there now."

I can't think of anything to say. I just hug her for a second. She puts fresh gel on her hair and we go out into the living room.

My brother nods toward the kitchen. I go in. The table top and every counter are piled with food. There's a two foot high stack of fry bread, four pots of stew simmering on the gas burners, two with chilis, two with corn, maybe a dozen different cakes, one of them with a frosting dirt bike and the words We will never forget, another with a fancy cross and roses.

I take fry bread, a little of the corn stew and find some pop in a cooler under the table. I'm not hungry. I'm more stressed, but if I don't eat, too many peoples' feelings will be hurt. I go out into the living room. Eddie pats the couch next to him. I sit down and take a bite of fry bread. It's all greasy in my mouth and for a second, I'm scared I'll get sick right then and there. I feel Eddie so solid next to me and see my grandma watching me from across the room, so I chew slowly, take a sip of pop and swallow.

"I think Wing's taking a fancy to you," Eddie says. "He keeps watching you."

I look up. Wing looks away. He shakes his head, lets his long hair flop over his right eye. He's even skinnier than the last time I saw him on the rez.

"I wonder what they meant," Eddie said, "about showing Auntie who they are."

"They probably didn't even know what they meant," I say. "Big talk."

Wing gets up and walks toward me.

"Ooooeee, here it comes," Eddie says.

Wing stands in front of us. "Hello, Eddie," he says. "Hello, Jinella. How you doing?"

"Not too bad," Eddie says. "Considering." One of the things some of the older people believe is that you don't say the name of the person who died or talk about it directly.

"Sad times," Wing says. He looks down at me. "Jinella. Could we talk a minute?"

"I guess so," I say.

"I mean more like private," Wing says. "Maybe go outside, get some air."

"I can do that," I say. Eddie looks at me, his face not showing anything. "It's okay," I say.

We wind our way through chairs and people and go outside. It's a bright cold night. The constellation Orion is hanging right over us. Wing slumps into a lawn chair. I sit on the stoop.

"There's something in the shadows," he says. "You remember that?" He stretches his legs out in front of him. He's wearing baggy shorts, white socks and scuffs.

"Aren't you freezing?" I say. I don't have a clue what he's talking about and I don't want to get into some weird tweaked-out conversation.

"I'm okay," he says, "but you remember that. That song about the shadows that Ricky babe sang that night we were all out by the Badlands with the fire?"

I nod.

"Look what I found," Wing says. "In the dirt where them dead plants is. Fucked my mind up."

He holds out his hand, palm up. I don't see anything. "Hang on," he says and moves his hand into the glare of the security light. I see a red sparkle, like the one I saw before.

"What is it?"

"One of the sequin things, you know, like the ones that

Ricky had stuck all over the ass of her jeans. Weird huh. Something in the shadows. That song. Weird."

He closes his fingers around the sequin and the sparkle is gone. "Pow," he says, "gone just like that." He laughs. "Bet you think I'm gonna say something deep about life and all. How it can go black. Pow. Fuck that shit."

I want to punch him. I want to say, "First off, you'd have to be able to think something deep." But Wing scares me. He's always scared me. I only came out here to talk because of Kyrin.

"I better go in," I say. "You know how my brother is."

"Fuck him. Fuck the old ones too. What'd they ever really give us? What'd they give Kyrin? Just a bunch of dead old stories and bible bullshit."

My heart hurts. I know he's whacked out, but he's talking trash about my relations.

"Stop it," I say. "Just stop it." I feel the deer breathing so fast under my hand.

Wing pulls his head-rag down over his eyes. "Get outta here, Jinella," he says. "I ain't gonna hurt you, bitch. Not now. Not ever." He raises his hand. I back up. He tosses the sequin. A tiny red spark arcs through the air and disappears.

I go into the house. It's quieter. My aunts and girl cousins are passing around big slices of cake on paper plates. J5 and Cupid the Duck sit on the floor in front of the woodstove. Cupid shovels chocolate cake into his mouth like somebody's going to steal it from him. He's so fat he's almost as wide as he's tall plus he's got this weird little pink angel mouth and flat feet so big people say that if he ever got lucky enough to go water skiing, he wouldn't need skis. J5 pushes his cake around on his plate and looks sad.

Shana hands me some cake and nods toward her room. I follow her. We sit on the bed. My cake is pink with bright blue frosting and a squished purple rose. "I'm not really hungry," I say. Shana sets our plates on top of her little TV. "I know," she says. "God, I feel so useless. The guys are going out to build the sweat. Eddie told

Cupid and them that they get to be the fire-keepers. We chicks get to hand around cake."

I can't think of anything to say. We sit there for a long time in the silence. I'm so tired my bones feel like they're made of glass. Shana puts on some music and turns the volume down. "I wonder what he was listening to," she says.

"Maybe the cops kept his iPod."

"Yeah. Then we'll never know."

My aunt knocks on the door. "Girls, come on out. The fire's going. Grandma's going to lead the sing."

Shana and I follow my aunt out into the field to the north of the trailer. Somebody's turned off the security light, so the only light is from the firepit. Everybody's standing around the glowing coals, even Wing. Cupid and J5 are leaning on their shovels. The covers on the sweat lodge flicker in and out of the orange light. I can make out the ragged tarp Eddie uses to cover tools in the back of his truck and the edge of my aunt's best Pendleton blanket.

My grandma takes the hands of the people next to her. Wing stands back a little, his arms down at his sides. "Wing," Grandma says, "you too. And when we're done, you grab a shovel. Them rocks aren't going to get in there by themselves."

Wing looks down at the ground. I think we are all holding our breath. He looks up, then over at me. "Okay, Grandmother," he says, steps into the circle and takes my hand. Grandma closes her eyes and begins to sing. Soon everyone is singing, even those who don't know the words.

CYNDRA WON'T GET OUT OF THE TRUCK

If Cyndra had known how completely crazy J.B. was—
even before he shipped over to Iraq—she would not have married
him. Even if she had been seventeen and him twenty-one with pale
blue eyes, shoulders that wouldn't quit and a manner of kissing that
said, "I completely respect you girl, and I completely want you."

But it was too late to take it back. There was Kelli who was
two and cute as a puppy; and there was L'il J.B. who was too little
for anybody to tell whether he was going to be cute or not. Kelli
was at her mom's. L'il J.B. was attached to Cyndra's left boob on
which he was sucking as if his life depended on it. Which it did.
Which was why it was too late to take back that dumb second when
she had looked up into J.B.'s eyes and said, "I do. I surely do," even
if the fool kept roaring up to her on his dirt bike and hollering,
"Come out and sit in the sunshine." Mojave Desert burn-you-to-a-
crisp sunshine.

Cyndra and L'il J.B. were in the front seat of J.B.'s King Cab
on a Sunday afternoon in June. The air conditioner was blasting
and Cyndra was squinting into the dashboard TV. She could barely
make out the picture because the light was a glare from hell. J.B. was
not in sight, but Cyndra could hear the bad boy roar of his dirt bike,
even though the windows were closed and she had her earbuds in
so she could listen to a duet between Faith Hill and Tim McGraw
that was causing her to drip tears on L'il J.B.'s tiny bald head.

She and L'il had been stuck in the King Cab for two hours.
J.B. would zoom up every now and then and say, "How ya doin',
baby? I'll just do this one last run and we'll head in for pizza, beer
and who knows what."

As if. As if all she needed was another baby boy nuzzling

her boobs. As if by then he'd have sobered up enough to be able to do the deed. The TV flickered and went black. Her cell battery was dead due to her listening for an hour to her sister Tyra bitch about how there was nothing to do in this totally boring place. Which meant now there really was nothing to do. Nothing.

She had a pile of her mom's magazines next to her on the seat because she had planned to leave them at her sister's salon. She glanced down at the top one. "How to Welcome Your Soldier Hubby Home." Right. There would be—she didn't have to look—a recipe for The Most Outrageous Triple Chocolate Torte and tips on how to lose weight. For your soldier hubby. Both so stupidly hopeless, the cake which J.B. would not eat because he would have slammed eight Dos Eq longnecks during dinner; and gorgeous skinny her if she was ever gorgeous skinny her again, because if J.B. did actually touch her, it would have everything to do with his boner, and nothing to do with want or respect.

Her sister's salon? Three stations and an ex-biker chick who called herself an aesthetician coming in about once every six months to do some old lady's toenails. Tyra herself was the sister from hell. No details thanks, except for how the bitch had managed to steal away Cyndra's first boyfriend when they were teenagers. Cyndra all perfect boobs and butt and heart-shaped face and Tyra the Tyrant ha ha, two hundred pounds with boobs that would be hanging to her knees by the time she was twenty-three. Yeah, and now Cyndra was pushing one-ninety.

L'il's mouth had fallen away from her breast. She set him on the magazines and pulled down her blouse. She was a mess. She was a slobby mess. Once she would have wiped off the milk and tucked herself into the nursing bra. Now she didn't even wear the nursing bra. She looked down at her top and saw the tiny star of wet spreading out.

If it weren't for the air-conditioner she would...what. She would who knows what. The last time J.B. had cruised up to the truck he had smelled like a brewery. He'd taken a twelve-pack out with him strapped to the back of the bike. He was drinking every day; sometimes he'd already popped a few on the drive back from the marine base. And it seemed like the only time he ever wanted to fool around was in the morning when he had a hang-over woodie. Cyndra could not figure out why guys had to give such ugly names to the act of love.

Suddenly she had one of those lousy memories, the ones that made her skin crawl, the ones that she thought had gone away when she was first in love with J.B. Back then when he put his arms around her, she knew she had escaped her past. Everything was new. Everything was magic. Like normal people. Like normal love. Not like her mom and dad when she was little—her mom crying, not mad crying, but pitiful crying; her dad bellowing, "Who puts a roof over your head? Who puts clothes on the god-damned kids? Who deserves a little pussy now and then—not twice a year?"

Cyndra cranked the volume on the iPod. There was a new singer, a woman singing quietly with only a guitar behind her. She had no idea who it was. She'd downloaded a mix from a website. The song was about making mistakes and running away and Cyndra wondered if it had been written for her.

She thought about just starting the truck and driving off, but she knew J.B. usually rode the damn bike till he was running on vapor. Pissed-off as she was, she didn't want to kill him, which is what pushing a dead dirt bike back to where he could hitch into Twentynine Palms in hundred and ten degree heat would do. She checked the gas gauge in the truck. There was a good half tank left. But she turned down the air conditioning just to play it safe.

Seemed like that was all she ever did now—play it safe. Make sure J.B. and the kids ate more or less right. Try to watch her weight while she felt so empty all the time. Listen to her sister bitch about the salon—how Gennifer was a bitch and Margo was a bitch and D'wanne was nothing but a bitchy faggot—and never tell her sister what she really thought, that Tyra was the real bitch. And why couldn't she just tell her that? Because sometimes, if Cyndra was realllly understanding, Tyra would offer to babysit and Cyndra could take a long luke-warm shower, go out on the patio in her wet t-shirt dress and sit in peace while the hot air evaporated the water from the dress and her skin, and she could pretend it was March in Phoenix, Arizona, where she and J.B. had gone for their honeymoon. The air had been perfect. Soft little night breezes. If she closed her eyes the evaporation felt like that kind of heaven—or maybe even how J.B.'s fingers had once been all delicate on her face.

What had happened to wild Cyndra? What had happened to the girl who didn't hardly drink or smoke pot, but who would walk away from the Luna Mesa full moon keggers on the BLM land, out into a silver desert where if she lined herself up just right with the big fat moon, her shadow would walk ahead of her? Or the girl who would run into the heart of a thunderstorm when one slammed in, like a miracle you could be terrified of and love how your heart pounded in your chest? What had happened to the girl who was going to be the first person in her family to go to college—right over at Copper Mountain College where she wasn't going to get some dumb girl degree, but major in computer programming?

Gone. Vanished in the instant it took for her to welcome J.B. into her body and whisper, "I'm going to drive you crazy, bad boy." Ten million years ago.

L'il J.B. snorted, whimpered and clutched his tiny hands in the air. Cyndra pulled him up to her breast and plugged him in. She heard the giant mosquito whine of the dirt bike. There had better be something new pretty damn soon.

"So how long were you stuck out there?" Tyra said. She had that "snooping for gossip but pretending she really cared" tone in her voice.

"Three hours all told." Cyndra shrugged. "At least I had my music. And I could just think for a while without somebody nagging me about something or other."

"You need a break," Tyra said. She'd got her gossip so she could afford to be charitable. "I sure do," Cyndra said. She figured Tyra was going to offer to watch the kids for an hour so she could take her shower and sit on the patio.

"I've got a surprise," Tyra said. "Tell J.B. you and me are going down into Palm Springs to get some stuff at Target. Call him so he doesn't get shit-faced on the way home from work. He can watch the kids. He owes you. You deserve to have some fun."

Cyndra thought of the heat in Palm Springs and the old people who all looked like they had never made a mistake in their lives. Plus a hundred and fifty bucks had disappeared from their savings and she didn't want to spend money. "We're almost broke till the end of the month," she said.

Tyra laughed. "You don't need money, baby sister. And we're not really going to Target. I hit it big over at Morongo last night and I've got five hundred bucks free money and a postcard from one of those fancy Palm Springs casinos that's good for two buffets, free drinks and fifty dollars in free slot play. We're gonna get wild."

"Play it safe" was hovering in Cyndra's mind like Casper the Cautious Ghost. It smiled its cutesy-poo smile. She wanted to strangle it. Cyndra straightened her shoulders, looked her sister in the eye and said, "Pick me up at seven."

"You won't regret it," Tyra said. "I left out the best part. I got tickets for Tim McGraw. He's playing there tonight."

"Without Faith?"

"Without Faith. It's some kind of benefit dealie. You put on that sparkly black dress, we get ourselves in the front row and when you stand up to cheer, stick your chest out and he's gonna tell Faith bye-bye, baby!"

"Like I said, pick me up at seven."

"See you later, mamagator."

On cue, L'il J.B. hollered from his crib in the kids' room. Kelli raced in from the dusty patio and grabbed Cyndra around the legs.

"Let me go, babygirl, I gotta feed your brother." Kelli clung tighter. Cyndra pried her away and crouched down next to her. "I'm sorry, sugar," she said. "Let's get you an ice cream and then you come help me get him up and you can sit next to me while I feed him and you can have your ice cream. L'il's gonna be all jealous of you."

Cyndra never knew if Kelli really understood what she was saying to her. She just tried to keep her voice all momsy and loving. Kelli reached up and patted her face. "Okay then, good girl," Cyndra said, "let's get going."

It was mid-afternoon by the time Cyndra got L'il back to sleep, the ice cream off Kelli and the couch, Kelli down for a nap and herself charged up enough to call J.B. He didn't answer. He'd always been like that—blah blah no woman's gonna be the boss of me blah blah. She left a message, dug through the back of the walk-in closet and found the black dress. She hung it in the bathroom with the shower on to steam a few wrinkles out. When she tried it on, the zipper almost didn't close. She sucked in her breath till it hurt and felt the zipper close. There would be no more ice cream bars. None.

When J.B. finally called his voice was all puffed-up and important. "What's up? I got a short minute." Cyndra rolled her eyes. "Honey," she said, her words racing to get everything in before he could say no, "I was hoping you could come straight home tonight. Tyra's gotta see a doctor down in Palm Springs and she's scared. I told her I'd see if you'd be willing to watch the kids so I could keep her company...see that way, she owes us and maybe you and me can get a little alone time on the weekend while she watches the kids as a favor. You know, we haven't had any alone time in too long."

J.B. laughed. His voice softened. "You mean special alone time? Real special my-girl-knows-what-I-like alone time?"

Cyndra grabbed an ice cream bar from the freezer. She did it quiet so he'd never know. "Uh huh," she said, "real real special alone time." She held the phone away and ripped the wrapper from the ice cream bar with her teeth.

"I can come right home," J.B. said. "You bet I can. You got yourself a deal."

Cyndra bit off the first inch of the ice cream bar and damn near swallowed it whole. "That's real sweet of you, baby," she said. "Bye-bye."

She still couldn't believe it had been so easy. J.B. had screeched into the drive, shoved open the door and stopped dead in his tracks. "Damn," he'd said, "you look good. You look damn hot. You gotta promise me you'll wear that dress when we have our real special time alone." Cyndra hadn't said anything. She'd just walked up to him slow, pressed up against him for a second, backed away and winked. Tyra had pulled up, beeped the horn and Cyndra was gone gone gone.

And now, right this minute, she was sitting on the most comfortable chair she'd maybe ever sat in. It had a seat that seemed to be made just for her butt, a nice high back and it was exactly the right distance from the glowing rainbow screen of a Cleopatra slot machine. She'd just bet forty nickels and three golden lion things had bounced down in front of her and there was music playing and a bunch of free spins about to happen at THREE TIMES THE NORMAL WIN and her damn sister was tugging on her sleeve, saying, "Come on, we gotta get to the seafood buffet while the crab claws are still there...plus Tim's on in forty-five minutes. Come on!"

"Wait up," Cyndra said. "Just give me two more minutes..."

It should have been easy. It looked easy when Cyndra did it. Taking care of two kids, a baby and a toddler, not like the seven kids in his family, plus he kinda liked both of them. But L'il J.B. was yowling and Kelli was tugging on his pant leg, whining daddeee daddeeee daddeeeeeee and he hadn't had a beer since the stashed one in his office at the Base. Which had been two hours ago, two hours that felt like two centuries. J.B. was not a happy boy.

He'd fed L'il J.B. He'd settled Kelli in front of the TV with a bowl of SpaghettiOs which was one of the three things she would eat. He'd even nuked the bowl of tuna casserole Cyndra had left in the fridge and made himself eat it. He wasn't used to solid food this early in the evening. He'd usually go for the three basic food groups: beer, beer and more beer. J.B. thought about putting the kids in their car seats and heading into Ranch Foods in Twentynine for a case of basic food group, but it was one hundred degrees and fuck and he couldn't figure out what he'd do with the kids while he ran into the store. He wasn't scared of much, but thinking of kids cooking in a car in the Mojave heat made him want to go back to being a hard-shell Baptist.

J.B. picked up L'il J.B. and held him close to his chest with the kid's head on his shoulder. He'd seen Cyndra do that. "Hey, Mini-me," J.B. said. "Give us one of those big guy belches." L'il kept yowling. There was a stink in the air. J.B. patted his baby's butt. Yep. J.B. sank down onto the couch, hollered and jumped up. He'd landed on one of Kelli's friggin' Barbie dolls—and a half-eaten bag of pork rinds. He held L'il out in front of him. "Okay, you little booger, I know what we'll do. We'll call Mom!"

Kelli hadn't let go of J.B.'s pant leg the whole time he'd been standing and sitting and jumping up. "Mommeeee," she whined. "I want my mommeeeee."

"You and me both," J.B. said. He saw Cyndra's cell phone lying on the kitchen countertop. "What the fuck! You sneaky bitch. Sorry, Kelli, Daddy said a bad word—make that two bad words." He swiped the Barbie doll onto the floor. Kelli shrieked. J.B. dropped down onto the couch with his daughter attached. He tried to think of how hot Cyndra had looked as she went out the door. All it did was piss him off. That's how she'd hooked him. That's how he'd landed in Marine housing in the middle of hell, drier than the sand around him, with a poop-stinking baby and a sobbing little girl for company. "I'll never have sex again," he said to his kids. They just kept stinking and sobbing.

Cyndra vaguely remembered something about how they were going to see Tim McGraw and eat crab legs and celebrate Girls Night Out. It seemed like a dream she'd had a million years ago. Her life with J.B. seemed like a nightmare she'd been living even longer. People said gambling was self-destruction. If sitting in front of a friendly slot machine drinking from a bottomless glass of diet pop and vodka was self-destruction, it suited her just fine. People ought to try living in a cheap shit two-bedroom apartment with three whiny kids, your husband being one of them, in the middle of a scorched-out Marine base, if they wanted to know real self-destruction.

Tyra appeared at her side now and then. Each time they were both more loaded. The last time she'd shown up she'd just laughed and plunked herself down next to Cyndra. "Hey, if you can't beat 'em, join 'em." She shoved a twenty into her machine. "Look," she said, "it's all cool and spiritual." Cyndra glanced over. There were Aztec pyramids and heathen gods. Tyra drove her nuts with all her back-dated New Age bullshit. When two moons and three suns popped up on the screen, Tyra shrieked, "Fifty free games!" Cyndra watched the credits rocketing up and figured maybe there was something to the ancient Indian powers.

"I just love this," she said. She and Tyra watched the bonus round spin gloriously. "You know," Tyra said, "when you get the little thingies that say you hit the bonus round, it's just like the seconds right before a guy you want to kiss comes forward to kiss you. You just know all you gotta do is sit back and EN-joy!"

Three golden lions dropped into place on Cyndra's screen. Bonus round! She remembered the first time J.B. had kissed her, and watched the memory wash away in a rising flood of credits—at a nickel a credit! "I don't ever want to go home," she said. "This is the most fun I've ever had."

Tyra stared at her slot screen. "That says a lot for romance, doesn't it?"

It had to stop. It flat out had to stop. Yes, the kids were finally asleep. Yes, J.B. had logged into his favorite Girls Gone Wild site. Yes, he'd had two nice intimate experiences with the girls. Yes, for once Cyndra wasn't nagging him about something. But it was 1:30 a.m. and no Cyndra. More important, he hadn't had a drink since the last hit of NyQuil, which had finished off the bottle. The crappy supermarket stopped selling booze at two a.m., meaning that if Cyndra didn't get her butt home in the next ten minutes, there was no time to head into town for a beer or twelve.

J.B. logged off and checked on the kids. They were both sound asleep. He considered the deep crap he'd be in if he left to buy some beer and Tyra brought Cyndra back and they both walked in to find the kids alone. It wasn't like he'd never been in deep crap before. But Tyra had a voice like a chainsaw and as ragged as his last nerve was, he didn't need that.

He stepped out into the backyard. He loved that damn Mojave sky. He hated all the rest of the friggin' desert, but he loved the big black above him, the way the stars looked like diamonds, the way the flares from the bombing runs to the north burst orange like alien spaceships. He locked the back and front doors, climbed in the truck and headed into town. The kids would be okay. He'd be a hot fifteen minutes to the store, five minutes grabbing a couple six packs and fifteen hot minutes driving back. No way any tragedy would happen. Especially since he'd busted his ass at the job all day and been a real sweetheart about Cyndra taking off.

Cyndra slid the card into the ATM. The message flashed. "Funds unavailable." Tyra looked over her shoulder. "You hit your daily limit, sistuh. What is it?"

"Five hundred bucks," Cyndra said. She stared down at the card. "What the fuck do I do now?"

"You borrow a few bucks from me," Tyra said cheerfully. "And we just hunker down for a little longer."

"But, what if…?"

"No 'what if', you been losing so long on that machine, it's gotta hit."

The beer run had gone smooth. Market open, the cute Philippina chick at the register. J.B. popped a brew as soon as he'd cleared town. That big sky was laughing down at him. Desert wind poured through the truck windows. He slid a Merle Haggard CD in the player and cranked it up. Life was sweet again. Then he saw the flashing red and blue lights.

J.B. checked his speed. Five miles over the limit. He grabbed a rag off the seat, shoved it into the beer and dropped the can on the floor. He saw the future like you were supposed to do when you were drowning. The cop's face in the window. The faint whiff of brew in the air. The bust. Cyndra and Tyra storming into the house. The end of his life—as crummy as it too often was. Merle was singing, *The way I am don't fit my shackles…* "Merle," J.B. hissed, "what do I do now?"

"I'm going out to the car," Cyndra said. Tyra looked up. Her eyes were like Night of the Living Dead. "Huh?" she said. Cyndra slowly stood up. Her feet were numb, her legs shaky and there was a hot-cold lump in her stomach. "I'm going out to the car. I don't have any credits left and I think I might have died in front of that machine and this is the after-life."

"Whoa," Tyra said. "You are such a drama queen. Take this." She handed Cyndra a handful of twenties. "Sit down! You're not leaving me here. Besides, it's still body temperature out there and if you open the car windows, the midges from the pool will eat you alive."

Cyndra couldn't remember the last time Tyra, or anybody else, had given a flying fuck about her comfort. "Okay," she said, "but it's three a.m. and I can't feel my legs and I think I gotta pee, so I'm going to go to the john. Save my machine." Tyra tilted

Cyndra's chair up against the machine. "Woo hoo," she said, "I just hit another bonus."

There was nobody in the ladies. Cyndra sat in the handicapped stall. All of a sudden she felt like she never wanted to be closed in anywhere ever again. She opened the stall door and rested her head against the tile wall. It felt sweetly cool and when she peed, she decided that peeing when you were about to explode was possibly the best feeling in the world—except maybe seeing the five gold pyramids drop into place on the slot screen. Which they had. About six hundred bucks ago. Which they might again. As the drink girl had said when she brought the last round of free pop and vodka, "If you don't play, you can't win!"

"I'm dead meat." J.B. realized he'd said it out loud. Who the fuck was he talking to? The sky? His pal, the open twelve-pack on the seat? It sure wasn't god, not the god of his childhood, not the god he'd stopped talking to when the IED took out Jackson and Martinez and his best wingman, Mr. Strac himself.

Something was listening. The blue-red dazzle zoomed by. He watched the cop's tail-lights fade into the dark. He wondered if you could have a heart attack at twenty-three even if you were nothing but muscle and beer. "Thank you, Jesus," he said to the god he didn't believe in and headed home.

"Hey." The voice was familiar. "Hey. Wake up." Cyndra jolted out of a dream of spotlights and sequins. Her head rested against her machine. Tyra shook her again. "We've got to go. It's four a.m."

"Holy shit, we won't be back till morning," Cyndra said. "J.B.'s gonna kill me."

"Undoubtless," Tyra said. "Has he called you even once?"

"The phone's on the kitchen counter. I left it there on purpose."

"No worries. I got it figured out. Come on, let's get outta here."

Cyndra checked around the machine. There was nothing

there. All she'd left behind was eight hundred and sixty-five bucks. She patted the machine. She'd seen other players do that. "I'll be back," she said. "I don't get mad. I get even."

"Dad-DY! Dad-DY! Wake up. Little phone ringing."

J.B. pulled the pillow over his head. Tiny evil fingers poked his stomach. Poked again. It wasn't the dream he'd been having that had been a whole lot like some Hobbit-nightmare. It was his real life. "DAD-DY! Mommy's on the phone." J.B. peeked out from under the pillow. "Ha ha," Kelli giggled, "Daddy play hide a seek. Here." She handed J.B. Cyndra's cell.

"What?" he said. "Oh hi, Cyndra, gee I'm glad you're okay, honey. Glad nothing happened."

Cyndra said, "Weren't you even worried?"

"Worried about what?" J.B. checked the clock. 6:10. "Hang the fuck on. Where the fuck are you?"

"Tyra's tire went flat out in the middle of who knows where. She had to take a short-cut home which just happened to go by this guy she like's house up on the mesa. Of course he wasn't home so then we got lost. There wasn't any phone reception. We've been sitting in the car waiting for somebody to come along since about ten. Finally, some old rancher drove up on his ATV."

"Jesus," J.B. yelled. "Can you just cut to the chase?"

"No yell, Daddy." Kelli climbed up on the bed and snuggled next to him.

"I'll be home in a half hour. Can you get the kids breakfast?"

J.B. pressed the cool phone against his forehead. It was already ninety in the bedroom. He felt like he'd been boiled. The cool spot on his forehead felt like rapidly fading hope.

"Yep," he said.

"You're not mad?" Cyndra's voice went little girl.

"Nope."

They said goodbye. "How the fuck," he said to Kelli, "could I be mad when now I've got time to clean up the living room and haul the cans out to the desert?"

"No say bad word," Kelli said.

Tyra pulled into the driveway and leaned her head on the steering wheel. "Oh! My! God! That was sooo much fun. Just leave me out here for a few minutes. I'm not going home. I gotta get to the spa by eight and set out my stuff. I'll just sit in the air con."

Cyndra picked up her purse from the floor. "We have to go back, you know that? I told my machine I don't get mad, I get even."

"I'm sure," Tyra said. "As if we wouldn't go back again. I've still got food comps and a room comp, so next time if we perhaps underestimate our enthusiasm and all of a sudden it's four a.m., we'll just crash in our room."

"If we make it to the room," Cyndra said. "I could play slots forever. I think I found a reason to go on living in this hell-hole." She opened the door and stood. The sun was already cooking all living anything out of the air. "Thanks, sis."

J.B.'s truck was gone. Cyndra let herself into the apartment. It was such a shack. You walked right into the living room/dining room/kitchenette and if you moved too fast, you were heading out the back door into the patio which was dirt, more dirt and one shriveled creosote bush. There were two beer cans under the coffee table. "Heh heh, we should call this a beer table!" was one of J.B.'s favorite jokes. A crushed bag of Doritos poked out from one of the couch cushions. There was, of course, no coffee brewing in the maker. There were no kids. There was a note on the kitchen counter.

Welcome home, party girl. I took the kids to Sally's. She doesn't have to go to work till 1. Try to get your fat butt over there before she leaves.

Cyndra laughed. Once upon a time, once upon a very long time ago yesterday, the note would have hurt her. No more. She made a pot of coffee and heated up a couple waffles. Then she sat at the breakfast bar in her fancy dress, drank three cups of coffee and ate a whole box of waffles—with butter and maple syrup. "I've got my own thing now," she said to the empty apartment. "Nobody's the boss of me anymore."

A month later, somebody decided to be the boss of J.B. He had stashed four long-necks in the locked drawer in his desk for emergencies. Monday had seemed to be the start of a week of boring and stupid. He figured that qualified as an emergency. He tucked the beer into his duffle bag, went into the john, locked the stall door and slammed down the brews. They barely wet his brain cells. No matter, there was a twelve-pack in the fridge at home.

He didn't really want to go home, but Cyndra had some dumb mommies' meeting so he figured he'd better be a good boy. He signed out and headed for the gate. The guard looked at him funny when he pulled up. J.B. smiled. The guard smiled.

The guard asked to see his ID card, nodded and said politely, "You been drinking tonight?" Before J.B. could answer, the sentry told him to pull his car over to the search lane. "Please get out. We're going to take a little test here."

J.B. knew better than to do anything but shut up and wait. The sentry made a call. Ten seconds or ten years later, another MP arrived and put him through the sobriety test. The guy shook his head. "Sorry pal, gotta cuff and stuff ya." The MP van pulled up and J.B. was on his way to a holding cell.

It had happened to him. Not him. Not lucky J.B. who'd skated when his buddies had gotten nailed. Later, after the Sergeant Major had showed up and the real shit-storm had started, after he'd been given his one call, after Cyndra had said, "Fuck you, you can rot in jail" and he knew there was a bigger shit-storm ahead, he had a little chat with the big whatever. "You win. Get me out of this, pal, and I'll stop drinking for a while."

It was a late Sunday afternoon. J.B. was slouched down in the couch, channel surfing. "Shit. Crap. Shit. More crap. Why the fuck did we even bother to get cable?" Cyndra heard him through the screen door. She sat on the back stoop. The kids were in bed and she was watching heat lightning flicker in the west.

J.B. groused on. Cyndra dug her toes into the cooling sand. She almost wished he was still drinking. Sober, he was more evil than ever in that feeling-sorry-for-himself way that guys were so good at, as though she could fix it, as though it was her fault. Her cell jingled. She checked the number. Friggin' Tyra. She got ready for a bitch bitch bitch session.

"Hey, sister. I got some interesting news and I got a fabulous idea."

Cyndra knew the interesting news would start off with, 'I think I met a man,' and the fabulous idea would require Cyndra to meet Tyra some-friggin'-where which would involve leaving the cooling air of the backstep and the almost hypnotic ripple of the lightning over the mountains.

"Yeah?"

"So I think I met a man." Tyra paused to let the full impact sink in. There weren't many single guys in Twentynine and over full-figured as she was, what ones there were weren't interested, or even desperate enough for a blow job.

"Yeah?"

"Come on, don't be a bitch. I'll tell you all about him while we drive down to Palm Springs for a little shopping—heh heh."

"I'm broke."

"You know what to do. Go on a jacket safari. Check the couch. I'll spot you forty bucks. That'll give you enough to play for a while. Then, you'll hit and have your stake."

Cyndra's mouth went dry. Her heart jumped. "You know, I gotta watch it. There's J.B.'s fine and plus he has to have money for his alcoholic meetings even though they don't charge anything."

"Get off the phone and start going through your jacket pockets. Tell J.B. to get his ass off the couch—I know he's there, I can hear the stations switching. Look down between the couch pillows and tell him to give you twenty bucks. He's all guilty now. You got some leverage."

"I've got a jar of nickels and dimes. Let's stop at Vons on the way over. I'll run them through the Coinstar."

"Fine. Get moving," Tyra said.

"Yes, ma'am," she said. "But first, is the guy married?"

"What guy?"

"For chrissakes, Tyra, your new punch."

He'd been sober for five whole months. Cyndra was gone off with Tyra for one of their Palm Springs runs. She'd come back with some useless crap from Target and be all relaxed and cheerful. But what about him? What was J.B. supposed to do?

Kelli climbed up in his lap and smeared PB and J all down the front of his t-shirt. L'il whimpered in the bedroom. It was seven p.m. and nothing but bad TV and whiny kids lay ahead of him. What possible harm could come from a couple beers? His brother owed him a baby-sit and there was the twenty bucks he'd stashed underneath the creosote bush.

"Honey?" he said. Kelli pouted. "You go out, Daddy?" Christ, she was already turning into her mother. She had the same belly on her. "How about you go over to Uncle Fred's and play with Amber and Shayla?" Kelli slid down off his lap. "I put on my dress-up, okay, Daddy?"

"Sure, honey," J.B. said. "You do whatever you want to do."

Cyndra thought she would go crazy right in Vons. The line at the Coinstar machine was damn near out the door. Once you decided to play, you wanted to be walking in the casino door that second. She stepped into a line that seemed to stretch forever. Everybody must have been on oxy. You couldn't have moved slower without being dead. Finally, it was her turn. She dumped Kelli's piggyback into the hopper. $16.25. She knew that by the time she left the casino, that $16.25 would be $1,625.

Dawn gleamed in the duct-taped window of the Midnight Mission. J.B. opened one eye, moaned and rolled away from the glare. There were voices near him. Chick voices.

"Ohmygod, that's Cyndra's hubby."

"Is he dead?"

"I don't think so, but the way he smells he might be."

J.B. curled himself into a ball. His shorts were wet and there was burrito-puke down the front of his t-shirt. One of the chicks poked him with her toe.

"He's alive."

"We should say his name, see if he's conscious. What's his name?"

"Hey, numbnuts." She nudged him again. "Numbnuts, you conscious?"

"Numbnuts? That's his name?"

"That's what Cyndra calls him."

J.B. wondered if he could exert ninja control and stop his breathing long enough to die—or at least look like he had. He held his breath and heard a third voice.

"Move along, ladies. There's nothing to see here."

It was the creep cop, Arlington. The wimpy punk the guys called Darlington.

"Exhale pal," the cop said. "Then suck it up. You're one more step on the slippery road to the end of your glorious military career."

Cyndra was hot. She couldn't lose. Sun Moon handed over five hundred bucks. Cleopatra told her she was a rascal and gave her three hundred. Tiki Torch was being a little coy, but then she jumped her bet to max and watched the credits take off. She almost missed the cell ring. "Oh shit," she muttered to Tyra, "it's J.B. I gotta take it in the ladies room."

She looked at herself in the john mirror. Her face was flushed, her eyes glittering like a speed freak. She hit Answer.

"Babe," J.B. said. "I got bad news."

Her heart jolted even faster. "The kids?" She leaned on the counter and closed her eyes.

"Nope. They're fine. They're at Fred's."

"What are they doing at Fred's? Hang on, what time is it?"

"It's seven a.m. They're at Fred's because I needed a break. And where the fuck are you?"

"Nope," Cyndra said, "you're not putting it on me. What happened?"

"Look," J.B. said, "I can't talk long."

Cyndra heard a metal door clank somewhere behind J.B. "You're in jail, goddamn it," she said. "This is your one phone call, right? Tough shit, pal. You can just sit there. You ought to be getting pretty good at it."

"What?"

"What what?" Cyndra said. "I'll be home in forty-five minutes and pick up the kids. You figure this one out."

J.B. leaned his head against the cell wall. He tried not to think about whatever speckled it. He knew he should have talked different, said a little lovey stuff, said he was sorry, said he was going to up the alcoholic meetings. He'd been a dumb fuck to think Cyndra was going to buy his bad boy talk. He'd been an even dumber fuck to think a couple beers would have nicely taken the edge off things.

It had been better lying on the scummy sidewalk in front of the mission. At least the stink had been his own. J.B. tried to inch away from a guy who must have taken a dump in his pants. The guy grabbed J.B.'s ankle. "Motherfucker. Jive-ass racist motherfucker. You too good to sit next to a Af-ri-can A-mer-i-can?"

J.B. sat tight and kept his mouth shut for once. It had been supposed to be a short relaxing evening and here he was sitting on the concrete floor of the Twentynine Palms men's holding cell, stinking of piss and in the grip of a big-ass nigger with only two front teeth.

"Thass better," the guy said and fell asleep, his huge fingers still tight around J.B.'s ankle. Where the fuck was Cyndra? She'd come down to bail him out. She had to. He figured it was later in the morning. They'd taken his watch and none of the other guys in the cell had a watch—not because the cops had taken them, but because the guys were either nuts or sleeping-on-newspapers homeless.

J.B. bowed his head and tried to rest his forehead on his knees.

"Do not move, motherfucker." The Af-ri-can A-mer-i-can didn't so much as open his eyes. J.B. heard footsteps outside the door.

"Bartlett." It was Darlington. "I got somebody here to see you."

J.B. wondered if he could swallow his tongue and choke to death before the footsteps got any closer. He knew the footsteps. It was his C.O. In ten seconds he was going to be pinned by the anti-bullshit stare of the man who was about to fuck with his entire life.

A Mexican leaning against the toilet looked up. "Ai, pende-jo, you screwed the chihuahua, brother."

J.B. dropped to the floor and sat. "You got that right, my friend. I truly did."

Cyndra tucked L'il into her shoulder and stepped out into the patio. "Kelli, you get on out here right now." The sun had finally dropped to just above the mountains. The house threw a blue shadow over the sand, over the pile of Barbie doll parts, the deflated wading pool and the busted gas grill. Cyndra hooked a plastic chair with her foot and pulled it into the shade. "C'mon baby, come sit with me and L'il. Mama's tired. She didn't get any sleep last night."

"Don't want to. Want my daddy. Where's my daddy? Where's my funny daddy?"

Cyndra pulled down one side of her tank top and plugged

L'il in. Kelli's lips trembled. "Don't start," Cyndra said. Kelli thumped down on the steps. "I want my daddyyy."

Cyndra pulled her cigarettes and lighter out of her shorts' pocket and one-handed lit a smoke. "Daddy's okay," she said. "He's nice and safe. I bet he's thinking about you."

Kelli butt-scooted down the steps, crawled to Cyndra and grabbed her leg. L'il snuffled. The blue shadow stretched out toward the wire fence. How am I going to get out of here? And if I can't, what are we going to do if J.B. has gotten himself booted out of the Corps?

L'il's mouth fell away from her nipple. Cyndra wiped his mouth and buttoned herself up. "Kelli," she said, "how'd you like to go back over to your uncle's again?" Kelli perked up. "Babygirl," Cyndra said, "here's an important true thing: when the going gets tough, the tough go gambling."

She called Tyra. No answer. "Well then, I'm going on a solo trip. Just me and my good luck."

It was six by the time Cyndra pulled into the casino parking lot. She felt strange without Tyra, a little like one of the lonely old ladies they'd see there every time, always by themselves, never talking to anybody, rubbing and loving up the screens of their slots for luck. Plus, there was a weird light over everything. The sun was copper. Dust had blown up from the Anza-Borrego, the guy on the radio had said. A crazy storm out of nowhere. Palm Springs was coated with grit, cars in the parking lot sand-blasted, the high rollers on their cells, probably to their insurance agents.

Cyndra headed for the gleaming casino doors. The big Indian security guard stood in front of her, his arms spread wide. "No. No entry," he said. Cyndra paused. "Not you, lady," he said. A lean-muscled woman in a tank top and shorts sat on one of the big fake boulders.

"Fuck you, chief," she said. "You gotta let her in. And when you let her in, I'll be past you slicker than snot." She turned to Cyndra.

"Chief here eighty-sixed me. Just because I took a forty-two cent pay-out slip that was on the floor under Wheel of Fortune."

"We've got our rules," the security guard said. "Not just for you, Mickey, for everybody."

Cyndra shivered. She'd never seen anything mean like this happen at the casino. The waitresses and pay-out guys were always friendly. She wondered if it was bad juju. Maybe a sign this wasn't the night to play. She started to go back to the car. "Come on in," the guard said. "Me and Mickey go through this about every day."

Mickey looked up at Cyndra. "Yeah, honey. Don't mind us. Besides, I left five hundred bucks in Sun Moon for you. I seen you playing it before."

The five hundred bucks the chick left never did show up. Neither did any of the five hundred Cyndra slid into Sun Moon, into Magic Mermaid, into Cleopatra and, finally, in a suicidal gesture of optimism, into the five dollar machines. It was three a.m. by the time the ATM told her that she'd exceeded her daily limit. She thought about using her cards without a PIN, but the money guys charged ten bucks a hundred for that privilege. She might have been a loser, but she wasn't a fool.

The parking lot was nearly empty. The lights of the casino and Palm Springs shone up into the sky like a reverse Milky Way and washed out the stars. Cyndra leaned on the truck. She didn't feel so good. The five hundred bucks was a hole in her gut. By the time the ATM machine had eighty-sixed her, she hadn't had a decent hit in four hours. She'd had to make herself keep punching the Max Bet button.

She climbed into the truck and fanned the five last ATM receipts out on the front seat. There must have been something wrong with her eyes or the machine. The balances didn't seem right. They were way too low. She tried to remember how many times she and Tyra had gambled. Twenty, maybe thirty—could have been, since they were heading down the hill a couple or three times a week.

She turned on the truck and checked the dashboard dials. There was just enough gas to get back up the hill and over to Twentynine. Damn good thing. Her eyes felt sandpapered. She couldn't figure out why she wasn't hungry. The last thing she'd eaten had been a bag of Doritos driving out of Yucca Valley. Even more, she couldn't figure out why she wasn't worried about J.B. The only thing she was a little worried about was where she'd get the money for her next gambling run.

Cyndra didn't see one other car between the turn-off from Palm Springs till she crested the top of the long hill into Morongo Valley. She hadn't played any music, just let the soft air blowing through the window calm her down. Driving alone always did that. Even when she was a teenager.

Twentynine was quiet, Ranch Market closed for the night. It seemed like a year since she'd driven west through town. She pulled into her driveway, walked slowly to the front stoop and sat down. She wasn't ready to go in. The house would be an oven still and maybe sitting under the huge uncaring sky would make her feel better. It wouldn't give her shit about all the money she lost. It wouldn't tell her she was a loser.

The stars glittered. There was nothing out here to wash them out. She kicked off her flip-flops and dug her toes into the sand. If J.B. saw her he'd call her a fool. "There's rattlers out here and scorpions and those friggin' camel spiders. You get bit and that's it. Your foot turns black and you lose it." For the hundredth time he'd tell her how they had those camel spiders in Iraq, how he and the guys would put two camel spiders in a box and bet on them.

Guess we're both gamblers, Cyndra thought.

Meeting twelve, only one hundred sixty-eight meetings to go. Some spaced-out chick was having her first sober birthday so there was cake and everybody was going to have to sing. J.B. slouched down next to his sponsor, Jackson, and pulled his hat over his eyes. Jackson poked him. "Sit up straight and take your hat off, friend. You can at least look like you want to be here."

J.B. did what he was told. "Good," Jackson said. "You're making progress." J.B. had to kind of admire the guy. He was career Marine, with a scrumptious wife—even if she was at least forty—and some kids who actually liked him. Jackson had arrived in the alcoholic rooms by way of a lost two months in San Diego.

He'd told his story at J.B.'s first meeting. "So finally one morning I woke up in somebody's backyard with a bottle of Captain Morgan's between my legs. There was an inch of rum sitting right there, waiting for me to start the day. I was broke. I stunk. I looked at the booze and knew there wasn't enough to fix my head. I poured it out on the lawn." People in the meeting had groaned. "Oh yeah," Jackson said, "you better believe I regretted it the second I saw it soak into the grass. But I knew. That was it. I got my ass out of that stranger's backyard and called the hotline. That was seven years ago and I'm still here."

The first time J.B. heard the story, he'd thought *I'm not that bad. Maybe I can just do this kind of casually.* Then after the meeting, Jackson had told him that he'd had a chat with the CO and they were willing to give J.B. this last—as in final—big break. One hundred eighty meetings in one hundred eighty days, twice a week talks with a rehab counselor and daily phone calls to Jackson. Then, maybe, just maybe, J.B. could still wear the green.

The door opened. Blast furnace air seared the room. A big guy was silhouetted against the last glare of the setting sun. The guy stepped in. J.B. froze. It was the Af-ri-can Am-er-i-can from the jail. J.B. started to slide down in his seat. Jackson poked him in the ribs. J.B. scribbled on a meeting list, *That guy is gonna kill me. I gotta get out of here.* Jackson whispered, "At least you got another hour to live clean."

J.B. was off at his meeting. He was always off at his meetings. Cyndra put the kids to bed and turned on the TV. There was nothing. She checked her email. Nothing. Cell. Nothing. It was too hot to sit outside and she'd already had three showers. She checked the freezer. Even the box of ice cream sandwiches didn't look good.

It had been twelve days since she'd crawled up the hill with a five-hundred-dollar hole in her gut. The ATM had not been broken. There was nothing left in the credit cards and only enough in the credit union to cover the bills. Cyndra logged on to a so-called free Facebook slot game. It held her for about three minutes. Besides, once you lost the free credits, you had to buy new ones if you wanted to keep playing. She slammed the mouse on the desk. I've got one thing in my life that makes me happy and now I can't even do that.

She saw the future slogging ahead of her. J.B. would come home. At worst he'd be cranky. At best—and it was hardly best—he'd tell her some corny thing he'd heard in his meeting. He'd flop on the couch and watch TV till he fell asleep. L'il would whimper. She'd plug him in. Maybe she'd take her fourth shower and sit on the back stoop. The worst part was that tomorrow would be exactly the same.

"When the going gets tough…" she muttered, picked up the phone and called Tyra.

"Hey, baby sister," Tyra said. "What's up?"

"Nothing much. J.B.'s at his meeting, the kids are asleep, I'm about to climb out of my skin."

"What's wrong? Is your big baby being himself?"

"There's that, but mostly I just need a little break. Want to run down the hill? I'll call J.B. and tell him to get a ride home."

There was a long pause.

"What?" Cyndra said.

"I gotta slow down a little," Tyra said. "Business hasn't been great. You know so many folks are losing their jobs and things won't pick up till the winter tourons get here."

Cyndra hadn't heard Tyra be this serious ever.

"Yeah, but we can win a few bucks. That'll help."

There was another long pause. "Girl, when was the last

time you made a few bucks down there? I hate to say it, but seems like whatever juju we had going for us is jujued out."

"What is wrong with you, Tyra? Is that new guy making you be all practical and boring?"

"He's long gone," Tyra said. "I'm just watching what's happening around here, all these people out of work, losing their houses, one of the girls works at the salon is sleeping in her car. I will not let that happen to me. You don't know how it is. You got J.B."

They both laughed. Cyndra remembered one of her dad's sayings. "He's about as useful as tits on a boar hog," she said.

"Less," Tyra said. "You want me to come over?"

"Well, actually," Cyndra said, "how about if I borrow a couple hundred bucks and go down by myself? I can stretch that out a good long while. I'll hit, come right back home and pay you off."

It seemed to be the night for long silences.

"I can't do that," Tyra said. "I'm sorry. I just can't do that."

"I get it," Cyndra said. "But I guess you can be a bitch."

"How many years you been waiting to say that, baby sister? 'Cause you said it now and all I want to say is goodbye." Tyra hung up. Cyndra stared at the phone. Her one single lousy life-line had been cut.

She thought about calling Tyra back, but she knew how her sister was. There was going to be a long cold-ass silence for a while. With Tyra, it was one thing for her to say all kinds of shit, but if somebody dished it out, she was all the princess and the pea.

There was only one thing to do. Modern times, you couldn't just write a bum check. Computers had ruined everything. Cyndra opened the freezer and stared at the ice cream sandwiches. They weren't going to do the trick, but they were going to have to do.

J.B. was on closing coffee duty for the meeting. He dumped the old coffee in the sink and put the creamer, sugar, cups and spoons in the file cabinet they used for storage. Jackson would turn off the lights and lock the door. J.B. walked out into the soft desert night. He didn't feel too bad. The big black guy had left right at the end of the meeting. With any luck, the van from the treatment center had picked him up.

As usual these days, there was no luck. The big guy sat on the low wall at the back of the church. He saw J.B. and stood up. "'Scuse me, mister. Can I have a word with you?"

J.B. considered walking calmly toward Jackson's car or back into the meeting room. He looked away from the guy. "I know you," the guy said. "You was in the joint with me, right?"

J.B. thought of the old movie he and Cyndra had found one night on the late night channel. Dustin Hoffman. An old Indian guy. J.B. had liked the part where Dustin Hoffman had to sleep with three Indian chicks. What was it the old guy had said? "It is a good day to die."

"Yeah," J.B. said and walked toward the guy. "I was there. What's up?" He hoped he sounded kind of casual and serene.

"You here at this alcoholics meeting CO, right?" the guy said.

"You're a Marine?" J.B said. "You mean CO like commanding officer?"

"Naw, motherfucker. I mean court ordered. Whoa, sorry about that motherfucker. I didn't mean no disrespect."

"No disrespect taken," J.B. said. "Yeah, I'm CO. I gotta do one-eighty meetings in one-eighty days or I get kicked out of the Corps."

"Whoa, you a Marine?"

"For now."

"I just wanted to say something to you, brother. I'm here for now, see. These alcoholic people are good folks mostly. But, I know I'll drink again. That's just how I am. But, when I seen you in the meeting, I just wanted to tell you I'm sorry for my foolishness when we was in the joint. See, I was…" He stopped and shrugged.

J.B. laughed. "Fucked up, right?"

"You got it, whiteboy. And God willing, I'll be fucked up again."

Jackson locked the door and walked toward them. "Good to see you at the meeting, Roland," he said. "You need a sponsor, give me a call. J.B.'s got my phone number."

"Thanks," Roland said. "I was just telling J.B. here about my situation. I'll be honest with you. I did the crime. I'll do the time. But then, I suspect I'll be in the wind."

"I know how that is," Jackson said. "See you tomorrow night."

He and J.B. walked to Jackson's truck. "No real harm in that man," Jackson said. J.B. nodded. He wondered what it was like to be as mellow as Jackson. He wondered if he, J.B., had real harm in him. He wondered if he'd ever find out.

Jackson took J.B. out for coffee, then drove him home. The house was dark. J.B. wondered if Cyndra and Tyra had headed down for one of their shopping trips. He unlocked the front door and walked into the living room. The blinds were drawn and Cyndra sat on the couch in the gloom. It didn't look good. He had something he had to tell her she wasn't going to like and it wasn't going to help that she was either feeling sorry for herself or ready to make him sorry.

"You okay, baby?" he said. He turned on the light.

"I hate that glare," Cyndra said. "Why'd you do that? It was all nice and peaceful in here." She launched off the couch and stood in front of him with her hands on her hips. "How come everything's got to be the way you want it to be? You could have asked me if I wanted the light on."

J.B. ducked his head and glanced away. She knew that look. It pushed her buttons every time—her pissed-off buttons and her poor little baby guy buttons. It was the don't-get-mad-at-me look a little boy gives his mom when he knows he has to say what he doesn't want to say and he knows it is going to send her postal.

"What."

J.B. flinched. She was already mad. Whenever she said "what" flat like that, he was in for days of one-word sentences and nights of nothing at all.

"Well, sweetpea…"

Cyndra narrowed her ice-blue eyes.

"Okay okay, I shouldn't of called you sweetpea. I'm sorry. Jeez, baby, oh fuck I didn't mean baby…"

She folded her arms across her chest. Everything went quiet, real quiet for about ten thousand years. J.B. wished for the first time in his sorry-ass married daddy life, one of the kids would wake up and holler.

Cyndra nodded. She had a cold smile on her face. "What."

"My shrink says it would be a good idea if you came to a session with me."

Cyndra laughed. "What fuckin' for?"

Bad as waking up in jail covered in puke had been; bad as knowing he was one fuck-up away from being booted out of the Corps, bad as dry hour after long dry hour was—standing in front of his wife who had turned into Cruella De Vil was worse. Plus when he went back to the shrink and said no way was Cyndra coming in, the doc was going to go off into one of her endless spiels about how the alcoholic ("and addict of course, Mr. Bartlett") was only the symptom of a "broken family." And she was going to want to visit "the family" in its "natural setting" which would most definitely hang him up to dry even more. He could see all those quotation marks around the words the doc used when she was being professional. It was her who needed a professional.

"I said," Cyndra said, "what fuckin' for?"

J.B. needed a beer. He needed a case of beer. He needed a case of beer and his truck and the road running east back to West Texas. He was ready to dump the Marines and get the fuck out of Twentynine. The only problem was that Cyndra had the truck keys and the nearest beer was a two-mile walk away.

"The doc says," he muttered, "it's our whole family is broken."

There was a long silence more terrible than the last long silence.

"It's her nose that's going to get broken," Cyndra said. "That snotty fucking cow. I'm calling the bitch right now."

J.B. didn't say anything. He just walked to the big windows and pulled back the curtains. He looked past Cyndra and out the window and shook his head.

Cyndra poked him in the chest. "Are you listening to me? Hey! What are you doing?" She turned and looked out the living room window. "What's out there? I don't see anything. Are you tripping? Did Chaz sneak you some dope or something?"

"The colors," J.B. said. "See those colors out there? How can a mountain be pink and orange? How come I never saw that before? I don't know, babe, you were talking and all of a sudden those mountains go rainbow color."

"For chrissakes, J.B.," Cyndra said. "It's just the sun going down. It's a reflection or something. Don't change the subject, nature boy."

J.B. watched the pinky orange turn to gold. He wanted to tell Cyndra he hadn't meant to change the subject. He wanted to tell her that the mountain and that glow were nothing he could remember ever seeing. And they made him feel almost normal.

But her mouth was set in a straight line, so he said, "I'm sorry. I'm a little weird these days. I don't know. Things look different sometimes. Sharper, maybe. Colors or something."

Cyndra sat down on the coffee table and hugged her knees. "Weird these days?" she said. "The only weird thing these days is you're not drinking or smoking dope and we are supposed to be happier, right? We're supposed to be getting to know each other again, right? We're supposed to be getting back to normal. But how can we get back to normal if there wasn't any normal to begin with?"

He grinned. It sounded funny to him. Nothing normal to begin with. She'd got that right. God help him, he grinned again.

She looked up at him. "What's that stupid look on your face? Seriously, are you high? Stop it, I'm scared."

The grin seemed to have taken over J.B.'s face. It wasn't a doofus grin or the grin of a kid getting caught. He didn't know what it was. Then, he laughed. "Remember the time we left that kegger and were fooling around out in the Joshua trees and the lizard climbed up on my bare ass and fell off 'cause I was going at it so hard?"

"Oh shit," Cyndra said and snorted. She ducked her head so her hair fell over one eye. "What the fuck happened. What the fuck happened to us. What are we going to do, honey? This is a straight-up fucking mess and now all I want to do is laugh. Or go back five years. Or something. I miss you so much. I miss us."

J.B. grabbed her hand. "Oh, babe." They giggled as though they were stoned to the eyebrows. She started to cry. "Oh my god," Cyndra said, "there's nothing we can do. It's like we fell down one of those mine shafts and there's no light and nobody knows where we are and we gotta get out because if we don't, Kelli and L'il will be orphans. Plus we'll be dead."

J.B. leaned in and put his head in her lap. He was laughing so hard he couldn't breathe. She set her hand on his head. He couldn't remember the last time she'd done that.

"Plus," Cyndra said. Her voice was a little girl's. "I got to tell you something. You are going to be so mad. Baby, you're not the only fuck-up here."

J.B.'s heart jumped. He wiped his eyes on her shorts and looked up. "Who is it?" he said. "Who is he? I'll rip his junk off."

Cyndra leaned her head back on the couch and closed her eyes. "It's not a he, or a she, or a them. It's the five thousand dollars we had in the Credit Union Golden Days Vacation Plan."

J.B. sat up. "What are you talking about? You gave the money to your boyfriend?"

"There is no fucking boyfriend! I gave the money to the Indians."

"What Indians?"

"The Palm Springs Indians, whoever they are."

"Fuck me running," J.B. said. "The casinos. Your bitch sister. She dragged you down there to the casino. Five thousand? All five thousand?"

"More. You know our credit cards?"

"We have credit cards?" J. B. said. He'd never used a credit card in his life.

Cyndra laughed. "We had credit cards. That's what you get for making your wife handle the money just like your mom did for your deadbeat dad. Yes, we had credit cards. They're corpses now. No use at all."

J.B. sat up. "You maxed them out?"

"Duh. Chase, five thousand; Citi, twenty-five hundred, BOA, three thousand, credit union, five thousand. Gone. Dead. All we've got is your paycheck."

"And me," J.B. said, "right on the edge of being let go from the one thing I know how to do right."

"Drinking?"

"The Corps. Oh, fuck fuck fuck fuck. The pooch is truly screwed."

"You want a divorce, right," Cyndra said. "Just say it."

J.B. stood. "Are you nuts? We can't afford a divorce."

He pulled her to her feet and put his arm around her shoulders. "Come on, let's go outside and watch that old sun go all the way down."

J.B. stared into the cup of alky coffee. He'd never been able to figure out why the coffee at the meetings tasted like shit and even more, why he kept drinking it. It was meeting one hundred fifty. The white-haired dinosaur in the Pilot truck hat had been talking for at least six months. Everybody else was trying to look as though they were listening. J.B. checked out the tits on the newbie. Either it was colder in the room than he thought or she'd caught his stare and was attracted to him. Man, he loved those clingy tank top things.

Finally, the old guy reached the obligatory last two sentences of his monologue: "So, when people ask me how the twelve steps work, what do I say? I say, 'Just fine.'" J.B. saw Motormouth Mona winding up to talk. He jumped in.

"My wife is driving me crazy. You know how it says, '... became powerless over alcohol and my life became unmanageable'? Well, it should say blah blah, my wife became unmanageable."

He saw a couple of the middle-aged guys roll their eyes, but he didn't care. He had to get it out. If he didn't, he was going on the drunk of all drunks. And, it would be one thing to lose the Marines, but a total other to lose Cyndra and the kids.

"No, seriously," he said. "I'm gonna drink if I don't get this out."

The older hippie chick was looking at him. She drove him nuts. She was always so fucking calm and she had a way of looking into his eyes as though she could see right down to the bullshit. He'd tried to flirt with her once and she'd just laughed. He'd figured he'd soften her up, but no damn way had that happened.

"So. I love my wife, but we forgot how to have fun. It was different when I was drinking. Then it didn't matter. But now? On top of being a chick—sorry, ladies—she's gotten all Al-Anon, plus she stopped gambling so she's all the time yacking about understanding what I'm going through being almost a year sober. I am sorry. Only an alcoholic understands what it's like being a year sober."

A bunch of the old farts nodded. The hippie chick actually flashed him a peace sign.

"Here's an example," J.B. said. "My wife doesn't like to do anything I like to do. For example, I flat-out love to dune-ride. You know, nature and all that. Right before I got popped the first time, I took her out so we could be together dune-riding. At the last minute, she decided she can't take the baby to the sitter, so she brought him along.

"We were out near Cadiz. It was sure enough hot, but I

figured maybe I could rig some shade and she and the baby could just chill out, drink some pop, wave at me now and then and let me show her some of the fancy tricks I know. I checked it out with her. Oh no. No way.

"I got out and hauled my bike outta the back of the truck. Next thing I knew, my wife had rolled up the windows, turned on the air-conditioning and was sitting there with the baby in her lap. 'Hey,' I yelled, 'open the window.' She flipped me off and locked the doors.

"So I take off. I'm so pissed off that it isn't that much fun. I come back every half hour maybe, try to get her to open the windows so we can talk, but do you think she'll even try. We're out there probably two hours. Each time I come back and take off again I get madder. Finally, I'm so mad it is fun. Like I'm doing my thing no matter what.

"See? See what I'm trying to tell you? It's like my wife, my wife Cyndra just won't get out of the truck. She never gets out of the truck—not when she's in the truck, not when she's outside of the truck."

The older hippie chick laughed. J.B. said, "What?" The chick shook her head. Steve, the twelve-step nazi said, "No cross talk." J.B. felt like he was drowning. If they didn't get it here, who the fuck was ever going to get it?

"Wait," J.B. said, "give me a minute more." He looked down at the table. For some reason, he wondered how come his hands looked so young compared to everybody else's. "See, I love the girl to death, but…"

Mona nodded. "But she just won't get out of the truck."

Jackson looked at J.B. and raised his eyebrows. "Yeah," J.B. said, "I'm done. Thanks for letting me share." Jackson closed the meeting. They held hands and prayed. J.B. was still on coffee clean-up, so he unplugged the pot and started to dump the left-overs in the sink. The older hippie chick put the creamer and sugar away. "You want to know why I laughed?" she said. J.B. ducked his head.

He didn't want her to see he was embarrassed.

"Global warming," she said. "All I could think of was how when you were out there and Cyndra had the truck running, massive chunks of ozone were just waiting to fall down on your heads."

"Oh jeez," J.B. said, "don't start."

She grinned. "Just another perspective, friend."

Cyndra was in her sister's old Neon outside J.B.'s alcoholics meeting. J.B.'s truck had been repoed. It seemed like a thousand years ago instead of two that J.B. had driven the truck into the driveway and called her out to take a picture of him and it. "Pretty pony," he'd said and patted the front fender. She'd wished he touched her like that and she'd taken the picture.

Maybe it wasn't a thousand years since then, maybe it was a million. She thought of J.B. rubbing her back the night before, just rubbing her back and nothing else. She smiled. Things were still tricky, but they could have been worse. It had been almost five months since she'd driven up the hill with that black hole in her gut. They were crawling out of debt. And it was August, which meant the Mojave Hell Months were almost over.

L'il was asleep in his carseat. Kelli was at her mom's. The windows front and back were open. You could smell rain in the air though a thunderstorm was miles away. Kenny Chesney was going full blast on the old car stereo. Cyndra watched lightning flicker behind the far clouds to the east. Twice she saw fading animals and eyes in their cool shimmer.

Two of the older ladies in the alcoholics club walked out the door. They were like black paper cut-outs against the yellow light, but Cyndra could hear their voices. She knew who they were—Mona who had to tell you every little detail of everything, and the older lady who still dressed like it was the Summer of Love.

The hippie senior hugged her friend. She must have said, "...what's that music?" The words came right in between "Keg in the Closet" and "What I Need to Do"—which seemed like a miracle to Cyndra. She'd made the tape the old-fashioned way after the truck with the big sound system had to be sold and her sister took both her and J.B.'s iPods in trade for what Cyndra owed her. Kenny. She'd never told J.B., but Kenny looked almost like his twin.

The ladies went their separate ways. The hippie senior headed for her old truck, stopped in the middle of the street, looked up at the sky and walked straight toward Cyndra.

Cyndra's jaw went tight like it did when she figured she was in trouble. She thought about scooting down but the lady was too fast. "Hey," the lady said, "it's you. J.B.'s lady."

"Yep," Cyndra said. "It's me."

"I loved hearing that music, especially on a night like this. You know how the air is getting cooler, that little bitty moon up there. Hearing Kenny makes it like a movie soundtrack."

Cyndra felt her jaw relax.

"Hope you don't mind," the lady said. "I can't remember your name."

"That's okay. It's Cyndra."

"I'm Liz."

They were quiet for a second.

Cyndra pointed toward the lightning. "I'm just watching that."

Liz smiled. "I love that too."

"I've seen a couple faces already up there, like ghost faces." Cyndra almost put her hand over her mouth. Maybe she'd said a little too much.

"In the lightning?" the lady said.

"Yeah. See how the clouds make a veil or maybe hair?"

"How cool."

The woman and Cyndra looked away from each other. Not impolite or embarrassed but because the lightning was out there and they had to see what came next.

"You know," Cyndra said, "most people never get to see stuff like that. Really see it."

"We're pretty lucky," the woman said. "Back up northeast where I was born, we could see the northern lights. You know those?"

Cyndra didn't know but she figured she'd keep her mouth shut and wait.

"Ribbons dancing across the sky, all green and pink," the lady said. "You ever seen them?"

"Nope," Cyndra said. She watched the lightning and imagined if the colors went from silver to green and pink.

"You can find those northern lights on the internet," the lady said.

"We don't have that anymore," Cyndra said. "We did, but we had some financial troubles and had to cancel it."

"Well then," the lady said, "this is even better. Mind if I sit with you till your old man comes out?"

"I'd like that," Cyndra said and laughed. "I bet he was talking about how I won't ever get out of the truck, right?" She climbed out and opened the creaky passenger door. Liz laughed.

"You know," she said, "what we say there and what we hear there…"

"I do know," Cyndra said. The woman settled into the passenger seat. "Here's the deal," Cyndra said. "He might not have told you but I got so far out of the truck I almost didn't find my way back. Palm Springs. Slots. I go to a couple different kinds of meetings now."

"Your old man just came out the door," the woman said. "Can we keep that story for later?"

"You want to meet up some time?"

"I do." Liz took out her phone. "Give me your number. I'll call." Cyndra watched J.B. walk toward the car, his shoulders squared as always. He still had his gramp's cocky walk. He waved. Cyndra waved back. Liz held out her phone. Cyndra punched in her number.

"Thanks," Liz said and got out of the car. She and J.B. high-fived in front of the Neon. He slid into the passenger seat and lit a cigarette. Cyndra started the car, pulled a U-ey and headed toward Adobe. "Hang on," J.B. said. "I gotta tell Liz something." Cyndra pulled next to the curb.

"Hey," J.B. yelled out the window. Liz turned. "Yeah?"

"Hey," J.B. said, "I'll be sure and tell my wife about that global warming, okay?"

Cyndra couldn't hear what Liz hollered back. J.B. waved, closed the window and patted her thigh. "You want to grab a couple tacos at Edchadas before we pick up the squirt?"

Cyndra leaned in toward him. "Like a date, right?"

"Yeah," J.B. laughed. "But you're going to have to get out of the Neon."

NAUTILOID

The Bell is a madhouse on Sunday mornings. I take a deep breath and open the front door. The old Airstream diner is packed with big city hunters, hung-over before they've even headed out to nail their buck; red-eyed Cortez cops just off the graveyard shift and hordes of tourists in their brand new fancy-ass hiking gear. And now there's me. Little Ray. Little Ray by himself, Little Ray wondering if any of The Crew will show up. It's taken me six weeks to force myself to come back in here.

I sit at the counter and put my coat on the seat to my left. Bets hands me my coffee. "Hey, stranger," she says. "Long time..." The hunters explode in manly laughter. I can't catch the rest of Bets' words. I can barely hear myself think. That's what my Meg loved about the Breakfast Bell. "I can't hear myself think," she'd say, "and that is a real blessing. The last fuckin' thing I want to hear is that roller derby in my head."

"Little Ray," Bets says, "you alright? We haven't seen you in forever. I mean. Oh shit, you know what I mean."

"I'm good," I say. "Maybe starving a little. How about taking my order?"

Bets pats my shoulder. "You got it, kid."

I'm fifty-four. Bets's maybe twenty-three. "The usual?" she says. I nod. The usual is two eggs over easy, four hot links, hashbrowns (burn 'em), rye toast and a cup of sausage gravy. Meg used to look over at my plate and say, "Rayboy, you're gonna be dead before you're fifty." I'm not. She is. And there is not one iota of consolation in any of that.

The hunters pay their check, flirt with Bets and stomp out. The table that once was The Crew's is loaded with dirty dishes. I'd made myself sit at the counter. I'd put the coat next to me so nobody would take the seat. It felt crazy, but I had figured that when I looked at that empty seat next to me, it'd be like Meg was on her way in. She'd shove open the big front door, weave through the packed room, pick up my coat and dump it in my lap. I'd say, "And so happy to see you too."

Meg would ignore my subtle wit and open the menu. I'd glance at her. Who knew what she'd look like—one Sunday her hair would be yanked back in a rat's ass pony-tail and she'd be wearing an artfully ripped ZZ Top t-shirt. The next Sunday she'd bitch-step across the room in high-heeled boots, her jeans airbrushed on her perfect butt.

My heart clenches. I look over my shoulder to distract my brain. Rosella, the older flint-eyed waitress, has just finished bussing The Crew table. I grab my coat and coffee and sit down.

Rosella flips me off. "That's a six-top, Ray. It's Sunday. What can't you compute about those two facts?" Rosella is stick-skinny, but she's got the mouth of a much bigger woman. I pretend to duck. "I'll order another three specials to go," I say meekly. Rosella swats me with the damp rag. "You dick."

Bets brings my food. I break the egg yolks, dribble in Gunslinger sauce and dunk a limp toast corner in the puddle. I hear the front door open and heavy steps. Somebody grabs my shoulder.

"Little Ray," Dean says, "looks like you and me had the same idea this a.m." He sits down across from me. He's a tall guy with sharp gray eyes and a drinker's belly. Rosella brings him coffee. I grin at her. "Told you so."

"Told her what?" Dean says.

"That I'd buy three specials if none of you showed up."

"The both of you are spared," Dean says. "Jeff and Carly are headed here. They couldn't find a place to park outside because of the fuckin' tourons. They went up to the lot behind St. Barbara's. They'll be in quick. Hey, Ros, grab me a Virgin Mary, strong on the horseradish. It's November out there." He looks at me. "Where you been, man?"

I make like I'm concentrating on getting up all the egg yolk. "Around. You know."

"Not around anywhere I been," Dean says. "Thought I'd catch you at the Widowmaker at least once."

"I've been busy."

"Busy?" Dean says. "What are you? Some fuckin' soccer mom? Busy? You busy?"

Rosella sets Dean's Virgin Mary in front of him. "Easy on the language, big boy. We got other customers in case you didn't notice."

"My bad," Dean says. "I'll keep it clean. The usual, ma'am." Rosella scoots to the order window and right back with his food. "Minute I heard your truck I called in your order," she says.

Dean nods. "That's why you make the big money, darlin'." He cuts up his sausage and eggs, breaks up his toast and mixes it all into his hashbrowns. "Good food, good meat, good god, let's eat. If Meg was here, she'd say, 'Dean, if I may. You disgust me. Like my old dad used to say, What barn were you raised in?'"

We're talking about Meg already. I think back on those days. Dean would shovel a forkful of the mess into his mouth, chew once and grin at Meg with his mouth open. She would pretend to gag. None of that happens except for Dean shoveling a forkful of the mess in his mouth.

Jeff and Carly walk in and sit down at the table. Jeff looks like he's looked since he was twenty, wild black hair, a gold earring in one ear that's been there since long before hipster developers wore them. Carly's about five foot not quite. She's done something to her hair that makes her look like a bottle-blond Little Orphan Annie.

"Raymond," Carly says, "we thought you'd died." There is a long silence all around the table. "Oh jeez," she says. "Ha ha, Carly. Very funny, Carly."

"Je-sus," Dean says, "way to go."

We're all quiet for what feels like a year. Jeff studies the menu as though there might be something new on it, and puts it down. "What's that expression?" he says. "The elephant in the middle of the room. We got an elephant in the middle of the table—or more likely an elephant not sitting up in her usual seat at the counter right behind Ray."

"Tell us how you really feel, Jeff," Dean says. "Jesus, people. Can't we just kind of ease into this?"

Bets rescues us. "Hey, you two, what can I do you?" Jeff orders oatmeal. Carly orders french toast and bacon. Bets pours coffee all around. My palms are sweaty. I want to grab my check, pay it and get the hell out of Dodge.

"What the fuck," Carly says. "Let's get it over with. Any of you guys go to the memorial service?"

"Nope," Dean says. "Couldn't find my suit."

"Me either," I say. "Plus I don't have a suit."

"Me and Jeff neither," Carly says. "It just didn't seem right. All that family. People who didn't hardly know Meg getting up to say mushy things about her. I would have broken down."

"Yeah," Jeff says, "and we figured what we had to say about Meg the rest of the folks might not want to hear." He snorts. "Remember the time she signed herself up for the Animal Shelter Fun Run?"

Carly snorts. "And ran it drunk on her ass in her babydolls."

"And almost won," Dean says.

"And how about the night she cold-cocked that German tourist in the Widowmaker," Jeff says. "We never did find out what he said to her."

I'm quiet. I know exactly what the German asshole said to Meg. She had told me—the same as she told me almost everything. He'd asked her if she was an Indian. She'd told him that she was an Arapa-ho—which was the punch-line of a dirty joke one of her Navajo friends had told. The German had bowed to her. "I am here to meet you and your people," he said. "We Germans believe that we are all one people. All one great tribe. Do you know that the swastika came from your people?"

Meg had turned away. The guy said, "I am here to meet an Indian woman and blend our bloodlines," and grabbed her ass.

"Auf Wiedersehen, motherfucker," Meg said and popped him one on the nose.

"Okay," I said. "It seems like we're having the unofficial Crew memorial service? Look, I don't know if I'm ready for this."

"Scared you'll cry?" Carly says. She puts her hand on my arm. "Hey, it's okay. Modern guys cry."

I look at the kindness in her eyes and know I have to get out. "Look, you guys," I say, "I love you, but I think I've got somewhere to be." I pat Carly's hand, pick up my check and go to the cash register. Rosella gives me a look. "I need to pay," I say and hand her a twenty. "Keep the change."

I nod to The Crew and push open the front door. The sidewalk is spotted with raindrops, the air washed in soft morning sunlight. I take a deep breath, start walking and wonder again why I lied to my best friends about Meg's memorial service.

The first words Meg ever said to me were, "You look like that skinny chick in Pulp Fiction." It was 2008. I'd just moved into a room in a noisy SRO in Cortez. I'd slept badly and come down the stairs bone-weary, caffeine deprived and starving. Every horizontal surface in the common kitchen had been covered in grease.

I'd headed out to find food. Main Street was quiet, a lot of the storefronts empty. All the For Rent signs were why next Monday morning, I'd be putting on a blue denim shirt and a name tag that said, "Ray, Food Town." The economy was tanking everywhere. I'd had it made in Santa Cruz, the real estate market going nuts, with Silicon Valley young retirees pouring into the area, wanting ocean-front dream homes with granite counter tops and custom teak cabinets—and me a custom cabinet maker. Then, bam! The papers weren't calling it a slump yet, but there I was, walking down a near-empty boondocks street hoping there might be even bad coffee in my immediate future.

I was nearly at the edge of town when I saw a hand-painted wooden bell hanging in front of an old Airstream. Breakfast Bell: breakfast day or night. Dusty old trucks, shiny SUVs and one rusted-out black '82 Turbo Trans Am were parked on the street all around the joint.

I walked up the steps and into a full house. I took the one empty seat at the counter. A chubby teenage waitress dropped a menu in front of me and waved the coffee pot. "Yep," I said. "And cream." She filled my cup, said, "Hey, I'm Bets. I'll be your server today," and powered off toward the kitchen. I doctored up the coffee, slammed half of it down and shivered.

"You look like that skinny chick in Pulp Fiction," the woman next to me said. "You know where she hoovers up a couple of lines in the Ladies and goes, 'God Damn! God Damn!'" She reached across me for the creamer. "You must have had some night what with you needing your caffeine fix that bad."

I was spared answering by Bets coming back for my order. I checked the tariff on the steak and eggs. Not in my league. "Try the special," the woman next to me said. "It's good and there's lots. Eggs, sausage, home fries and toast. A local Basque guy makes the sausage. Choriza. It'll jack your heart rate." She shoved out her hand. "I'm Meg."

I shook Meg's hand and said to Bets, "The Special. And just leave that coffee pot on the counter."

"Now you're getting it," Meg said.

"I'm Ray. Usually get called Little Ray."

Meg laughed. "Suits you. At least you aren't a flabby gorilla like a lot of the guys around here. Me? Standard getting-by getting-older single chick in a one-horse town."

I looked at her more closely. She had frost-gray eyes, a wise-ass grin and long red-brown hair.

"Cinnamon," I said.

"What?"

"Your hair's the color of cinnamon."

"Oh great," Meg said. "A new guy finally comes to town who's even a little cute and he's gay. Right?"

"Because I said your hair was cinnamon?"

"There isn't a straight guy in the world who would say that," she said.

"Yep," I said. "But it's not like I'm constantly bursting into 'YMCA.' You've got some serious gaydar going on."

"Thanks. My first husband turned out to be queer."

"What a coincidence," I said, "so did mine."

Bets brought my food. I took a bite of the sausage patty and abruptly had a new relationship with my sinuses. "Hooee," I said.

"So what are you?" Meg said.

"Besides gay and a little cute? A wood worker. Custom cabinet maker. From Santa Cruz."

"How come you're here?"

"The real estate market tanked. I lost my house. And I met a guy in a bar. He said he was a cowboy. He had great cheekbones and an even greater butt. We got to talking. He said he was heading for Cortez, Colorado, and did I want to come along and could I drive and pay for gas."

"What happened?"

"Turned out he wasn't a cowboy."

A big guy came up to us. "Hey, Meg," he said, "me and Jeff and Carly just grabbed a table. Sit with us."

Meg looked up. "Big Dean, I want you to meet Little Ray. He's the new kid in town."

Dean shook my hand. "Bring him too. We got room."

Meg and I grabbed our food and coffee and followed Dean to the biggest table in the room. He sat down between a short woman in her late twenties with streaked brown hair and a skinny guy the same age with a mullet and a little gold hoop earring. The woman reached out her hand. "I'm Carly. And this throwback to the Eighties is my husband, Jeff."

Four hours later, the Bell was closing and I was one of

The Crew. We swapped phone numbers and emails and headed out into a blue-brilliant Colorado afternoon. I started up the street for home—as it were. Meg grabbed my arm and pointed at the Trans Am. "You need a ride? We could maybe go for a Sunday drive up to Durango. I could use a change of scene."

"That's yours?"

"Sold my soul for it."

"That makes two of us," I said.

"You've got a Trans Am?"

"I wish. I sold my soul for a cute ass."

Meg opened the passenger door and I got in. "I love stories," she said. "You can tell me the whole story on the way out of town."

Over the next year I told Meg the whole story. She told me hers. By the time we'd hung out at the Bell for nearly seven years, I felt as though I'd known Meg and The Crew my whole life. Every Sunday morning, Carly, Jeff and Big Dean sat at the table near the counter. Meg and I perched on the counter stools next to them. We five never stopped talking. We criticized everybody we saw who wasn't us—baby-faced Eurotrash tourists who tried hard not to look at the Navajos, or charged up to them and shoved their Hasselblads in their faces; middle-aged hippie chicks in swoopy skirts who'd discovered they couldn't afford to move to Durango to find themselves and settled for Cortez; rich émigrés who had built their eco-friendly four-thousand-square-foot houses on what used to be high desert and who prided themselves on knowing the "genuine" Cortez.

Meg found and quit eight different jobs. I moved up to Produce Manager. She had one date with the new math teacher at the high school. I had none at all, despite my almost middle-aged cuteness. We agreed that sometimes the excitement was unbearable.

Carly and Jeff tried to have a kid and finally gave up. Dean just moved through day after day, waking at five, running his dogs, working at the lumber yard and settling in front of bass fishing specials with a twelve-pack till he fell asleep. For almost six years, I was part of the family I had never had.

Then Meg started going out of town every couple weeks. One Friday night we were eating chile rellenos at Fiesta Mexicana and I asked her what was up.

"Hot date," she said. "I lie. I decided I needed to get serious about the smoking. I'm seeing a shrink in Durango so I can quit." She forked one of her rellenos on to my plate. "Only thing is, even thinking about giving up the smokes, I got no appetite." She patted her butt. "I'm down to a size eight."

The waitress Sara bustled over to us. "You want me to warm up that relleno for you?" Meg shook her head. "It's great. I was just telling Little Ray that I gotta quit smoking and I feel so shitty about it I don't want to eat much."

Sara patted her on the shoulder. When Fiesta Mexicana said it was a family restaurant, they meant it. Meg held Sara's hand. "Thanks, sweetheart. You can bring me another Milagro, skip the lime."

"Hey," I said.

"Shut up, pal," Meg said. "Tequila's a vegetable."

The Crew minus Carly rolled into the Bell early the next Sunday morning. Rosella grabbed the coffee pot and five cups and set us up fast. "Where's your old lady, Jeff," she said. "She finally wise up and leave you?"

"Nope. She said she had to check our box at the post office."

"Probably for the best," Rosella said. "It's not as if there'd be any alimony in it for her if she did wise up. You all up for the usual?"

Dean gave a thumbs up and Rosella walked back to the kitchen. The front door opened. Carly walked in, blissing like she'd had shrooms for breakfast.

"Hey, girl," Meg called out. "What's up?" Carly sat down, pulled a sheaf of papers out of her backpack and spread them out on the table. "Ta da!"

"What are those?" Dean said. "They look a little too government for me."

"Yep," Carly said. "We have our very own permit to run the San Juan in April. Two-day trip. Put in at Sand Island, take out at Mexican Hat."

"God damn," Dean said. "I'm going to steal you away from Jeff. That's the best time to be on that water."

"It's been years," Meg said, "since I paddled the Juanner. I was twenty-six. It was just me, this darling river boy, a couple ounces of Acapulco Gold and a case of beer."

"Remember anything?" Jeff said.

"Shoulders, broad tan shoulders with freckles on them."

"So," Carly said, "everybody in?"

Meg picked me up at six a.m. the morning of the big day. The air was damp, the April sky more opal than blue. A canoe was jury-rigged to the top of the Trans Am and the backseat was loaded with coolers and ammo cans.

Jeff's boss had called him in the day before, so Jeff had loaned me his big river bag. I'd packed it the night before and liberated a box of donuts from the job. Meg handed me a thermos of the Bell's finest joe. "Get wired," she said. "We've got a long day ahead of us. Too bad Jeff can't make it, but his boss is a real asshole."

We were quiet on the drive to Sand Island. We'd gotten good at that—just being in each other's company. The first green of spring was creeping up across the sand and rocks. Ute Mountain gleamed cobalt and fawn.

"Hey, Meg," I said, "you ever notice how the Old Ute is all cobalt and fawn in this light?" She snorted. "That's why you don't get picked up by manly cowboys out here," she said. "You still talk hair-dresser."

We bumped down the dirt road to the Sand Island put-in. Carly and Dean were on the shoreline pumping up their inflatables. Meg parked and we unloaded her canoe. We started packing coolers, ammo cans, tents and gear in the boats. I figured it was going pretty smoothly, until Dean leaned into Meg's canoe with a heavy ammo can. "Thanks, mom," she said. "I can load that."

"Fuck you," Dean said. "I was just trying to help. You've been looking a little peaked lately."

"And fuck you, Dean," Meg said. "I'm fine." Dean shook his head and stomped off up-river. Big and loud as he is, he can't stand when it gets weird between people.

Meg grabbed my arm. "Go find Dean. I can rig. There's not much left to do."

I pushed my way through the rabbitbrush. Dean was perched on a sandstone slab at the edge of the gray-brown water. He held a knife. I froze. "What the hell you doing, Big Man?"

He laughed and shook his head. "Lighten up, Raymond. I'm whittling. Take a look." He held out a willow branch. There was the beginning of a face carved into it. "Recognize that nose? I'm going to make Meg glaring at me, Carly looking worried and me staring off into space."

I sat down next to him. "So what's it for?"

"I finish it up. We toss it in the river for good luck, go back, get in our boats and follow it down this old muddy." He made a few more cuts and handed the stick to me. I ran my thumb over Meg's face. "You believe in this?"

"Can't hurt," he said. "I left the church a long time ago—all those damn candles and talking to invisible people in the sky—but they get you before seven, they got you. Mostly, carving stuff like this calms me down."

"Nothing much calms me down these days," I said. I wanted to tell him I was worried about Meg but I figured if she found out I was and had blabbed it to Dean, she'd kill me.

"You need to get your hands back on the wood," he said. "Make a bookshelf. Something."

"Seems like I've lost the heart for it," I said. "Plus my ass is whipped by the time I get home from fondling the cucumbers."

"Now that was crude, fellow." He took the stick from me

and resumed carving. We were quiet for a while. He polished the totem on his sleeve and offered it to me. "Want to do the honors?"

"That'd jinx us for sure."

He tossed the stick out into the middle of the slow current. We watched it bob along for a minute, then walked back to the put-in. Carly and Meg sat on a log passing a joint back and forth. Meg held the dope out to me. "Hey, boys. Toke up. And let's get this flotilla into the raging white-water."

Carly shivered. "Ooooooh, scary!"

The river worked on me fast. It wasn't just the easy pitch of the canoe in the gentle current or the way the sun turned the dry rabbitbrush to pale gold. As I slowed down, I realized that paddling felt a lot like those times when I was lost in carving a piece of wood, no thought, just movement, no Ray, just the work.

Meg and I let the others get ahead. We were about a half-hour from the take-out for lunch when Meg pointed to a little beach covered with cottonwood drift logs. "I've got a surprise for you. Let's pull over here."

"What about the rest of them?"

"We'll catch them up. And if we don't, our camp is at Eight Foot Rapid. They'll be there."

We beached the canoe, stepped into the ice-melt water and pulled the canoe up on the sand. "See that little canyon going up from the beach?" Meg said. "We're going there. Follow me."

She clipped on a fannypack and walked across the sand. A clump of bushes with feathery green branches cast shadows on the beach. Meg pointed to them. "I bet you think those are pretty?"

"I do," I said. "I'm trying to think of a sensitive color to describe them."

"They're tamarisk, they're not native and they're taking over. They drive out the native veg—the willows and cottonwoods."

"How'd they get here?"

"Meddling humans, that's how." She turned away and

walked into the mouth of the little canyon. I followed. The sand darkened, grew damp and became a stream wide as my hand. Meg sat and took off her sandals. "We can go barefoot the rest of the way." I kicked off my flip flops, stepped into the water and let out the breath I hadn't known I was holding. I shivered. "Where are we?"

"Ray," Meg said. "You cold? It's ninety degrees."

I stepped out of the water and over to the side of the wash. "I don't know. This place feels eerie to me. I need to recalibrate." I sat on a log. Meg hunkered down next to me and pulled out her cigarettes.

"What are we doing here?" I said. "Maybe it's just me being a former city boy, but there's something spooky about this place."

Meg dug into the sand near her foot. "Got one," she said and tossed me a pebble. "Check it out."

The stone was gray with streaks of black that looked like ferns. "It's a fossil."

"Yep," she said. "A chunk of a nautiloid. Maybe what you're feeling isn't spooky. Maybe it's just something really really old."

I studied the pebble to give me time to gather what I knew I had to say. "Maybe it's something new. Dean was right. You're tired all the time. And I've seen you go wobbly and stumble. Plus, you're losing weight—lots of weight. Are you doing that throwing-up thing?"

Meg looked away. "Guess this is the time—I sure as shit am throwing up, but not on purpose. You want to know the details?"

"No. I need to know the details."

"My pal," Meg said. "Okay. Colon cancer. I ignored what I knew was wrong. By the time I got to the clinic, it had spread. It's in my liver. Too late for surgery. I've been getting chemo in Durango. 'We poison you,' my doc says, 'so you can buy a little more time. You might want to think about cutting out the cigarettes.'" She lit up. "Right now, there's about four things that make me comfortable and my smokes are one of them."

We sat for a while without saying anything. Meg field-stripped her cigarette and got to her feet. "Come on," she said. "You're going to love this."

I looked up at her. "Don't give me that look," she said. "We talked. Now we walk." She tugged on my shirt. I stood and we picked our way up the wash. The walls narrowed till we had to walk single file. Meg went ahead. I loved watching her move easily over the red and gray rocks. She had broad shoulders for a woman and a narrow butt. The walls of the wash cast a cool shadow over her. I caught my breath. I knew in that instant that had she been a man I would have been in love with her.

Meg stopped at a blind curve in the trail, turned and held up her hand. "Stop. Wait till I'm around the curve. I'll let you know when to come forward." I waited. Time went funny the way it does when you suddenly think you might never see that beloved person again. I wanted to disobey her, run forward, find her glaring at me and saying, "Ray. I told you. Bad Ray. No miracle."

"Okay," she called. "You can come ahead."

I walked around the curve. Meg pointed at the wall of the wash. "Look," she said. "How's that for a miracle, city boy." A dark mineral galaxy was embedded in the pale sandstone. "What is it?"

"Look closer."

I leaned in and saw a scattering of discs and cross sections of articulated cylinders. "They're nautiloids," Meg said. "The last time they lived was five hundred million years ago. They're the ancestors of octopuses and squid."

"Octopi," I said and reached up to touch one.

"Wise-ass," Meg said. "Don't touch them."

I pulled back my hand. "Why?"

"I dated a rogue geologist for a while and he taught me a bunch of stuff. He figured maybe a hundred million years of people touching them might wear them away."

"You figure our species will be around that long?" I said.

"Maybe some of us. Let's go."

We walked till the canyon pinched out. Meg dropped to the sand and leaned against the end wall. "Look, Ray, I don't want to talk more about what's happening, okay?"

I hunkered down next to her. "Then you better stop making subtle references to It."

"It," she said. "Yeah. Well, sometimes my terrified takes over." She lit a cigarette and blew the smoke away from me.

"Thanks," I said. "I intend to stick around for a while."

"Thanks for the peptalk." She dug her toes into the sand. "Okay, here's the deal. I'm not going to tell The Crew till I don't have a choice. Carly'll try to get me to talk about my feelings and yap about some New Age happy horseshit. The guys will be embarrassed. I haven't told what's left of my family yet. Same deal. I'll wait till the last minute. So. You're my wing-man."

"I can live with that." We looked at each other and burst into laughter. "Ah shit," she said. "Everything means something different than it did before."

She hauled herself up. "Let's go. We've been away long enough that Dean and Mother Carly'll have supper on."

"Nice," I said. "Pretty sneaky."

"Yep," Meg said. "Coyote to the end."

It moved fast. I watched Meg shrink into the old lady she would never be and hid that I was watching. I never saw her without a lit cigarette and more and more often, taking sips from a flask she kept in her bag. I asked her what she was drinking. She smiled slyly. "It's a very special cocktail—verrrrry special. An old dealer pal of mine mixed it up for me. Thank god for friends in low places."

Finally the late August Sunday morning came when Carly looked up at Meg on her perch at the counter of the Bell and said, "Okay, girlfriend, what's going on? You're a toothpick—a toothpick that got knocked up. You're too tired to hang out. And you're the color of a hang-over. This might not be the time or the place, but inquiring minds need to know."

Meg leaned down. "It's not the time or place, but what the hell, when and where could be? Okay. I'm dying. I've got the big C. It's past the point where they can do anything. I've got a couple months on my feet, then who knows?"

Carly slammed her fist on the table. "And you didn't tell us till now? For chrissake, Meg. Maybe we could have done something." She looked down at her fist and unclenched her fingers. "God damn you. Oh, just god damn you." Jeff put his hand over her fingers.

"Meg, this sucks." Carly ducked her head. "Listen, there's all kinds of stuff you can take for this, you know, tinctures, herbs, there's that little shop that sells homeopathic remedies. Normal medicine doesn't know what the fuck it's doing."

"Carly, normal medicine gives me serious pain-killers. That's good enough for me."

Meg stopped the chemo. She and I spent most of our time together, either at the Widowmaker, the Ute casino or taking short walks. One afternoon, we took a break from handing money over to the Utes and walked out back to a little bridge over Navajo Wash. Meg perched on a low wall covered with graffiti. "I don't know how much longer I'll be able to get around," she said.

I looked down. I didn't want her to see what was in my face. Damn, if a bright red heart and the words Love Life weren't painted low on the wall next to her leg. "Meg," I said. "Look down by your leg."

She stood and looked. "Fuck sake, Ray. Thank you for being the friend who would never say sappy shit like that to me."

Two weeks later, I was working with the market's endless spread sheets when I got a call on my cell. "Is this Ray Hutchins?" My hands went cold. "That's me," I said. "Margaret Lawson asked us to call you," the nurse said. "She's at Emergency. The ambulance just brought her in. A neighbor found her at the bottom of Ms.

Lawson's front steps."

I didn't even bother to log off. I grabbed my car keys, told the manager a friend was in trouble and climbed in my old truck. The six blocks to the ED. took forever. I slammed into a parking spot and raced through the door. An intake nurse looked up. He was a young guy with dreds and paisley scrubs. "Hey, man," he said, "take a breath and tell me what's up."

"I got a call. My friend Meg Lawson. Where is she?"

The nurse nodded. "Hey man, she's okay. Let me get Sandy. She'll take you in."

A plump Navajo teenager took me to a cubicle and pulled back the curtains. Meg had IVs in both arms. She was surrounded by machines, their LED lights flickering on her gray-green face. She looked at me. "Beam me up, Scotty."

I pulled a chair next to the bed and took her cold hand. "Yeah," I said. "We gotta get the warp drive operational."

Meg closed her eyes. "So I got a little too enthusiastic about my cocktail and too unenthusiastic about eating. I was going for the mail, started down the steps and ended up here."

"Chicks," I said. "Girls just want to have fun."

"Here's the worst part," she said. "They insisted I give them a family name—you know, blood family, not real family. I was so spaced-out I gave them my sister Shannon's name."

"Shannon the Saved," I said. "Jaysus."

"Exactly," Meg said. "Jaysus who takes away all suffering, Lamb of God, etc. etc. What I want to know is where that long-haired freak is when I need him?"

She took a deep breath and let it out in a sob. I'd never seen her cry before. "I need a smoke," she whimpered. "I need a smoke and my cocktail and I need you to carry my skinny ass out of here."

The Navajo nurse pulled back the curtains. "Are you family?" she said.

"Yes," Meg said. "He's my half-brother Ray."

"Good," the nurse said. "I wanted to tell you both the

doctor's plan. We'll keep you here overnight and tomorrow morning for some tests. Then you can go home. The doctor's office will call you once the test work comes back." She turned to leave. "Oh, and your sister Shannon called. She wanted you to know that she's flying in this evening."

"Swell," Meg said. "That's real swell. Thanks."

The nurse checked a couple of the machines, made notes and left. "Ray," Meg said. "This may be the worst time in my life: my special cocktail is on the kitchen table, my smokes are on the couch, I've got a belly like a six-months pregnant chick, my born-again sister is flying here and my gorgeous best guy friend is still gay."

"Man," I said, "I can resolve the cocktail and smokes problems, but the rest of it is going to have to be in Jaysus' hands."

"How about you scamper out," Meg said, "and see what you can resolve."

Meg called the next afternoon. Her voice sounded strange. "Hey," I said, "are you okay? You sound funny."

"Remember that list of unpleasantries I gave you yesterday?" she said. "Add in that Shannon is praying over me. Please come over as soon as you can and maybe pick up one of those fake pagan tattoos the herb lady sells and stick it on your forehead."

I skipped the tattoos, but grabbed a joint from one of the baggers. When I tried to open the door to Meg's place, it was locked. Her door was never locked. I rang the bell. A willowy middle-aged woman opened the door just enough to see me.

"Yes," she said. "What can I do for you?"

"I'm Ray," I said. "Came over to see how Meg's doing."

"Bless your soul," the woman said. I was suddenly five years old, sitting in a pew trying to figure out what I needed to confess.

"No no," I said. "It's my pleasure."

She didn't make a move to open the door wider. "Uh, can I come in?" I said.

"Sis. Sis," Meg called from somewhere in the house. "Let

Ray in. He's the home health aide."

"Oh gosh," Shannon said and blushed. "I am so sorry. I'm Shannon. You come right in. Meg and I have a batch of oatmeal chippers in the oven."

Meg? Oatmeal chippers? "That's so kind of you," I said.

Shannon walked me into the kitchen. Meg sat at the table wearing shades and playing solitaire. She slapped the winning King of Diamonds down on the pile. "Gotcha," she said. "Raymundo," she said, "what's on our schedule?"

"How about a little R&R," I said.

"As in?"

"As in, we get you out for a little drive. Breathe in some fresh air. Check out the Ute, see if his Xanax is still working."

Shannon took the cookies out of the oven. "Now, just who is the Ute?" she said and began arranging cookies on a plate. She poured Meg and me coffee, sat down with us, bowed her head, mumbled something and yaffled down a substantial cookie in two bites.

"The Ute," Meg said, " is the mountain just north of the Ute Mountain Tribe casino."

"And, what is Xanax?" Shannon said.

Meg glanced at me.

"Xanax," I said—good home health aide that I was—"is a relaxant. It's used for anxiety."

"I see," Shannon said, "but I don't see how a mountain could be anxious."

We were all quiet for what seemed like forever. Finally, Meg patted Shannon's arm. "It's just a joke sis. A locals' joke. We call the mountain the Sleeping Ute because it looks like a big Indian guy lying down. You have to be from here to get it."

"Speaking of local," I said. "Let's get you in the Trans Am and head out for a while."

"You run along," Shannon said. "I'll tidy up and check my email."

Meg and I walked toward the Trans Am. "You want to drive?" I said.

Meg shook her head. "I just took a swig of my cocktail. Be safer if you took charge, what with me being pretty relaxed here. Which, by the way, is why I haven't killed my dear sweet sister yet."

I pulled out onto the highway and turned east. "The Ute is west," Meg said. I cut left onto a dirt road. "Stealth," I said. "That way Shannon can't find us when she calls the cops when we've been gone over an hour." I pulled to the side of the road and handed a pack of cigarettes to Meg.

"Oh thank you, blessed St. Philip Morris," she said, took out a smoke and lit it. "So what's the plan?"

"No plan. What do you want to do?"

"You mean aside from the Trans Am being a time travel ship and we're back three years ago?"

"Yeah, but then you'd have to go on the date with that nice teacher," I said.

"I'm not saying that dying is better," Meg said, "but that was a near-death experience."

"So?"

"Okay, my choice is we get big fat sundaes at Dairy Queen and drive up to Mesa Verde. I want to show you something."

We turned onto the park road that wound up the mesa to the ruins. "I bet you're wondering how I'm going to go on one of the tours, right?" Meg said. She tossed what was left of her Brownie Batter Blizzard out her window. "Yeah, yeah, I know. Littering. Tell that to the coyotes."

"I'm too sensitive and well-trained in health care to ask how you're going to go on a tour."

"We aren't going on a tour. Just turn where I tell you."

The road topped out on the mesa and ran along the edge, lush sage trembling feathery, dry rabbitbrush shimmering gold in a September breeze. We paid at the entrance station and kept straight on the mesa top road. Meg pointed at a left turn marker.

"Go down that road a few yards and stop, so we can change seats," Meg said. "I'm going to drive. That way you can close your eyes till we get there. Don't get that worried-but-hiding-it Ray look. I can handle this."

We swapped seats. Meg looked like a gleeful child with premature aging. "Close your eyes," she said. I did. The raw green scent of juniper and sage poured in through the open window. She drove for a few minutes, then pulled over. "Okay," Meg said. "Keep your eyes closed and let me walk you." We climbed out; she took my elbow and snuggled into me. She smelled faintly of the cancer. I pulled her closer. She led us straight ahead, then in a half circle and stopped. "Open your eyes."

I opened my eyes. There was NPS fencing around a crumbling two-story tower with a tall juniper snag to its right and a little roofless kiva in front. Fire-blackened forest lay around the ruin. "This is my favorite place in the whole world," Meg said. "Before the cancer started kicking my butt, I came here every week. I never told you about it—not anything about you—just because I learned long ago that I have to have some private stuff.

"People used to be able to go inside. There's an underground passageway from the ground floor of the tower into the kiva. It's all built from sandstone held together with local clay. I used to sit on one of the little benches in the kiva. The air smelled old, good old. If we could still go in, you'd see fossils in the stone and centuries-old fingerprints in the mortar."

"How come just the few rooms?" I said.

Meg pointed to a deep canyon a few hundred feet away. "It could have been a surveillance post, but I doubt it because a lookout wouldn't have had a kiva. I don't really care what the facts are. I like to think that an un-married woman or a widow lived here, away from the rest of the people. Maybe she was a healer. Maybe she could have visions here."

Meg walked to a fallen cedar and sat down. "I need to rest

a little. I need to be alone for a little bit. I'm going to go down into the kiva. Ray, would you feel bad if I asked you to go back to the car and play look-out?"

"Be that way," I said.

"Thanks, my brother."

I walked to the Trans Am and leaned against the back bumper. That half hour before Meg walked out from the kiva might have been the most alone I've ever felt in my life.

Hunting season was back. Meg called. "How about Sunday sunrise services at the Bell. Let's go early, so we can beat the Cabelaed-out deer slayers." I picked Meg and her new walker up at six a.m. and handed over a carton of smokes and a pint of Jim Beam.

"Oh yeah," she said, "thou good and faithful servant." She opened the JB and took a deep swallow. "You know, the only good thing about dying is you don't have to live healthy. It's a get outta kale jail card."

I parked in the handicapped spot in front of the Bell and started to help Meg out of my truck. She shook my hand off, hobbled up the steps and opened the door. "Let's go," she said. "The gang's all here."

Meg and I found our places up at the counter and ordered. "Hey, girl," Carly said, "how are..." Meg held up her hand. "Nope. We're not discussing anything to do with my health. That will not be a table topic. Watch this." She kicked out, spun around on her stool a couple times, stopped and gasped.

"What?" Carly said. "Meg, what?"

Meg grabbed my arm. "Ray," she whispered. "Something's wrong." Carly dialed 911.

A nurse settled The Crew and me into the ED waiting room and told us the doc would be in soon. We snuck the JB around. Carly picked up a magazine, flipped it open, flipped it shut and put it carefully back in the pile. After what could have been a year, a gray-haired woman came in.

"Hello. I'm Dr. Vitols." She shook each of our hands. "I don't have any news for you yet. We need to run some tests. You are welcome to visit with Ms. Lawson for a few minutes. Only a few. I hope you understand."

Carly nodded. "Is she..."

"She is fully conscious and more than a little angry, I think." Dr. Vitols smiled. "She has, how do you Americans say it, the fighting spirit."

The doc led us to the curtained cubicle. I wanted to get the hell out of there, but I made myself walk in. Meg looked up. "You guys," she said. "You know, I'm just fine with dying—but losing my mind wasn't supposed to be part of the deal."

"You're not going crazy," I said.

"Want to bet? You try looking down at a menu and all the letters are wobbling across the page. Then, the room starts to spin around and the next thing you know you're flat on your back looking up at these ugly fluorescent lights."

Carly took Meg's hand. "Maybe it's the drugs."

"It's not. I don't know how I know that, but it isn't."

Dean hunkered down. "Thanks, Deano," Meg said. "I was starting to feel like I'd been hit by a car and all the Looky Lous were staring down at me, waiting for something exciting to happen."

We all crouched at the sides of the bed. Jeff set the near-empty Beam bottle on the bedside stand. Meg looked at us, then at the opening in the curtains. She closed her eyes. "Oh shit."

Shannon stood just outside the cubicle. "What is that?" she said quietly, walked in and picked up the JB. "I should report the lot of you."

"It's okay, Shannon," I said. "Dean had it in his pocket from breakfast. We didn't give it to Meg."

"Be that as it may," Shannon said, "would you all please leave? Dr. Vitols is coming in to explain to Meg and me what we need to do next."

Carly started to say something, but I cut her off. "We were just headed out," I said. I leaned down and kissed Meg on the cheek. "Let me know what the doc says."

Meg called me at work later that afternoon. "I'm home. The doc said that she suspected the cancer was on the move and ordered tests. I had an MRI which was weirdly cool—I'll tell you about it later—but there's a patchy area in my cerebellum. That's why I got dizzy. Ray, please come over asap. There's more."

I hung up and walked into the boss' office. "You don't need to say nothing," the boss said. "You got mercy leave. Just show up when you can."

I grabbed my coat and barreled over to Meg's. Shannon opened the door. "Ray," she said, "I'm sorry about that little fracas in the ED. I'm kind of jumpy these days."

"Aren't we all? No foul, no harm."

Meg lay on the couch, her body barely a bump under an old quilt. "Hope you don't mind if I don't sit up," she said. "That room spinning deal is just like before you're shit-faced and you puke." She patted the couch next to her hip. "Sit down. You're going to need to be sitting when you hear what comes next."

I sat. I could feel her bones through the quilt. "Which is?"

"Nothing."

"Nothing?" I said.

"The doc said the only chemo that might work—might work—could take my memory and what's left of my hair. No way. My crowning glory is going with me."

Shannon brought me a cup of coffee and more damn cookies.

"Thanks," I said. She started to go to the kitchen. "Shannon," Meg said, "pull up a chair."

"I just thought maybe you and Ray needed some time alone," Shannon said.

"Are you kidding?" Meg said. "You and Ray are the pit crew." She shifted a little. Pain flashed across her face. She looked me in the eye. "So the doc thinks it's time for hospice. They can more easily give me steroids and pain-killers and monitor things than you and Shannon can here."

"What?" I said. "No."

Meg took my hand. "Ray, don't look so upset. That hospice is right across from Lotsa Pasta. They say that on their website. You can bring me a medium with anchovies. How crazy cool is that?"

I wanted to smack her. I wanted to say, "Meg, stop joking. Stop being so fucking tough. Ask me to hold you. Ask me to hold you while you cry and I cry with you."

I looked at Shannon. "Ray, she's always been like this. She drove our old dad nuts because she just wouldn't take anything seriously. Don't even try to talk sense into her."

"Excuse me," Meg said. "Kindly don't discuss me in the third person. I'm here—and I'm damn well going to be here until I'm not."

I visited hospice every day. Meg's voice grew weaker and weaker. She could only whisper when she told me about the MRI. "Ray, it was like being in a space ship on shrooms. There were these low hums that sounded exactly like those Tibetan Buddhist chants we watched on Youtube. I just listened and put myself in my boat on the San Juan and rode the sound downstream."

A week later, I watched Meg begin to draw into herself. She was always conscious when I visited, but the past was what we talked about. After a couple weeks, she kept a black sleep mask over her eyes most of the time. One afternoon she said, "It's my cave, Ray. It's like we walked up that little wash and found a cave and when you're here, we're sitting in it and smelling rain on the sagebrush instead of Lysol."

I sat with her a while till she fell into a restless sleep. "I'll be back," I whispered and left. I walked back and forth the length of downtown. I couldn't figure out how people could just buy lousy

Starbucks coffee, drop into the tourist boutiques and stumble out of the pretend Western bars like everything was normal. I wanted to shake them and say, "Do you know that death is real? Do you know that people you love will die?"

I could imagine Meg walking next to me and how we didn't need to say a word when some touron in a brand new Stetson sauntered down the sidewalk. "Fuck," I muttered. "I don't know how to do this alone." I wasn't even sure what "this" was. Then light glinted off something in a shop window. I scoped it out. The streetlight was reflecting off a little polished nautiloid, a dark brown spiral gleaming in rock the pure black of a winter mountain sky. I walked into the shop and bought it.

Shannon called me at work the next day. It was close to quitting time, the sky outside dark. "Ray, Meg's having seizures. The hospice sent her to the hospital. She asked me to tell you to come. The front desk guy will tell you where to go. I told him you're family."

I thanked her, drove to the hospital, checked in with the desk volunteer and took the elevator to the second floor. I walked out into the usual waft of disinfectant, ozone, the faint reek of incontinence pads—and something else, something sweet and terrible. My heart jolted.

There was a stairwell door next to the elevator. I stumbled through it. The stairs were concrete, the air smelled of good clean dust. I bent and leaned my head on the metal railing. "Meg," I said, "I'll get to you. In a minute I'll stand up and go back through that door. I'm scared. I'm scared you've already gone and I'll never see you again. Worse, I'm scared I don't have the guts to help you die right."

I couldn't cry. It wasn't that I hadn't gone through this scene a dozen times in AIDS-riddled southern California. That had been hideous, but it hadn't been Meg. I slowly opened the door and walked carefully into the hall.

"Just go," I muttered and headed for Meg's room. Her door was closed. I knocked and heard what sounded like the voice of an old man. There was a blurred cough, then another. I opened the door. The curtains on the big window were half open. The sky outside was platinum, a full moon hanging just above the horizon.

The room itself was gloomy except for the LED lights on the equipment. A machine beeped, another wheezed like painful breaths. I opened the curtains all the way. Meg's face and one bare arm glowed softly in the moonlight. I sat down on the bed.

"Meg," I said. "I'm here. I brought you something." I opened her left hand, put the nautiloid on her palm and closed her fingers around it. She sighed, pulled off the eyeshade and opened her eyes. "Ray. You are here." She looked down at the fossil and pressed it to her cheek.

"I am."

"I dreamed you were, but you weren't."

"I'm not a dream."

"Whew," she said. "It's weird here. The nurses are great, but they're telling me they're concerned because I seem low and would I like an anti-depressant?"

"Would you?"

"What?"

"Like an anti-depressant."

"How?"

"Tell them you could use a little fresh air. They fix you up in a wheelchair and your home health aide rolls you outside for a nice calming cigarette and a view of the Ute under the full moon."

"Oh, my Robin Hood," Meg said. "I'm afraid we've gone way past that. I'm too wobbly to sit up straight and too exhausted to do anything but lie here." She held the nautiloid up to the moonlight. "This will have to do." She ran the stone over her forehead. "Ray, the biggest thing they don't tell you about the pain is how boring it is."

There was nothing to say to that—nothing.

Meg waved toward the nightstand. "My purse," she said. "Get it for me." I handed her the bag. She took a deep breath, fumbled inside, pulled out the Trans Am's keys and dropped them in my hand. "Take these. Shannon's got the title."

"Girl," I said, "you really know how to cheer a guy up. You know I'll..."

"No sappy promises." She pulled the eyeshade on. "Let's go in the cave so I can tell you a story, Ray. A true story, a story you've never heard before. We are in a rubber ducky on the San Juan river in the mid-nineties. It's almost noon. The light begins to cool. The shadows of the rabbitbrush and tamarisk grow longer. We are on the far edge of the moon's shadow passing over the sun. We keep paddling. We float through a day in a few hours. Then the shadows begin to shrink and light that was moonstone goes opal, then blinding white.

"I was there, Ray. When that happened. On the northern edge of a full solar eclipse. With Shoulders. I don't have many regrets or many wishes, Ray. But I truly wish Shoulders had been you."

I tugged on the eyeshade. "Will you please take this off? I need to see your eyes."

Meg pulled the shade slowly away from her eyes. "Could you see how that light was?"

I took her hand. "As clearly as I see my best friend's face."

She looked at me. "Will you do one more thing for me? Please help Shannon with this next part. Make sure the memorial service I know she'll want to have, is outdoors. Be there. Next to her."

"I will."

We were quiet for a few long minutes.

"Ray," Meg said. "Can this please be our good-bye?"

I bent and kissed her forehead. She reached up, stroked my hair and whispered, "Down the river."

"Till then."

THE TALKER

For Sarah C. and John M.

I

To imagine how it was where we lived that Northern Arizona autumn, you might burn a little juniper, breathe in the gray-green smoke and picture ten ramshackle cabins gathered in a crescent, as though the young moon has fallen to earth and grown shelter in its light.

There's a two-hole privy set back from the cabins. There's a shower house with DO NOT signs posted on the walls. Just under the juniper smoke you can smell the half-dozen kinds of soap that have seeped into the damp wood, lemon and rosemary, the tarry kind for crabs, and stronger than the rest, the musky raspberry of Candy's shampoo.

You can hear a faint whine off the far highway and the scrawk of a raven. You stand on the porch of the privy, look north and see the sacred mountains, their colors ever-changing, so that when you go in to take a leak, they're dark purple and when you step out, they've gone burnt-orange or silver. Winter afternoons, there's a wreath of clouds around the tallest peak. You know that storms are coming, and there's deadly black ice on the highways.

If you're patient in your imagining, you'll see the trees that sheltered our home, tall mountain pine, green-gold at sunset, whose bark on a warm day smells like butterscotch. They stretch up into pure blue and their shadows hold everything, a cool inhuman embrace into which a person can enter and leave at will, no apologies, no regrets. At the entrance to the parking gravel, there is a sign: PRIVATE. DO NOT ENTER. OWNER WILL SHOOT. VISITORS!!! NO PARKING BEYOND THIS POINT!!!

Nine of us lived in this perfect ramshackle shelter. We

hadn't gathered on purpose. We weren't hippies. We weren't dreamers. We weren't true believers in any way. In fact, it was for each of us a raw miracle that we were alive at all. Any one of us, by all that's fair, should have been dead. So we'd worked out ways to be kind with each other. Sometimes that meant telling the truth. Sometimes, it didn't.

"Lower than whale shit, that's how far I sunk," was how Little Black up in the first cabin near the road put it. He was neither little nor black and he didn't remember how he'd got the name, but it had followed him for a good ten years. When I think back on our time together in that place now, I know Little Black had said it right. We were all walking time bombs. It had been weak and dangerous men for me, too, too many by the time I was thirty, too many in the dangerous years since the Seventies, ninety percent of them users, most of them hiding their distrust of a woman till the meanness surfaced and it was too late for me to say, "No thanks." It'd be no surprise if I'd been selling it. Hey, girl, use that money-maker. But I hadn't done it for money. I'd just done it. I'd escaped with my physical health—and memories that have been helping me keep my pants on.

Little Black didn't say much about his memories, but his arms looked like the hand-gun targets of a deadly shot. He'd done anything that revved his jets–speed, crack cocaine, anything zippy you could get into a needle. He was a sad, solid man with a gutty body, not a whole lot of brown hair and the class not to comb what he did have over the bald parts. He wore fine old broken-in cowboy boots that he kept in high polish. He'd earned them working on his uncle's ranch till he got shipped out to Nam, where he learned how it was to be so scared that you just didn't give a damn anymore.

Candy, in the cabin next door to me, was young and still cute. She'd had the Big Test maybe five years earlier, and as much as you could trust medical science, she knew. It was no surprise to her. She'd gone both routes, working girl and junkie. She had a round little butt and round little tits and fine slim everything else. With all those assets and an abiding desire for some peace and quiet, she'd taken to pulling her rose-gold hair into a bun and wearing floppy clothes. It didn't work, so she quietly put in her hours at her computer job and came straight home.

Shireen, in the rebuilt travel trailer near the shower house, had hung for years with a gang of born-again bikers. She still had the look: lavish tits, long scrawny legs, big scared eyes, and she still wore the ladies' auxiliary uniform: pasted-on Levi's and t-shirts with eagles belching fire. Jesus was her mechanic, but even if He was, there were too many days she could barely account for and nights she'd plain forgot.

"It wasn't drugs," she said the first time we talked. "See, Glynne, the Road was my drug. People don't understand that unless they've lived it. When the Road is good, it's the best. When it's bad... well, I was tearing up Highway One out of San Gregorio in that ocean fog and a big old horse stepped down into the road."

"I'm okay," she said, "but something's a little weird with my personality. People like me well enough. They just don't want to—well—be around me for long."

I was older than I looked. Always have been. I have long straight brown hair, a peasant face and freckles, a combination that fools people. I have good eyes. A blessing, my mom had once told me. Little Black called me the owl. He'd seen me watching, not missing a ripple in the shadows, the chill in a person's smile. I felt most times as though I was all eyes, hollow inside, the things I saw floating in, resting awhile and floating away—everything a movie shot: dawn, the bread I baked at my job, my fed-up and long-gone kids' faces, my last real lover gone long before that fall when everything changed.

That's only four out of the nine of us, so you can imagine why we might have been so gentle, as though mean-spiritedness or a cold face or a favor unnoticed might be the trip wire that set off chaos in the body or mind. Too, it was a time when people still danced around addictions and brain troubles, around the reality of AIDS, a time when there were rumors and confusions and it was best to go delicately, as though you could shadow-box a possible future.

Candy, L.B., Shireen and I had been there the longest and were, in a way, the core of the place. Daniel Deacon was our landlord—and fierce protector. He was a short guy, all honed muscle and fire. He was eight years without a drink, not because he particularly wanted to be, but because an Anchorage sheriff had once strongly urged him to leave Alaska. "You wear trouble as close to you as your long johns. I like you, Deacon, but you gotta go...or else."

In Deacon's rush to comply, he found himself sitting in his beat-up truck in Boise, Idaho, with a nine-milli in his mouth and the realization that the shit had to stop. In the rosy glow of early sobriety, he bought our place for peanuts from some worn-out hippies in the late Seventies. He re-named the thirteen acres, run-down cabins and piles of Ripple bottles Deacon's Last Stand. He'd brought the cabins up to a little less than code, his place no fancier than the others. It sat snug against the fenced-off heavy equipment lot. "Takes a thief to know a thief," he'd say. "If anything goes down, I'll hear it and be all over the scum before they know what hit them."

"This is not a halfway house," Deacon told you when you moved in. "This is full-tilt It. You got one chance...just like I got. Mess up once and you're out."

He had posted rules in the shower and outhouse: No pot. No hard drugs. No booze except for official Last Stand parties - Previous notification to me required. Keep dirt clear of junk. Rake up pine needles. No asshole boyfriends or girlfriends. No dogs. No firearms except mine.

"The first week I owned the place," Deacon told us at least once a month, "I hauled fifty-two truck-loads of trash to the county dump—and eight so-called vehicles." He'd look around the place, at the big sweet ponderosa, at their delicate shadows, at the cabins that looked like they'd grown up out of the rocky red earth. "When I finished," he'd say quietly, "what you see is what you got, no broke-down bikes, no hippie vans sitting on their axles, no busted glass and dog shit, nothing but trees and cabins and peace and quiet. Medicine, pure medicine for what ails us. I intend to keep it that way. I will fight to keep it that way."

Deacon ran his scrap iron business as fiercely as he guarded his home. He cut up skeletons of old shopping malls, bankrupt mom-and-pop stores, abandoned buildings and eighteen-wheelers gone down in flames on the midnight interstates. Our little red-neck/Mexican/NavaHopi/aging hippie town had transmuted a few years ago into second homes nobody but rich Californians could afford, so Deacon was at it six days a week.

Some nights, the zircon glare of the cutting torch burned into the early a.m., the roar of the generator jarring us out of sleep. We never complained because the next morning, you'd meet him by the shower house, both of you bundled in bathrobes and galoshes, your breath rising like angels into the diamond air.

"How you doing?" you'd ask.

He'd peer at you out of red-rimmed eyes. "A hell of a lot higher than whale shit." Sometimes that started a conversation about how the resident ravens are a loud pain-in-the-ass, but, man, did you ever see them play tag at twilight? Or maybe how it was colder than a witch's tit—no offense—but where else could you wake up to ice sequins on your bedroom windows?

Deacon, Little B., Candy, Shireen and I were the only residents of the Last Stand that worked steadily. L.B. was an old-for-it roofer. He was forty-three with the body and brain—courtesy amphetamine—of a sixty-year old. Most summer days, after he came home from a day up on some hilltop trophy mansion, he'd be frog-belly white. He'd disappear into the shower house and stay a long time, running cool water over his aching body.

Candy ran a computer for the town's one real industry, a bio-tech research place. It pissed her off. She swore the computer gave her migraines. The Voc Rehab people had placed her there, told her she didn't have enough business skills for much of anything else. "My business skills were fine," she'd told us. "At one point, I had eight people running coke for me."

Shireen believed herself to be the property manager. In fact, Deacon had inherited her when he bought the place. He hired her to clean the shower house and dump chemicals in the privy and make sure water and propane were delivered on time. She'd amended the job description to include taking care of morale. She was always trying to organize monthly potlucks and theme parties and barbecues. Sometimes she succeeded, especially in the summer when there was more sun and consequently, our brains were a little more optimistic.

I baked in a little coffeehouse, the kind of place where no one can spell, they call vegetables "veggies" and the pastries could bring you to a happy death from hyperglycemia. My boss would let me bring home day-old goodies for quarter price. Little B. wouldn't touch any of it. "Sugar ain't good for a man," he said. "It dilutes the male hormones."

The full and part-time unemployed filled out the rest of our semi-circle. There was Leon, a bulky gray-skinned veteran of indeterminate age. He was fine as long as he took his meds and you didn't let him maneuver you into a chat about contrails. He was on full disability and self-appointed keeper of the resident cats in the luxury to which they had become accustomed.

Jacques lived in the south-most cabin. Its former tenant had painted a mural of a mountain stream on one side, with a garish sunset that Jacques finally painted over with wispy clouds. "I cannot stand the banal," he told us. "It reminds me too much of my former wife." He was sixty-four, an ex-doc due to some missing Demerol in the clinic he had worked in. He saw a new-age shrink who had convinced him that he had to reclaim his dreary childhood. Jacques shot marbles in the driveway and he'd begun to pester Deacon for a basketball hoop. In his kitchen, there were posters of Mr. Toad and Mr. Ed and Mr. Rogers. Deacon would stop by, look at the posters and shake his head. "Can you say Mr. Crazy, Jacques?"

Tyree bunked in the one-room cabin by the shower house and worked off and on, sometimes with Deacon, sometimes wherever he could get it. He was half-Navajo and half who-knew-what. He looked like a skinny guy till he turned sideways and you saw his belly. When he was in a good mood, he'd pat it and say solemnly, "Resting place of a million fry breads."

"My drinking days are over," he'd say. "My people are afraid of death. I'm afraid of death." He'd told me and Little Black stories of his father's people and how they abandoned a hogan if someone died in it, locked it up tight, with cook pots and bridles and the TV set sealed inside. "You don't say the name of the person who died. Bad luck. Not everybody believes this stuff. Jesusway Navajos, Mormons, the young gangbangers—they're different, but me and my grandma, we pay attention to this stuff."

The outpost cabin on the south curve of the crescent was Part-time Billy's. He worked in Show Low and only made it in about once a month, though he was almost always with us for holidays. He had once honest-to-god ridden the rodeo and he walked like something was half-killing him. That was how he'd gotten into pain-killers. His yen for young cowboys was another story—that he didn't regret.

An empty shack sat in the western curve. "I don't like that place," Tyree said. "Don't know why, just don't want to go near it." The cabin wasn't truly a cabin, but an old trailer with a busted-out wall covered in plastic. It was an unaltered artifact from the Late Biker Period of the hippies, the living room carpeted floor, walls and ceiling in mottled orange shag. Deacon guessed that you could probably vacuum up enough dope to live on for a year. We called it the House of Usher and were all grateful we hadn't sunk low enough to have to live in it. "You'd have to wonder about anybody who could live there," Candy said. "Seriously wonder."

We were given our chance to wonder. It was a green-gold September afternoon. Little Black had brought out his coffee pot. I unpacked a fat bag of cookies. Candy was still in town, Leon at the VA. L.B., Shireen, Jacques, Tyree and I settled in on L.B.'s front porch. Deacon ambled over from his office.

"What a day," he said. We figured he was going to launch into his The-Good-Lord (or Lady, Glynne) -in-his-her-infinite-wisdom-has-brought-us-sick-sumbitches (Sorry, ladies) -to-this-beautiful-slice-of-Heaven speech.

"Well," he said, "The Good Lord has found us a new sick sumbitch (Sorry, ladies) to join our little family."

We looked at each other. We sick sumbitches liked the population just fine as it was.

"I met this guy at the ten a.m. meeting," Deacon said. "If he walks his talk, he'll do just fine."

"What's his story?" I asked.

"Decade on booze, five years on crystal. He's clean as a whistle, been that way for five years."

"Aw jeez," Little Black said. "Sorry Deacon, but you sure about this?"

"Yep," Deacon said cheerfully. "He goes to meetings, he can look a man in the eye and he'll pay me two hundred bucks to live in the House of Usher. That's good enough for me." He grinned. "Whatever it takes."

"You bet," Little Black said. Deacon tipped an imaginary hat and headed back to his office.

"Crystal," Little Black said. "Oh shit."

That night I had a dream, one of those that are so clear you believe you're awake. I was in my kitchen, perched on the bar stool by the counter. I was playing solitaire. As I shuffled the cards, I saw a feral cat under the sink. She was gray, her fur silky and long. She was playing with something, slipping in and out from beneath the curtain I'd hung over the pipes and cleansers and busted linoleum.

I kept cutting the cards and laying them out, one at a time. The same card came up again and again. I couldn't see it clearly. It was as though I looked at it through one of those old swirly hand-blown window panes. On the eighth deal, something shot out from under the sink. It was a juvenile flicker, unharmed, clear-eyed, its orange and black and white feathers like plumes of light. It flew straight to the broken kitchen window and out. Two orange and black feathers drifted back into the room.

I cut the cards a last time and turned one over. It was a face card. That was all I could tell. And then, though I've played solitaire almost all my life, I could not, for the life of me, remember what any of them meant or even why I was dealing them. I woke up, my heart fluttering against my ribs. I made myself lie still and fell back to sleep.

Next evening, a pearly Indian summer late afternoon, we had a cook-out on Part-time Billy's grill. We loaded up our plates and went over to Shireen's big front steps, which were the best place to watch the sunset. Shireen perched on the top step like a mother crane. The rest of us ranged below her, except for Tyree who squatted back on his heels like the good old Navajo cowboy he was. I told them the dream and asked them what they thought. Shireen went tight around the lips. She didn't approve of following any guidance that wasn't stamped with the Jesus H. Christ Good Soulkeeping seal.

Little Black had just nodded his head and cleared his throat, the sure sign he was going to say something wise, when Leon wandered in with a plateful of something nasty pale that turned out to be charbroiled soy cheese. All he had to hear was the topic and he held forth for half an hour on "this illusory world which is, after all, revealed to us as nothing but a dream." The poor man would never be at risk for any STD because, even when he took his meds, he talked so much and smelled so bad that he was a virgin at thirty-one, which was truly awful when the Sex God part of the manic hit. We all listened and didn't say anything, so he finally stuffed six of Shireen's double chocolate chip cookies in his pocket and walked away.

"That lithium," Shireen said, "I hate it worse than thorazine. It gives you the sugar fits and then you just blow right up."

Tyree nodded. "I tried that shit once. You can't get no kind of buzz off it at all."

"Well now," Little Black said, as though the last half hour hadn't occurred, "tell me about that cat again. I knew this chick down in Bisbee. She'd learned all these theories about dreams, especially if there were animals in them."

"The cat was silver-gray," I said. "Long-haired, green eyes. She was just going on about her cat business. When the flicker got away, she came out from under the sink with that look cats get, you know, like, 'Hey. No problem.'"

"Did it mess with that flicker?" Tyree asked.

"I don't know. It had the bird back where I keep the laundry soap. I didn't see. But when the bird came out, it looked fine."

"That dream gives me the creeps," Candy said. "L.B., what'd that chick say about cats?"

L.B. shook his head. "She didn't actually tell me none of them theories…but, cats…could mean hunting, could mean taking a nap. I don't know."

We were all semi-mental health professionals, full of bits and pieces of hope and psychobabble from long damp discourses with bar philosophers, thirty-day treatment programs and involuntary funny farm stays where you mostly played ping pong and flirted with the psych aides. I'd once had a shrink who hadn't spoken more than five words of English. He'd just smiled nicely and written me prescriptions. I had actually felt pretty safe with him. I had actually told him the truth of my story. At least forty percent of it.

Shireen jumped up and disappeared into the trailer. In a minute, we could hear gospel music rocking away. She had a knack for it, picking the stuff that thumped right into your bones. I started sit-dancing. Candy was shaking her shoulders and doing bad little street moves with her hands. Shireen came out and glared at us.

"It's not dance music," she said. "I put it on to clear the devil talk."

"I'm sorry," I said. "My dancing was more like a celebration."

Candy ducked her head and sat very very still.

"Why don't you two just come with me some day and get sanctified?" Shireen said gently. "Then the Lord won't mind. He'll look down with joy at your dancing."

"I can't," I said. "I've got what I can live with. Maybe the music's enough."

Tyree and Little Black lit cigarettes and studied the ground. Shireen and I had this discussion every time she put on gospel and my body heard the back-beat and couldn't resist. She shrugged and turned away. I made myself shut up.

When she turned back to me, her eyes were soft. "Have you prayed on that dream?" she said. "I mean in your own way." I looked up at her. She's almost six foot tall and as scrawny in the arms and legs as a ten-year-old.

"I know," I said, "you fear for my soul."

She nodded.

I patted her slender foot. "I will pray on that dream. I promise."

Next morning just before dawn, Tyree tapped on my window. I heard him go around to the front door. I felt surly, always do first thing in the morning. I put the coffee water to boil and glared at Tyree through the big kitchen window. "It's open," I said.

He didn't come in. He stood there in his camo jacket and scuffed paratrooper boots, holding a dish of smoking juniper and staring at my door. I opened the door and waved him in. He was shaking and wouldn't meet my eyes.

"Please open the back door," he said quietly. "And all the windows." The eastern sky behind him was washed in lavender. He seemed big and solid against the fragile light. "Move," he said. "Please. I gotta clean your cabin. I gotta smoke out the bad."

I stepped back. Tyree walked through the cabin, moving east to north to west to south, from door to window to door, the thick gray smoke trailing behind him. He prayed, unfamiliar throaty words weaving up with the smoke. The tea kettle rattled on the burner. I turned it off and set up the coffee fixings.

After Tyree had gone around the cabin four times, he walked outside and stood in the pale light, his lips still moving. I stepped out beside him and we watched the light go rosy, go gold, till the sun crested the tattered tops of the pines. I finished making coffee, Tyree hauled out a couple chairs and we sat in the morning cool, drinking coffee, watching steam rise from our cups.

"I dreamed that flicker," Tyree said, "and it turned into a goddamn owl." He shuddered. I relit the juniper the way he'd taught me and stood in front of him. He stood and washed himself with smoke, his hands moving like wings, beating the smoke from the top of his head to his feet. I didn't watch him too carefully. It wouldn't have been good manners. Besides, he had a way of making what he did private. He shook his head the way you do when you're shaking off fogginess or pain. I brought out the last of the coffee and some evaporated milk.

"Good. Fresh milk's got no taste," he said. "I don't like that dream. Maybe I'll head up to Chinle, see what my grandma has to say."

"Sounds good to me." I had to get to work. I went inside, put on my sneakers, tied up my hair and slipped my silver raven hoops through my ears. Tyree was still drinking coffee when I walked out. I touched his shoulder once and climbed into my truck. As I pulled onto the dirt road that led to the highway, I looked back. He was hunched over his cigarette, his wide shoulders carrying worry like he'd once carried his grandma's sheep.

Tyree was gone when I came home. Candy said he'd set out about noon with his duffle and five bucks she'd loaned him. He'd make out fine. He'd get picked up by a family in a Chevy double-cab out on 89 North. They'd pass some Taco Bell and soda pop back through the open vent. He'd hunker down next to the gothed-out teenagers and about Tuba City, chip in on some gas.

Candy hung around and helped me carry in groceries and

water. She wouldn't come right out and visit, but she had a way of hanging out until you realized she'd been there two hours. I liked it that way. No written-in-concrete date in a day planner. It was her half-day off, so she was wearing sweatpants and a t-shirt.

"You piss me off, girl," I said. "You'd look good in a thirty-gallon garbage sack."

"Girl," she said, "you sure have a poetic way of putting things."

She'd tucked her hair up in a trucker hat and hadn't put on make-up. Standing in my kitchen, illuminated by the afternoon light coming through the big window, she was soft and golden, no hard brightness to her face.

I made a fresh pot of coffee and we took it and some café plunder to the wood pallets and cinder blocks that served as my back porch. Two big pines rose on either side, their arching branches a feathery roof. If you didn't look to the right, where the suburb lurked behind the trees, you could believe you were living in the middle of the forest. I'd put in a garden to the left of the porch, digging out dozens of what seemed to be constantly upwardly migrating rocks. All that was left of my work were three scraggly tomato plants, a few peppers and a vine full of monster zucchini.

The meadow beyond the garden still bloomed with wildflowers: lupine, penstemon, shooting stars and magenta four-o-clocks. Mountain jays and ravens perched in the tall pines and made fools of the cats. There were still a few Rufous hummingbirds proving their mighty manliness around the feeder. When I'd first moved in—after two years of thinking I might be dying and wishing I was— I'd sat for hours on the back porch with binoculars and a bird guide, learning the names: Steller's jay, hermit thrush, common raven, flicker and mourning dove. I'd look for feathers and try to guess which bird had dropped them. I stuck the smallest feathers in a big ponderosa cone, set it in the window by my bed and decided to live long enough to fill up the cone.

Candy sat on the porch steps, rolled up her pant legs and

stretched her bare legs and feet out to the sun. I pulled off my sweatshirt. The sun was like warm honey on my face. "Tyree sure was spooked," Candy said. "He told me to tell you it was okay for you to tell me his dream."

While I told her, she shook out her hair and began combing it with her fingers. Her sitting there, in sloppy clothing, with a bare face, hanging out with another woman was an ordinary miracle. She should have been dead—from drugs, from booze, from the beating, from the time her old man had dumped her in an Upstate New York field, wearing nothing but a powder of coke on her upper lip on a night so cold trees exploded. When I finished telling Tyree's dream, she stared out across the garden.

"Damn it, Glynne," she said. "This is the first time I've felt uneasy out here."

I nodded.

"Your dream. Tyree's. They're a mystery to me. I don't remember mine. I have them, I'm pretty sure, but by the time I'm half awake, they're gone." She shook her head. "It's probably better that way."

By the time Tyree came back with a chunk of mutton and a shirt with satin ribbons on the sleeves, the new guy had moved in and Shireen was lost in love. It was a mystery to Candy and me. I'd seen him a couple times at a distance and he was no big deal—coppery gray hair and beard, maybe six foot, walked like he wanted you to know he was one bad rooster. He drove a brand new silver Cherokee, which didn't quit fit it seemed to me, with living in a shack you'd have to demolish to make livable.

Shireen saw it differently. She started wearing skirts, not short ones, but her old semi-hippie patchwork numbers. She'd dug up a series of blouses that hung low on her impressive chest and, as if that didn't thoroughly make the point, she'd hung a silver cross from a velvet ribbon so that it glittered right between her boobs. She developed a funny walk, a cat-like sidle that seemed to suggest that she was a hot item but too much of a lady to show it. And she made, as Candy noted, an unusual number of trips back and forth to my cabin, requiring her to pass smack in front of the new guy's place.

"I think," Jacques said thoughtfully to Candy and me, "that we are seeing here a re-creation of a childhood dream, Rapunzel, perhaps, or the Little Mermaid." He'd had his gray hair cropped close to his head. It had a silvery light to it, so he looked like a monk. I could see him sitting in a sheltered garden, gossiping pleasantly with the ladies of the castle.

"Could be," I said, "anything's possible these days." It paid to respond to Jacques with vague affirmations. He could really get going on his shrink's theories that we all needed to reclaim the childhoods we had never had. Little Black said that was his idea of pure hell. "My childhood was simple," he said, "shot at and missed, shit on and hit."

I finally met the new guy face to face. Shireen had already come over to my place five times since noon, once to borrow the paper, once for coffee, once for sugar, twice because she thought she might have forgotten something the other three times. On her sixth run, Tyree and I were leaning on my truck, drinking coffee, soaking up sun and not saying much. He'd brought some fry bread back from his grandma's. We dripped honey on it and dunked it in our coffee.

The new guy's front door was open and we could hear hammering. He sounded like a pro. My long-gone true love Michael had sounded like that when he was working. I'd seen him measure, cut, match and nail up the walls of a room in one day, the crack of his hammer steady as a heart beat. My heart still jumped at the thought of him, his hard carpenter's arms and hands, his delicate touch. He'd been nothing but a good man—so, of course, I'd left him.

Shireen undulated over and perched on the splitting stump. Tyree coughed and looked away. She had on one of her low-cut blouses. The soft flesh of her breasts shimmered when she caught her breath. I tossed her my sweater.

"Spare us," I said. She blushed, the pink coming through the rouge she'd dabbed on her cheeks. I was surprised at her. One of the unspoken kindnesses we gave each other, as deep-hungry for touch and loving as most of us were, was that we didn't flaunt whatever we had.

"I've been thinking," Shireen said. I could tell a party scheme was in the works. Halloween, maybe, long-range Thanksgiving blueprints. She lit a cigarette and exhaled slowly. You could tell she was making every effort to not look sideways to where the hammering was sounding solid and true.

"We ought to have a little potluck to welcome McCain," she said.

"Who's McCain?" I asked as if I didn't know.

"Our new neighbor," Shireen said.

"We never did that before. I like to take my time to get to know people before I party with them."

"Well, then you don't have to come," Shireen said calmly. We all fell quiet.

"What's the big deal about the new kid?" I said. Tyree nudged me. The hammering had stopped and for a second it was totally quiet.

"No big deal," an ultra-cowboy voice said in my ear. "Keep it simple, right?" The new kid stepped around in front of me and nodded at Shireen.

I shaded my eyes and looked up at him. "You got it."

"You must be Glynne," he said.

"I must be," I said and made myself stop. Some old battle cry was sounding in my gut. He was too handsome. He knew it. His eyes were steel-gray. There wasn't a touch of color in them, none. The longer I looked, and I couldn't seem not to, the more I saw that steel was too warm to describe them. They were asteroid gray, outer space icy. He made them go warm and studied my face for a second.

Heat rose in my throat. He winked and turned to Tyree.

"I'm McCain," he said.

Tyree held out his hand. McCain shook it. I could see that McCain had avoided the white man's mistake. He held Tyree's hand lightly in his, no conquistador bone-crusher, just peaceful stranger to peaceful homeboy. Tyree scanned the guy for a second. You would hardly know it, just a quick lift of his chin, a quick sweep with flat mahogany eyes and he was looking casually over McCain's right shoulder as though he'd spotted something out in the meadow that had caught his attention.

"Tyree. Good to meet you," he said.

McCain nodded and stepped back. Shireen looked up. She'd let the sweater fall open a little. McCain suddenly crouched next to her.

"I was looking for you, darlin'," he said. "Hopin' I could borrow some milk for my coffee if it won't run you too short."

Shireen wafted up from the stump. She and McCain started to walk away. There was something about how he held his body in relation to her, something I don't think can be defined—a hovering, a yearning. I imagined she could feel it. McCain turned back to Tyree.

"Catch you later, hosteen," he said.

Tyree nodded.

"Glynne," McCain said, "come over some time and I'll make us the best damn cowboy coffee you ever tasted."

"Yee-ha."

He glanced at my cup. "You like coffee, right?"

"Yep," I said, "but I'm pretty busy."

He didn't move. You would have thought it was high school. You would have thought he was the king jock and I was the pudgy chick nobody ever noticed. Any moment, he was going to step forward, take off my glasses, let down my pony tail and say, "Why, Glynne Anne honey, you are beautiful. May I take you to the prom?"

McCain swung back to Shireen. She seemed to tuck herself into his shadow, to round the sharp lines of her thin body.

They moved away.

"Hosteen," I said.

"Aw, lighten up, Glynne," Tyree said. "He's okay. A little overeager maybe. No big thing."

"He's weird," Candy said. "He doesn't look at me. And, he's so careful, like he researched all of us before he moved in." It was Sunday and we'd gone up to the Dream Eagle tavern for breakfast. The place smelled of fresh coffee and bacon and home baking. The owner made the best biscuits and gravy you ever ate, and there was a pool table and never anybody playing. Candy and I had gotten in the habit of eating, then shooting quarter pool till the Sunday papers came into the grocery next door. It was always peaceful, the families and couples in the dining room reminding us that there was normal love out there, if only for two hours on a Sunday morning.

"A guy like him," Candy said, "a little older, losing his steam. Usually they're the worst around me. You know that pathetic, I-am-one-swinging-dude way they have." She poured gravy over her biscuits and started to eat. "But McCain acts like I'm not there, like I'm a piece of furniture or a guy or something."

"I wish he'd see me as a chair," I said. "This old woman blues singer, Ma Rainey, once said, 'Don't want nothin' from an old man unless it's a message from a young one.' That's how I see it." The waitress refilled our cups and set down homemade salsa. "Of course," I said, "that's how most older guys see me, so we're even."

"You're not old," Candy said.

"Old enough," I said. "Old enough that McCain shouldn't even see me."

"Speaking of seeing," Candy said, "he's got truly scary eyes. They remind me of a computer screen, that twilight-zone gray. Cop eyes. That's it!"

"Listen," I said, "maybe he's okay. Maybe he's one of those sensitive guys they used to talk about in chick magazines. He's always running on about his kids."

"Sure," Candy said, "but have you seen them? No way." She stirred some salsa in the gravy and poured it over what was left of the biscuits. "I'll tell you something, Glynne," she said. "My old man used to beat the shit out of me—he was a cop and knew how to do it so there weren't any bruises—but every now and then I'd meet a john like McCain and I'd take that whipping from my old man for turning down the john, and be glad for it."

We told the waitress we wanted a piece of blackberry pie and two plates. Candy poured half the pitcher of cream over the pie. A weary old cowboy played one of Willie's hang-over anthems on the jukebox. A little kid climbed down off his booster seat and bounced down the aisle. That minute, there in that company, there was nowhere else I'd rather have been.

"Know what?" Candy said. I shook my head.

"I want to tell Shireen how we feel."

"She won't listen."

"Yeah," Candy said, "we never do."

"Nonetheless," I said.

She grinned. "Nonetheless."

We came home to Jacques and McCain nailing a basketball hoop on the big dead pine between Jacques and Candy's cabin. Jacques was up on the ladder pounding away and McCain was holding the ladder steady. Candy nodded to them, a quick stiff little head-bob, and walked on to her cabin. She was holding her body absolutely straight, the way teenage girls walk when they don't want anything to wobble. I started to follow her.

"Glynne, you got a minute?" McCain called out.

I stopped. He smiled. A fool fascination stirred up in me—and a challenge. I wasn't who I'd been. Two years alone. Two years looking deep inside. A long time. A long look. And he had no way of knowing my past. I decided to close whatever drama I'd been making up with him.

"Sure," I said.

"Hold the ladder a minute," he said. "I want to show you something."

I set my hands on the rungs and watched Jacques finish fussing with the hoop. He started to back down. I stepped away. He hated to be touched, especially by women. He set the ladder flat on the ground and looked up at the hoop.

"I've always wanted one of these of my own," he said. "I'm short, you know."

It was easy to imagine him always watching from the sidelines. It was easy to see how surgery, with its delicate precision, might have let him be any size he wanted. The Demerol would have soothed any whispers of memory. He flashed me a quick smile and spun suddenly in the pine needles. Quick and nervy as a squirrel, he dribbled an invisible ball to the foot of the pine, paused and leaped into a perfect shot.

"Whoosh," I said.

"Nice shot," McCain said from behind me. Jacques shouldered the ladder and left. McCain slipped a pine cone through the dead center of the hoop. I noticed I had shoved my hands in my pockets and was hanging on to my thumbs. Not a good sign. McCain reached inside his denim jacket and pulled out a feather.

"You collect these," he said.

"Not that kind." It was an eagle wing feather, long, curved and shimmering. He handed it to me. I smoothed the barbs till the feather was a sleek dagger of reflected light.

"Where'd you get it?" I asked. "It's a felony to have one."

"Not for people like us," he said.

"What do you mean us? Hosteen."

His smile didn't change. "Those laws only apply to people who aren't right in the heart. I'm right in the heart. Are you?"

I turned the feather in my fingers. It was easily one of the prettiest things I'd ever seen. I coveted it and what went with it. I knew it would never be mine. I'd watched Tyree once with a peyote feather his cousin had fixed up for him. He'd been fanning himself with it, standing in pine shadow on a warm day, and smiling. I'd heard the whisper of it. It seemed that I had always been lonely for that sound.

"Here," I said to McCain, "it's beautiful."

"Keep it," he said. "Add it to your collection, you know, that collection in the big pine cone in the windowsill?"

"Were you looking in my window?" I handed him the feather. There was a cool slender empty space between my fingers where the spine had rested.

"Lighten up," he said. "Check this out." He walked on the path toward the west side of my cabin. Sure enough, without snooping you could see everything in the window right from where we stood.

"Sorry," I said. "It's not a collection. I just take them where I find them. I like to find them myself."

He laughed. "Hey, Glynne, you got any other collections I might be interested in?" He didn't move, but I felt he had stepped closer. "Anything I could add to?"

"Nothing," I said. I looked him straight in the eye as I'd learned to do and smiled. He smiled back and held the feather behind him. I wished I had it, that blade of light. Right then, right that instant, with my body suddenly achy hot, I could have cut his throat with it.

I jolted awake around two a.m. My tabby cat Harold was at the window above my bed, frozen in a shaft of white light. I pulled the sheet up around my shoulders and knelt to look out. Everything was sharp-edged: the cat's green eyes, the old Mexican bottle next to the feather cone, my fingers splayed on the sill, the slice of arctic light across the clearing. I could hear Deacon's generator roaring from the steel yard. The tops of the ponderosas seemed etched in frost against the black sky.

My throat was tight. I rubbed the tabby's ears. He curled into my hand and began purring. "It's okay, Harold," I whispered.

"It's nothing new."

I picked him up and crawled back under the quilt. I could feel the first serious chill of autumn moving in. The cat settled next to me and we fell asleep.

Shireen won out. We had the welcome-the-new-boy potluck. Even Deacon came. Shireen observed what a remarkable coincidence it was, the very first day of fall landing right on a Saturday, so we could celebrate two things at once. She fixed up a plate for McCain. He'd brought two six-packs of Corona and a Fuji mum for each of us women. Candy's was pale yellow, mine was peach and Shireen's was ivory and pale green.

"Flowers," Little Black said. "Why didn't I think of that? I gave a girl flowers once. It wasn't even any special occasion. We were in Reno and this rose vendor lady came by. I bought the girl a whole dozen, set me back eighty bucks, plus tip. The lady told the girl to kiss me and she took our picture. I used to have it. Somewhere." He looked puzzled.

"Are you alright?" Candy asked. That was the most consecutive sentences any of us had ever heard L.B. speak.

"Well shit," he said. "I was just trying to make conversation."

"Where'd she go?" McCain asked. He was tilted back in Shireen's lounger, his boots off, his belt loosened.

"Go?" Little Black asked.

"That girl you bought flowers for," McCain said. "She ain't with you now. Where'd she go?"

"Shoot," Little Black said. "You know. I got bored. Dime a dozen, chicks like that."

I'd never heard L.B. do that old man-to-man horseshit before. Candy glanced at me.

McCain pushed back the brim of his hat. "Come on, Little," he said. "You can fool the fans, but you can't fool a player."

Little Black looked down at the ground. Candy stepped between him and McCain and stuck her fantastic butt about a foot from McCain's face. "'Scuse me, gentlemen," she said. "Let me clear up those plates. It's time for dessert."

Shireen took one look at the scene and perched on the arm of the lounger. McCain patted her ass. Candy turned around and smiled at me.

"Nonetheless," I said.

"Nonetheless," she said. "Let's clean up some of this mess."

Deacon rose out of the sway-backed couch a former tenant had hauled in. "I'll help."

We were all pleasantly smooth-faced, our voices neutral. Leon was oblivious, yammering away with Jacques near the charcoal grill. Deacon tapped Little Black on the shoulder. They looked at each other.

"Come on, Mr. Black," Deacon said. "Help me empty the ashtrays."

Little Black didn't move. He was looking dully at McCain, a muscle jumping in his jaw. "Hey, Mr. Black," McCain said, "no offense. Shireen's been telling me this was a no-bullshit place, you know, people talking about their feelings and all. I didn't mean to push or nothing."

"No offense taken," L.B. said, "but I will take one of those beers."

He popped the cap and drained it fast. I'd never seen him drink before. Deacon's face tightened. He'd never say anything. He was no buttinsky. Only once had he come to my place after Tyree had smudged it with black sage, and asked me what I was smoking. All I'd had to say was, "Marijuana hates me," and he'd let it go. Sometimes he wore a hat that said Instant Asshole: Just Add Alcohol. We'd suggested he get a slightly different one: Instant Asshole: Just Add Advice.

Candy nudged me and we went into the trailer's tiny kitchen. There wasn't much but plywood cupboards between us and the living-dining room, so we whispered. She set the water to boil. There was no running water in any of our places, which made doing the dishes a ritual or a pain in the ass, depending on what mood you were in. Mostly for me, it was a ritual, like when you're camping and each step requires thought and you can slow down and notice all the pleasures: soap bubbles like opals, how clean everything smells, how good it feels to start something and finish it, all of it.

Candy slammed a couple pans into the sink. "Tell me this, Glynne," she hissed, "how the hell are you supposed to welcome someone you want to go away?"

"What is it about McCain?" I hissed back. Then I realized I wanted to talk about him. I wanted his name on my lips. I realized I was semi-lying to her and that it was for the first time. First Times and Never Befores. Those were bad signs. I couldn't tell her about the heat he fired up in me. That was a worse sign.

"He's a scum bag," she said neatly. "I can't believe I stuck my butt in his face, but I figured it would shut him up. I went right down to his level. Gack."

He popped his head around the corner of the door. "Hey, ladies, the days of women in the kitchen are over, didn't you know? Come on out where the party is." He bowed and backed down the steps.

"Shit," Candy said. She picked up her mum and pulled clumps of petals off. "Go away, you make me sick, go away, you make me sick," she sing-songed. When the stem was bare, she held it up. "Good, it ended on go away. Maybe we'll be rid of him."

I picked my flower out of the water glass, looked at its cool beauty and put it back in. Candy looked puzzled. I was hoping she'd ask me something, give me an opening to spill my guts. She was quiet. "No big thing," I said. "It's just a gorgeous flower." I should have told her the truth right then and I should have told her that the mum was the first flower a man had given me in twenty years.

I went home early, right after the raspberry pie and ice cream. The party had slowed—to be expected when most of the partiers had avoided the beer. Little Black had only the one and Deacon looked relieved. Tyree never showed. As I crossed the dark yard, I saw a shuddering glow in his cabin. I guessed he was sitting alone, lights out, the woodstove door open, him staring into the coals. I wondered why he was there and why he'd stayed away from the party. I'd never known him to turn down home-made pie. Still, there was something about the silence of his place, the clean thread of smoke rising from the chimney that kept me steady on the path home.

A few weeks later Shireen talked most of us into driving up to Hart Prairie to see the trees. In early October, the mountain aspen are beaten gold with a silvery undertone, their trunks dappled moon-white. The leaves shimmer in even the most delicate breeze. To lie on your back in a bed of leaves under that delicate light, in air so thin you know that each breath really is a miracle, is to be filled with grace.

"We'll take a picnic," Shireen said.

"What we?" Candy and I said. "This time the guys can bring the food."

We drove up to the edge of an old meadow and parked. There were a few wildflowers left, purple and orange glowing like fallen meteors in the dry grass. Jacques tossed a tarp down on the ground and the gentlemen spread out their idea of a feast: pizza, pop and rosé wine. Jacques pulled two crystal candleholders and two white tapers out of his backpack, set them between the pep-peroni pizza and the Hawaiian ham and pineapple and lit them. I shuddered. "How can you people eat pizza with pineapple on it?"

"Hey," Candy said, "go back to Chicago if you're going to mock the glorious New Southwest."

I picked the pineapple off my slice and held out my glass. I can handle alcohol—it's the bozos that so often went with it that fogged my mind.

"Hey, hosteen," McCain said cheerfully, "come on over and join your neighbors."

"I'm okay," Tyree said. He was a few feet away, sitting on a deadfall at the edge of the meadow, drinking water from his old army canteen. McCain turned to me. "Anything I can do you, Glynne?"

"I'm set," I said. I looked up at the most northern peak of the mountains. "Here's to you," I said and took a sip.

"Why thanks," McCain said. "Can't remember the last time I was the subject of a toast."

"Wasn't you," I said.

"Who then?"

"Not who. What."

"Deep," McCain said. "You must be one of those New Agers."

Candy poked my leg with her foot. "Nonetheless," she said. "None the less."

"Women," McCain said. "Like the gentleman said, 'What the hell do they want?'" He stretched out next to Shireen with his head in her lap, a glass of water balanced on his chest.

"No wine, McCain?" Candy said sweetly.

He laughed. "No way, darlin'. I don't want to miss a moment of this lovely day."

"Me either," Jacques said. He lay under an aspen, eyes closed, his face dappled with light and shadow. "Did any of you ever do acid?"

Candy snorted. "Oh heavens to betsy no. Not me. How about you, Glynne?"

"I don't remember," I said, "but it must have been acid. It was that brain-busting old-time acid."

Candy picked a handful of dry milkweed pods and shook them over Jacques' face. A breeze caught the feathery seeds, drifted them up around her, spiraled them down toward Jacques.

"Open your eyes, Jacques," she laughed. "It was kinda like this, right?"

"No," he said. He looked up at her. "I only did it once. It would have been beautiful if I hadn't been so frightened." I wanted to tell him to shut up. I could see the water glass rise and fall with

McCain's even breathing. His eyes were closed, but I knew he was listening and that he would remember everything Jacques said for future use.

"I'd read up on it," Jacques said. "It was 1967. Other scientists had tried it. I read about the theoretical neurological pathway. That was my big mistake. I thought if I knew how it worked I'd handle it well. When the stuff hit, I became a molecule. All I could do was go for the ride. It was like being in the final space war of all time."

McCain laughed. "You're a cheap date, Jacques."

Candy sat down next to Jacques. "I thought everybody loved it," she said. "Once when I was dancing, I dropped a tab of the old stuff. I had this back-dated Dead tape and breakaway retro hippie outfit that ended up being nothing but beads and fake dope leaves on the floor. I was stripping and tripping, and for once I loved every loser in the place."

She flopped on her back and shook the rest of the milkweed down over her and Jacques. "Oh goddammit," she said. "I miss those days."

"That must have been a sight to see," McCain said.

Candy sat up. "That was a long time ago. Another time, another life. I shouldn't have said that. Erase the last two minutes, please."

I walked over to her and waved my arms as though I was wiping out the moments. "Gone," I said. "What two minutes?"

"Glynne," McCain said, "you are one drama queen." He held up the jug. "Have a little more grape. Be fun to see what comes next."

I walked over to him and Shireen. He had his shirt open to his flat belly, so that his red-blond chest hair was shining copper in the sunlight. "I know you," I said. "I know more than you could guess."

"Jesus Christ," he laughed, "lighten up."

I turned and walked past Tyree into the aspen grove. I felt

the trees close around me. There were silvery deadfalls and dark boulders shining with mica. Moss speckled everything. Pale vines twined up the cool white aspen trunks and I could smell damp earth. "I know what he is," I whispered as though it were a password. I walked till I couldn't see or hear anybody. I pulled down my jeans and squatted over the dead leaves. Steam rose up from my piss, the leaves darkened and washed away. I'd made a tiny channel in the forest floor.

"There," I said. "I was here. What I know matters."

I pulled up my jeans and sat on one of the big boulders. There was a tiny pool of water in the rock. I dipped my fingers in and thought about my old love, Michael. I saw him walking the boundaries of his winter wood supply, cords of pine and oak, two thousand miles away, twenty years gone from this earth. I saw him piss on each corner of the stack. "Just to let 'em know," he'd told me. "Just to let the local dogs know who's boss of this woodpile."

I sat at the base of an old aspen and watched the light change. When I felt less likely to make a fool of myself, I went back to the picnic. Shireen and McCain were picking up the empty pizza boxes. "Peace," he said and held up two fingers. "No problem," I said and sat down with Jacques and Candy. They were telling stories. They kept on as though I'd been sitting there the whole time. What little wine high I'd had was wearing off and I felt like a fool. I'm not an alky, but booze can make me Big. And when I'm Big, everything is more glorious and awful than it really is—and I can handle it all.

We drove back to town through the deepening twilight, Candy, Jacques, Tyree and me in truck. McCain drove Shireen's truck ahead of us. She was snuggled next to him. Suddenly we saw him say something to her and she dropped toward his lap.

"Oh nice," Candy said. "That's real class."

I tried to pass them, but McCain hugged those nasty curves and that white line as though his life depended on it. We tried not to watch.

"Maybe she just got tired," Jacques said.

"Oh jeez," Candy said. "I think I'm going to be sick." She looked at me. I hoped she couldn't see that my face was red. I wasn't embarrassed. I couldn't not imagine—as I knew McCain knew I was imagining—how whatever was happening in the truck might have felt to both of them.

"Nonetheless," Candy said. I was quiet.

McCain went out of town on unspecified business in late October. I felt light enough to fly. I got a curly perm and even let Candy play around with make-up. I took long showers and walked slowly back from the shower house, watching my breath cloud up in front of me, studying Orion as he drifted silently above the eastern trees. I'd glance back at McCain's cabin, no lights, no smoke, no thump from the Top-20 country-western hunk-slop he listened to. Sometimes, there'd be the little beacon of somebody else's flashlight, maybe Candy on her way to the privy or Shireen moping over to Deacon's to complain about something that was just a cover-up for her missing McCain.

I was nearly at my door the last Saturday of the McCain reprieve when I felt a light touch on my wet hair.

"There's starlight in your hair," a man whispered.

I turned. It was Leon. Even by the no-light of a new moon, his eyes glittered. When he smiled, which he was doing non-stop, his teeth were pure white.

"That's so beautiful," he said and moved in closer, his hand tangled in my hair. "Your hair and the stars." A smell rose from him, a pungent, almost metallic smell. I tried to back away. His hand tightened on my hair.

"It's okay," he said. "I'm not poisoned anymore. I'm a man again."

"Leon," I said, "it's me, Glynne. Your friend."

I figured he had overdosed on the lithium or something, maybe gotten into what had been left of the picnic rosé. His smile became more brilliant.

"I know," he said, "and I think of you as more than a friend. I always have. It wasn't until the poison had gone that I could tell you."

I stepped back a little and felt one of the pines pressing into my back. "What poison?" I kept my voice calm.

"You know," he said. His smile became soft and conspiratorial. "McCain told me about the poison. He told me the shrinks are trying to kill our brains with the poison. He said that I was fine without it."

"You stopped taking your lithium," I said calmly.

Leon nodded. "There's a book. McCain gave it to me. It's about curing yourself with herbs. I've been doing them for a week." He pressed himself against me. "I'm a man again," he whispered. "And it can be our time now." His smell was thick in my throat and nose. I kept my face still, but I could feel tears running down my cheeks. "You must be so happy I'm a man again," he said.

I froze. He touched my throat gently. As I started to bring my knee up, light flooded us. Deacon took Leon's wrist in his two hands. "Hey pal," he said, "I've been looking for you." He let the flashlight fall.

I pressed myself against the tree's cool bulk. I smelled the bark and breathed as deep as I could: delicate scent of caramel, clean night air, my own fear rising harshly off my skin.

Deacon led Leon off. Leon was telling him how wonderful it was to be a man again, how strong he felt, how happy I was for him now that we could be together on God's mission of teaching people about the poison. I let myself slide to the ground and looked up through the branches to the diamond stars. I stayed a while, shivering in my bathrobe, counting the stars and naming the ancient creatures of light: Cassiopeia and Pegasus; Orion, the Hunter and Lepus, his prey. That was how it should be—the two of them, hunter and hare, and after long aeons, when both of them knew there would be no capture, no death, they must have known they were linked forever.

Shireen drove Deacon and Leon into town that night. She said Leon had talked constantly, about McCain, about me, about how lucky he was that we had all reincarnated as a group. She said he shook so hard she was afraid he'd slide off the seat. Deacon had sat on the window side. Something about him, Shireen said, had seemed to gentle Leon. The ED shrink told them it would be a while before they got Leon in balance again. So, the cabin up by the road stayed dark, and we faithfully fed his cats.

A week later, on a gray November afternoon, I stopped Deacon on his way home. We stood in the shadow of the basketball tree and I told him what Leon had said about McCain and the book. We both shivered. Deacon put his arm around my shoulders and guided us out into the last of the day's soft light. He looked at me. He had a way of making his eyes go neutral even if he was smiling. When he got that look, you knew to be careful and you almost wanted to pinch him and say, "You still alive?" He kept one hand on my shoulder. I understood he was trying to calm me.

"I just want you to know," I said.

Deacon hated it if any of his tenants even hinted at how he might better run the place. But he also believed that we were family. He nodded. "I know, Glynne," he said. "Let me think on it. You notice anything else, feel free to tell me."

I was reading by the woodstove that evening when Deacon knocked on my door. "I asked Leon. He said McCain just had that book lying around," Deacon said. "Leon picked it up and asked if he could borrow it. McCain didn't say 'do it' and he didn't say 'don't.'"

"If that's good enough for you," I said, "it'll be good enough for me. For now."

Deacon shook his head. "For now, you take care of Glynne and I'll take care of this place."

I looked away.

"Listen," he said, "I'll keep my eyes and ears open. You can count on that."

"Leon gone," Candy said, "one down, eight to go." We were on our way into town to do our weekend shopping. She had started smoking again. The passenger window was open and the icy air felt clean.

"Do you think it was deliberate?" I asked. "Slick Mick leaving that book out and inviting Leon in?"

"Do I?" Candy said. "Listen, Glynne, I'm not one of those suckers who believes we are all One. There are evil men in this world. And women. In my former line of work, you meet the worst. There was this couple who wanted me to tell them stories of an uncle molesting me while they got each other off." Candy hunched down in her heavy sweater. She looked like that little girl she might or might not have been.

"I won't tell you the worst of it," she said. "Let's just say I'd do that couple for free rather than let McCain so much as touch me."

I thought of one of my last men, the unspoken agreements, the exciting humiliations, how I'd imagined that in submitting I had the power, how he'd gotten it all for free. I started to tell her about it, but she had that hundred-yard stare, so I shut up.

"I wonder who's next?" she said. "It better not be you."

The days were shrinking, the nights stretching out cold and dark. I could feel my animal heart cringing into itself. We all retreated. After the long summer evenings on each others' porches, after walking home under a ceiling of stars as though we lived in a big house whose rooms were connected by hallways of night, it began to seem a long lonely trek across the frosted pine needles from a warm cabin to a neighbor's door. It didn't stop McCain. I turned around one afternoon and found him standing behind me in my kitchen.

"You could knock," I said.

"I thought we had an open-door policy out here," he said cheerfully.

"Some do. For some people."

He nodded, brushed past me into my living room and sat on the old wicker chair in front of the woodstove. He stretched out his hands and long legs to the fire. I watched him.

"Cold," he said. "It's getting real cold."

"Christ, McCain," I said, "do you ever just say something out straight?"

"Hey." He raised his hands in innocence. "I'm a nice guy once you get to know me."

"You can fool the fans, McCain," I said. "You can't fool a player." The moment the words were out of my mouth, I wished I could breathe them back in.

"You a player, Glynne?" he said.

I turned away. "What?"

"Just sayin'. You're the one that said it."

"What do you want from me?" I said. "I don't get it."

"Whoa," he said and looked me up and down. "You might be assuming. How old are you anyhow?"

"Forty-five." I felt myself slipping past the point where I could be who I'd become, where I could tell him to get out, and if he didn't, leave and find Deacon.

"You don't look it," Mccain said quietly. "You know you got the legs of a teenage chick."

"Oh please," I said and knew my eyes had given me away. I tried to do Tyree's trick, scan McCain while I seemed to be looking past him, but I couldn't force my gaze from his lanky body and calculator stare.

"All I want from you," he said, "is maybe a few spoonfuls of sugar. I ran out and I don't like my coffee bitter. Just a neighborly request, right?"

I didn't move.

"You know how some guys are," he said. "They chase after a chick until she gives them what they want. Then, bam, they lay off, so to speak. Maybe they even get the hell out of Dodge. So, if you loan me some sugar, I'll put on my coffee pot and make you that cup of coffee we discussed back awhile."

He walked into the kitchen. I dumped some brown sugar in a cup and handed it to him.

"This all you got?" he asked. "No white?"

"I think," I said, "that when you borrow something, you run the risk of having to settle for what you get."

"Tell me," he sighed. "Take Shireen…" I knew what would come next. "Hey, don't get me wrong. She's a sweet gal, but 'settle for'. That says it. What I want doesn't want me."

"Stop right there," I said. I grabbed my coffee mug, pulled on my parka and started toward the door. He followed me out. "Close it," I said. "I'm coming over because I figure it's the only thing that will get you out of my house and off my back."

"Yes, ma'am," he said and closed the door behind us.

I walked straight from my cabin door to his. He stepped in and gestured. "Welcome. My first real home in five years."

The place was immaculate. He'd ripped out the orange shag and put linoleum down on the floor. There were a few good photographs on the walls and vintage rock posters and a bumper sticker that said More Will Be Revealed.

"Charming," I said. I kept my coat on. He poured me a cup of coffee. "Here it is, McCain. I have a PhD in guys like you. All you get to know is that I knew you before I met you. You want what you can't have and what you have, you don't want. You fuck up everything."

"Prove your theory," he said. "Let me touch you."

I raised my coffee mug to him. "Salud. You proved my theory. No coffee for me."

"Not even one cup?" He raised his eyebrows and grinned.

There were twenty answers chasing themselves in my brain. "None," I said. I wished Candy was home. I stepped out into the cold air, turned back and faced him. "One more thing, if you trash Shireen, you trash my friend. I don't like that. The next time you do it, I'll tell her."

"I see that sisterhood is alive and well. But, just remember this: Whenever you're ready, punkin', you know where to find me." His laughter followed me halfway across the yard.

Tyree went out on a drunk. He hitched back home a few days later, hid in his cabin till morning and went out again. None of us would ever have known except that he managed to bum a ride back home and lurch over to my cabin. He steadied himself on the counter with awful dignity. Carefully, he took his hat from his head and set it on top of the fridge, moving it slowly into place, so the eagle on the beaded headband faced front.

"There," he said. "I still got my hat."

I'd been cleaning my kitchen to early Clapton. Tyree's face brightened. He did a quick dance step and looked at me.

"You didn't know I can dance, did you, Glynne? I can. We can go dancing sometime. We could go fishing, too. Maybe I'll teach you how to track rabbits on foot."

I looked at him. "Tyree, it's me. I fall over things that aren't even there."

"Well," he said, "we could just go for a walk. We could do that, right?"

He pulled a paper bag out of his jacket pocket and tilted the bottle to his lips. "'Scuse me. I just need a little swig. Kinda steadies me." He looked down into the bag. "Want some?"

"I'm set," I said. "You hungry?"

"I could eat," he said. "That'd be good. Maybe some coffee too. Then we could talk."

I made us hamburgers. Tyree ate a few bites and kept pulling on the bottle. "I got drunk last night," he said. "Night before too, come to think of it. Not tonight though."

He touched his big broad face, as though he was trying to make sure it was still there. I knew better than to give him helpful advice. Instead, I made us both coffee and loaded his with honey and canned milk. He gulped it down and sat quiet for a long time. "You mind if I piss off your porch?" he finally said. "My legs are a little shaky."

"Just stay downwind of the cats."

He laughed and staggered out. When he came back, he had a new bottle. He held it up to the light. It was that sugary soda pop fruit wine the kids drink.

"Lotta vitamins in here," he said. "Raspberries. Fruc…tose."

"You want a glass?" I said. "Maybe a chunk of orange in it or something?"

"Sure," he said cheerfully. "Don't you worry, though. You know 'bout drunk Indians? I'm not one of those. I'm just drunk."

I brought him a glass with a two-inch slab of orange in it. He set it on the counter. It sat there for the rest of the evening while he pulled steadily on his bottle. He put on his hat and leaned back in the rocking chair. "Damn, I feel good. See that's the holy truth, sister, this stuff is the only thing that makes me feel right. I'm the only one in my family like this. Everybody else is good—well, kinda. My brother can get pretty mean."

I sipped my coffee. I felt safe and warm, almost peaceful, the peaceful of nothing to do, nothing to fix. Tyree tilted his hat over his eyes and seemed to fall asleep. I put more honey in my coffee. When I looked up he was watching me.

"You're pretty," he said. "Did anybody ever tell you that?"

"Once that counted, somebody did," I said. I remembered Michael's tough hands tender on my face, holding me so I couldn't move and looking at me as though I was beautiful scenery.

"I didn't mean anything boy-girl by that," Tyree said. "You're my sister."

"Understood," I said. "And appreciated."

"I made up my mind about something," he said. He twisted the cap off the bottle and took a deep swallow. "I'm leaving. I'm going up home."

"No shit." I laughed. "If Deacon catches wind of the last three days, he'll personally escort your butt out."

Tyree looked at me hard. "Well, that's cold," he said.

"Come on, Ty, you know it's true."

He settled back into the chair. "Yeah. He's an honorable man. He can't do nothing else." He slugged more wine and sighed. "Ooooweee, that feels good. Makes me all warm inside." He pulled his hat down and peeked at me from under the brim. "I'm gonna tell you something. It's a secret. Only person you can tell is Deacon."

"Promise."

"I got a gramma up in Chinle," he said slowly. "She's only part Navajo. Her daddy was from one of those tribes down south, a married guy. She says he came to see her once when she was nearly grown. A nice guy. Soft-spoken. He told her some stories from his people."

Tyree studied my face. "I'm gonna tell you some rules about stories like these. You keep 'em." I nodded.

He drank more wine. I refilled his coffee cup and set a juniper log on the fire. He bent forward, took sage from his pocket and sprinkled it on top of the stove. Green-scented smoke drifted up.

"Makes it nice for telling stories," Tyree said. He stretched. "So, my gramma told me this story. It's almost winter, so I can tell it." He drained the bottle and touched my wrist gently. "If you ever have to tell this story, do it in winter. Be careful. You can't mess with these things. You could get hurt. The people who hear the story too. They could get messed up."

"I promise."

Tyree's soft speech had gotten even softer, the slurring out of it, the goofiness. He leaned forward in the chair, clasped his hands in front of him and said—more to the fire than to me:

"Way back, a long long time ago, there was only Indian people. What was even more different was that they were all different colors. Some of them was brown. Some of them was black. Some of them was yellow. Some of them was even white. They were all living in a kind of heaven. Lots to eat. Lots of pretty ladies and handsome men. The kids was all good. Nobody got sick. Nobody got old. They was all getting on good with each other.

"Then one day this thing who'd got himself up to look like a guy came along. He was real smart and he could talk real good, so they called him the Talker. He knew stories nobody else had heard and he knew how to make people feel important. So these Indian people didn't notice at first when he started doing this thing.

"He talked to the brown people and told them had they noticed how they were smarter than the black people. He talked to the men and told them they were better than the women and he asked the women had they noticed how foolish some of the men could be.

"Pretty soon the people weren't getting on so good. The black people weren't talking to the brown people and they weren't talking to the yellow people. The ladies were off by themselves. The men weren't even talking to each other. That Talker talked and talked and next thing you know everybody was off by his lonesome. Nobody talking. Nobody laughing. Nobody singing or dancing. Nobody taking proper care of the little babies. That Talker, he sure made a mess."

Tyree looked up at the ceiling, where the fire was throwing gold and shadows on the rough plaster. "It was pretty bad."

"Why'd he do that?"

"Cause he was the Talker," he said. "He had to do it."

"What happened?" I was scared to hear the answer, but I knew I had to ask.

"My gramma got a little mixed up about this part, but I think this is how it goes. God looked down at the big mess and got mad. He hunted up Old Lady Spider. 'Hey, God,' she said, 'I been waitin' for you.' She got God to squinch all down and come into her house. He yelled at her a little for letting that old Talker be down there. She said she was sorry, but it was too late. So her and God told the few good people who were left to go someplace safe and God spun that world out into space, everything flying off except the mountains and the desert and the good people.

"Then God stopped the spinning and Old Lady Spider

reeled the world back into her web and the good people got to start all over again." Tyree unfolded his hands and leaned back in the chair.

"That's it?" I said.

"Yep." He stood up fast and grabbed the back of the chair. "Whoa," he said, "gotta go slow."

"You want more coffee?"

"Nope. Gotta get my things together, get a little shut-eye. I'll be heading out tomorrow morning."

I held out my hand. He shook it gently. "Been good knowing you, Glynne. Watch out for that old Talker."

"I will." I kissed his cheek. "Nothing boy-girl there," I said. "I'm just glad I know you. That's all."

Tyree closed the door carefully behind him. I picked the glass up off the floor and emptied the orange chunk into my mouth. It was warm and clean tasting. There was a plastic bag on the old bar stool that is my dining table. I thought he'd left some dope behind. Then I saw the black and orange feather lying on top of the leaves. When I opened the bag, the dusty green scent of sage drifted up. I sifted some on the stove top and tucked the flicker feather in my pine cone. I poked up the fire and settled back, the sage working its magic till I was peaceful enough to sleep.

II

"Two down," Candy said. "Leon. Tyree. We've got to do something." So she and I grabbed Jacques, L.B. and whoever else was willing and we played basketball every day, even when the first snow made the ball hop even worse than the pine needles. In fact, "play" was a weak word for how we went at it. The game played us.

A lanky kid from up in Washington State moved into Tyree's cabin. He said his name was Jeff and there was nothing he'd rather do than smoke dope and play pick-up ball. "What with dope off limits here," he said, "when I'm not out carpentering,

I'm ready for a game."

Most of us, at least a few of us, were out there whenever there was enough light to see, Jacques a blithe wizard in our midst, Jeff, McCain and Shireen handicapped for height. The ground underneath us handicapped the rest of us. No matter how often or deep we dug out the rocks that poked up through the pine needles, they came back.

There is a steady upward underground migration in the North Country, rocks moving like moles, tunneling up to the light. The Colorado Plateau is full of stony stories and mysteries. If you drive up the nearest mountain outside of town, there is an overlook from which you can see for miles. Black and ivory and sienna spread out below you, the black the blackest you have ever seen. There are cinder cones and canyons and basins, and you see that this was once ocean bottom. A great inland lake, the guide books say. From the overlook, you look and breathe deep and you can't help but fill in the air between you and the earth with water and shimmering fishes. You don't even wonder that you do this.

Sunset Crater, a local volcano, is two hundred years overdue. Its peak is burnt orange, the long slope of it black. On the hottest day, there are ice caves in its guts. Its lava tubes run for hundreds of miles under the heart. In the heart of one of the old Hopi ruins there is a blow-hole. You bend over it and air rushes up into your face. You breathe earth. Once, scientists dropped powdered dye into the opening and it drifted up from a cave fifty miles to the southwest.

And the rocks move. You have to have something solid in this shifting land, so we got organized for our tournament. Three weeks to play-offs, then the big game on Thanksgiving. We switched the teams around, girls against guys, drunks against junkies, young against old. Deacon nailed a scoreboard on the shower house and we kept careful score.

Looking back, I know I was watching McCain a lot by then. He wasn't that particularly graceful. He hot-dogged no more, no less than any of us. He stayed out of my face. Shireen fussed over him, making sure he had Gatorade, massaging his shoulder after each game. Things stayed calm. I figured maybe I had made my point, and I wondered how much it had actually had anything to do with me personally.

We were playing with cut-off gloves on by the time the second big snow hit the week before Thanksgiving and turned the ground to mud. It didn't stop us. We put ourselves through the junior high misery of choosing teams and hunkered down for that last week to practice. One warm afternoon, one of those pure opal days the high desert can spring on you, I watched Jacques shoot baskets. He wore a bright red t-shirt and cut-off jeans. His cheeks and legs were rosy from the work-out. He sunk twenty-three out of twenty-five and jogged over to where I was leaning against my car.

"Glynne," he said. He was breathing hard. He said my name again and hugged me. For an instant I felt his wiry body, smelled his clean soapy smell, and he was back a step, smiling sweetly.

"It's like home here," he said. "It's the first time in my life I ever felt at home."

I looked around. In that shimmering light, with smoke rising from chimneys and the smell of peoples' suppers in the air, it felt closer to home than I'd ever been. I tapped the basketball out of his hands and dribbled to the foot of the pine. I was tired from work, giddy with the light, my bones felt like silver, my muscles silken. I jumped into my shot, watched the ball kiss the backboard and drop in.

"It's better," I said.

I'd clearly forgotten the flip side of home. Wednesday evening before Thanksgiving, there was a knock at the door. I looked out the kitchen window. Candy stared fiercely at my door. I pulled it open and she stomped in. She looked like every pissed-off little sister you've ever seen, blizzard and thunder in her eyes, up yours in the set of her shoulders.

"Whoa," I said helpfully.

"Glynne," she said, "I was going to let this pass, but I can't stop thinking about it and my social worker says stress is very bad for me and holding things in makes stress and I can't afford to mess with that because it could maybe trigger you know what."

My mind kicked into overdrive. I realized we hadn't spoken for a week. True, we'd been out there at the basketball tree, practicing, hollering, stretching out our sore muscles together, but we hadn't really talked. That Sunday, she'd had some reason to skip breakfast and I hadn't thought much about it.

"We gotta get this cleared up," Candy said and burst into tears. I was so stunned I started to cry. I grabbed a dish towel to wipe my eyes. She grabbed the other end. We just stood there wiping our eyes and not looking at each other.

"I hate for people to be mad at me," I said. "Hurry up. Get it over with. What did I do?"

She dropped the towel, walked into the living room and sat in the chair at the big old desk. "Do you really think that..." she said and her voice rose to a squeak. "Do you really think I show myself off?"

"What?"

"You know, show off like a chick? Go for the guys' attention? Act sluttish?"

I sat in the rocking chair. She shoved her hands into her jacket pockets and stared at the floor. "Well, do you think that?"

"Oh sure," I said. "I never took a penny for all the loving I gave away. That gives me the right to judge you? If I judged you. Which I don't. Girl, you are simple."

She shrunk down into herself. "It wasn't me thought it up." She looked into my eyes. I'm not sure what she saw, but it made her grab my hands and say, "Glynne. Jesus. I'm sorry. You're the first real woman friend I ever had. Back in the day, how it was, dancing, hooking, dealing, it was all he say she say, backstab and bitch this, bitch that."

She let loose my hand. I got us coffee. We sat quiet for

what felt like forever. I wanted to let it end there. I wanted to run. Move out. Find a crappy studio apartment somewhere and listen to the neighbors' TV through the wall and let that be all the humanity I'd need to know.

"I have never ever, not once, had those thoughts about you," I said. "You are a true lady and I study you to learn how to be one."

"Well," she said, "thank you. I should have come to you right away."

"McCain," I said.

"McCain."

"How?"

"He came over one evening after supper. I was wiped out from work and it seemed easier to just let him sit on the porch with me. I kept thinking he knew I was tired. He said he had to be honest with someone. He copped to loaning Leon that book. He said all this shit about how he'd been a real taker in the past and he was trying to change that. Like learning how to give. Like thinking the book would help Leon and maybe be a step into a better future."

"I'm sure that's how Leon is seeing it these days," I said. "A step into the future at warp speed."

"He asked me if maybe I could talk to you," Candy said, "ask you to give him a break, cut him a little slack. I'd never seen him look sad before. He said he figured you were just trying to fix people, help them—that's why you were kind of controlling. Even me. He said you had told him that you loved me to death, but did he wonder if I hadn't caused some of my own troubles—you know, kind of played up my attractiveness."

"Let's kill him," I said. "Not fast. Something slow, something involving delicate body parts."

"You'd have to find them first." Candy laughed.

We went into the kitchen and made chili-cheese scrambled eggs and toast and hot fudge sundaes. "Women's ancient wisdom," she said. "Protein and chocolate." We lit candles and sat in the living room eating.

"I think I'll always remember this time," she said. "I didn't run."

I looked at her generous face. "You know how I told you life is like a movie to me? I told you that, right?"

She nodded.

"Not tonight," I said. "This is real."

We hugged and she headed up the path. I put wood on the fire, damped it, turned out the lights, gathered up a couple cats and crawled into bed. My mind was clear. I looked out the window into the black and all I saw was a bright November night, the stars wild diamonds above Candy's cabin. As I drifted off to sleep, two sentences whispered in my mind. *I will sleep like a cat tonight. I will dream like a cat.*

Next morning, we had donuts and coffee on Little Black's front porch. The air was warm, the light sweet and clear, teasing you, making you think that maybe we'd already made it through the winter. Shireen had dug up an industrial-size coffee pot and she was smiling and pouring and smiling and pouring. "All of us together," she kept saying. Part-time Billy was coming in from Show Low. That was enough to get her through till Christmas Eve. Deacon had brought real cream for the coffee. Jacques had put the turkey in at four a.m. and you could already smell it.

Little Black opened the donut box as though he was a magician. The donuts were covered in chocolate and sprinkled with orange and brown jimmies. "Thanksgiving special at the Donut Den. Goofus is working there, you remember Goofus used to live in Jacques' place?" Deacon and Shireen nodded. "He gave me the Deacon's boys' discount. They had him dressed up like a turkey. Funniest damn thing I ever saw."

"C'mon," McCain said, "you expect us to believe that?"

Shireen, Deacon and L.B. grinned at each other. "You don't know Goofus," L.B. said. "For him, that's normal."

We finished up and headed out to the court. Billy pulled

in just as we were flopping around in what passed for warm-up moves. He ambled down the cinder path with a big cardboard box in his arms. A guy walked behind him. More accurately, the most gorgeous soul I'd ever seen in Levi's walked behind him. The jeans were gun-metal gray and stonewashed so they looked like crushed velvet. They were cut loose and it didn't matter. The guy was all bulge and cheekbones and eyes. He wore a black jacket, an orange sequined bandana around his neck and the only classy pair of white cowboy boots in existence. Candy's mouth dropped open.

Billy bowed. "Meet Rafe," he said. "Rafe, meet my family." We said "Welcome," and "Where did you get that bandana?" and "Do you play ball?"

"Hey," Jacques shouted. "Let's do it." He tossed the ball to Jeff.

McCain and Jeff went up against each other. There was me, Little Black, Candy, Jeff and Rafe's fine self on one team; Shireen, Deacon, Jacques, Billy and McCain on the other. We played our hearts out. By half-time, the score was 46-38, them over us. We broke for cider. Jacques went to his cabin to baste the turkey. Deacon disappeared. We were diving into the hot cheese doo-dads L.B. brought out when we heard the rumble of heavy equipment coming toward us. Deacon had clamped a sturdy ply-wood sheet on the front-end loader and thrown a fancy white table-cloth over the wood.

"Here you go," he said. "Fine dining at its best." He climbed down from the machine and grabbed a couple of the cheese doo-dads. "L.B.," he said, "these are elegant."

"Used to be a sous-chef," Little Black said, "after I got back from Nam."

"Sous?" Deacon grinned. "Doesn't that mean under?"

"Hell," Billy said, "somebody's gotta be on the bottom."

L.B. shook his head. "Buncha pervos. My talent is wasted on you."

"My old dad used to call things like these horses doovers,"

said Billy. "He figured they were what rich people ate." Billy was never afraid to be corny. He been broken so often and scarred so bad, he wasn't afraid of anything. "Glynne," he'd once said to me, "you die when you bull-ride. It's just like being in the worst kind of best love."

"Well here we are," Shireen said, "just like I was hoping." She and McCain were snuggled together on the porch swing. She kept touching his hair and the cross between her breasts. His jaw looked like it was wired shut. I was delighted that something had his shorts in a severe bunch.

Billy bent over the cardboard box. "Pears," he said. "My pap sent 'em down from Washington State." Shireen ran to her cabin and brought back a bowl. "You can put them in here," she said, "so people can grab their own." Billy put the pears in the bowl and offered it to McCain. McCain shook his head.

Rafe laughed. "I respect a man who knows what he doesn't want."

I bit into a pear. It tasted of Northwest light and sleeper waves and gray-green hillsides disappearing in the fog. Jeff hauled a bucket of warm water from the shower house. We finished our pears, washed the juice off our faces and fingers and walked back onto the court.

When I think back, I know the first fifteen minutes of the last half of that game were the happiest minutes I've ever lived. My team danced. We forgot who was male and who was female, who was tall, who was short, who was middle-aged and tired, who was young and damn near airborne. We could not make a mistake. We brought the score to a tie and rocketed steadily ahead.

McCain's face went pink, then red, then volcanic. The mad The madder he got, the worse he played. I was gleeful. I kept my face perfectly blank and passed and shot, my moves gorgeous, the ball soul-kissing the net on every try. Rafe guarded, his arms and shoulders perfect protection. Candy twisted in between the men and stole the ball, quick and smug as a cat. Again and again we made our moves as though we were seventeen and had played together forever.

The timer ticked away. McCain started nagging his team. Billy ignored him. Deacon kept bouncing around like a super-charged puff of milkweed. Shireen got scared. You could see it. The ten-year-old girl in her started to run her long arms and legs and did a piss-poor job of it. Jacques seemed to catch the clumsies from her. Jeff fouled McCain. We called time out. Little Black went into his cabin and put Bob Seger on loud. "Fire Down Below," he said. "Let's get this slaughter over with."

Candy and Rafe started to bump and grind, faking shots and lust in perfect time. Ya watch 'em come and watch 'em go. Jeff had a joint hanging from his lips and an angel's smile behind it. Deacon tried to look stern and gave up. "This is damn near about perfect," Jeff said. "Thanks."

McCain stepped up to the foul line. "Turn that music off," he said. "I need it quiet."

Little Black smiled. "Sir, yes, sir," he said and didn't move.

McCain looked around. Half of us were dancing.

"Get serious," he said. He tensed for the shot. Jacques stood next to Shireen, shifting nervously from side to side. He mis-stepped and came down hard on Shireen's foot. She yelped and McCain blew the shot.

It didn't really matter. The score was 74 to 50 and the timer almost run down. McCain turned and stared at Shireen. She stepped back. He walked past her to Jacques and stood over him. "Stop the fucking timer."

Deacon started to move forward, Candy and me close on his heels, but before we could get there, McCain grabbed Jacques by the collar of his t-shirt and lifted him off the ground.

"Christ," McCain said. His face was blotchy. He kept his voice cold and even. "Are you tripping? You're the sorriest son-of-a-bitch I ever knew. If you're gonna be useless, you half-pint asshole, you could at least stay out of the way."

He carefully set Jacques back on his feet. Then he walked

into Little Black's cabin and shut off the music. In the silence that fell, McCain stomped up the path to his Cherokee and climbed in. Shireen ran after him, but by the time she reached the parking gravel, he was gone. The Cherokee's engine roared once, then faded out toward the highway. Shireen watched him go.

Jacques tugged at the collar of his shirt till it lay neat again. I looked at Deacon. "Seen enough?" I said. He could just go right ahead and ask me to leave. I didn't care. I'd be Number Three if that's what it took. "Heard enough?" Deacon picked up the basketball.

"Enough," he said. "He's got till the first. I'll tell him tonight if he comes back. If not, tomorrow morning." He tossed the ball to Jacques. "We get a second try."

Jacques stepped forward and neatly sank the shot. We played out the last four minutes. By then it didn't matter who won. I wondered if we'd skip the Thanksgiving feast, retreat to our cabins, do what we were all so good at: isolate, as the treatment shrinks called it. Candy looked at me. She mouthed a word. "Nonetheless."

"Right," I said. "The sweet potatoes are keeping warm next to the wood stove. I'll just dump a can of fried onions on the green beans and bring it all out."

There was a long silence. L.B. spun on his heels. I didn't know whether to chase after him. "I'm going for the bird," he hollered back over his shoulder. One by one, as though we'd been released from a spell, each of us headed off to get food to lay out on the festal plywood.

McCain came back and straight to my cabin that night. I'd been standing at the big kitchen window, waiting for the coffee to warm up and looking out at the candle flame in Shireen's back window. I imagined the clenched fist her heart might have become. Been there. Done that. Sorry sister, but better you than me.

McCain didn't knock. He stepped in and walked up to within a few inches of me. My house was quiet. I'd burned sage and there was a steady low fire in the stove. "Nice," McCain said. "Cozy."

"I know what you are," I said. "I told you that." He shrugged off his down vest and walked into the living room. "Takes one to know one," he said quietly. He started to unbutton his shirt. "I'll be gone before morning," he said. "You'll be rid of me."

"Did Deacon talk to you?" I said.

"No. But it wouldn't have made a difference. I'm almost done here." His fingers hesitated on the third button. I walked up to him and slipped the button completely free. I was seeing things— my fingers, the buttons, the pulse in his throat—the way you can see things when your car hits black ice, everything brilliant, everything somewhere between beautiful and terrifying.

"Yes," I said. I was calm. I wish I could say that I did what I did to finish things off and keep him away from us forever, but that would not be entirely true. In his cruelty, I saw mine. In the private movie he occupied, I saw my relentless stories. My life, in too many ways, was his business.

With the lightest pressure of my fingers on his naked chest, I pushed him down into the wicker chair. "This is going to be different," he said. His voice was thick. I unzipped his jeans and kissed his belly. Then I went into my bedroom, undressed and pulled on a silk nightshirt.

I walked out into the living room. The fire burned rose-gold in McCain's eyes. I added pine to the stove and opened the damper. The flames roared up the chimney. McCain sat motionless, his arms hanging at his sides, only his eyes shifting as he watched me. I lit three candles, one on the bookcase, one on the desk and one in the window by my bed. The feathers in the pine cone trembled in the candlelight.

"By this light," McCain said, "you're damn near pretty."

"By this light," I said, "you're damn near human."

I took his hand and led him into bed. He murmured something about being nervous and took off his clothes. His body was quite beautiful, pale, the muscles long and supple. I stayed clothed.

He put my arms around him. The silk moved along my skin, then his, like water. He lay down on his back. As I bent over him, he sighed once.

His face was gentle in the candlelight. I could hear the fire roaring in the other room, the pine exploding with tiny sharp sounds. I did what I knew to do so well. Once, he tried to touch me and I pushed his hand away. He tried to take hold of my hair to guide me and again, I pushed his hand away.

There was a fine heat and clean scent coming off his skin. I drew back for a second and watched him turn his head from side to side, his eyelids fluttering, his mouth open and seeking. There was no question in my mind, right there, right then, who was hunter and who was prey.

I moved in to finish it off. Glacial light flared in the window. McCain coiled away from me. I turned toward the light. Just beyond the glass, I saw Shireen, her hair tossing like a wave in the violence of her turning away.

The light died. The noise of Deacon's generator faded to a whine, then nothing. The window was black and in it, I saw the translucent shadow of my face.

McCain stretched out flat. He grabbed my hair and pulled me to him. "Finish the job," he said.

I woke alone at first light. There was a note taped to the mirror. "Glynne, I'm gone. We hurt someone I loved. It was a fluke. Last night. That's all it was."

I tossed the paper into the ashes in the stove and added pine cones and tinder. By the time the fire was leaping and my coffee hot, I was dressed. I almost tossed the silk nightshirt onto the flames and stopped.

I looked out the kitchen window. The Cherokee was gone. Shireen's truck was parked in its usual place. No smoke rose from her chimney. I wondered if she'd gone with McCain, or just couldn't bring herself to face the day.

Dawn moved up from the pines, frost going to mist. I

opened all the doors and windows and carried a bowl of smoking juniper from room to room. I breathed in the green scent, drew it deep into my lungs. I'm no wannabe, but for those moments I could feel Tyree's words moving through my body: "I gotta smoke out the bad." I wanted to smoke out not just McCain, but the kinship I had told myself was there.

There was more. I knew I'd live with a hard not-knowing for at least a few months. Though we had not had intercourse, there had been no protection. McCain had told me he had done cocaine any way you could: up his nose, free-basing, off a woman's flesh, and in a needle. He said that he had always used clean works. I would never know.

What I could guess was that when the necessary time had passed and I sat in the green plastic chair in the women's clinic while the lab tech pierced a vein, I would watch my blood fill the vial and I would know I was taking back my pleasure, my passion and my self. Positive or negative, the test results would not alter what I had learned.

I took the juniper ashes to the red dirt in the back of the house and scratched them into the earth. Morning threw long blue shadows over the forest floor. Ravens swerved through the pine branches. As peaceful as the moment was, I felt uneasy.

I left the back door open and took my coffee to the rocking chair in front of the woodstove. The coffee's pure bitter heat soothed my throat. The fire warmed me, my back was chilled by the cold that moved solid as a wall through the open back door. I thought about how I might already be dying, how the virus might have set out on its long-range patrol in my blood. I thought about surrender, about fighting back, about the body turning on itself as though caught in friendly fire. I knew I had rarely felt this alive. And I knew I had something to do.

I finished up the coffee and walked to Shireen's. She hadn't gone with him. Her suitcase and an old backpack were in the front hall. I stepped over them, walked in and called her name once. There was no answer. Her cat nosed my boot. Its plate was empty. I carefully opened a can of food and spooned it into the dish. "I don't want to go down the hall," I said. The cat bent its head and ate.

Shireen was in the bedroom, half off the bed, an afghan twisted around her. There was an empty pill bottle on the floor. Her face was gray. I touched Shireen's hand. It was warm. Then I sat on the edge of the bed and screamed and screamed until there was no breath between the screams, and the sound keened straight up from my bones.

Candy came in first, her old chenille robe wrapped around her. She looked, turned and was gone out the door. I put Shireen's head in my lap and tried to smooth her hair. By the time Candy and Jacques were with us, I had her hair unsnarled, a web of brown and gray across my thigh.

Jacques bent and pressed his ear to Shireen's chest. He held a mirror to her mouth. A faint mist spread across the glass. My thoughts ran fast and slow. I remembered the black glass of my window, the blurred candle flame wavering against the light of Deacon's arc welder. I knew then I'd seen more than the silhouette of her head. I'd seen the anguish in her eyes.

We carried her to her truck and set her in the seat between Jacques and me. I cushioned her head on my shoulder. Candy ran out to the truck, waving the medicine bottle. It was Leon's lithium and it was empty.

We drove out of the parking lot. I looked in the side-view mirror. Candy stood barefoot in the icy dirt road. She was still standing there as we turned out onto the highway and headed north.

Shireen came to on the way into the examining room. She grabbed her cross, then my wrist. "Don't leave," she whispered.

"I won't," I said. "I promise."

They cleaned her out, ran saline and meds through an IV into her veins. Once they'd finished their work, Jacques and I were allowed to sit with her.

"You saved my life," she said and touched Jacques hand. "A

child couldn't have done that."

I held tight to her other hand and when she looked up at me, I made myself not turn away. She touched her cross again. "You made him leave," she said. "Even if Deacon banished him, he would've kept coming back. I know him."

"I wish I was that noble," I said. "I wish it was that simple."

"I maybe understand," she said. "I don't know whether him gone is a blessing or a curse for me." I kept my mouth shut.

"I'll miss him," she said. "He thought I was pretty. By the candlelight. He said so."

Jacques and I sat with her till she fell asleep.

"Would you drive?" Jacques said. "I'm exhausted." We climbed into the truck. Jacques seemed very small and contained next to me. "I guess I wasn't so useless," he said. "I guess McCain was wrong."

"Not useless at all," I said. "He was jealous, that was all. You were having so much fun—and you were a better player than he was."

"I'm pretty good, aren't I?" Jacques asked.

"On the court?"

He nodded

"You're a wizard."

I turned on the radio. I was so tired I felt translucent. About two miles from the turn-off, we saw a woman hitchhiking along the highway. She wore skin-tight jeans and a black leather vest that had ridden up so you could see every quiver of her perfect ass. She was stomping along on backless four-inch heels, dust puffing up at every step, her long earrings glittering, a sequined trucker hat jammed on her head. Without bothering to turn around, she stuck out her thumb.

"Our neighbor," Jacques said.

I pulled over and Candy climbed in. She had glittered her curls, pasted feathery eyelashes over her own and painted her mouth apricot. She smelled great, wood-smoke and expensive perfume. She hauled her purse up, punched Jacques on the arm and glared at me.

"Don't worry," she said and peeled off the eyelashes. "I didn't do anything. I was going to. I was going to find that son-of-a-bitch and any guy who reminded me of him and I was going to fuck 'em to death. I couldn't do it. So I went to the 7-Eleven and bought breakfast and headed home. Then I got so scared I didn't try to hitch till you saw me. My feet are down to bloody stumps."

She pulled her foot up into her lap and started rubbing it. Jacques and I were quiet. I felt tears slipping down my cheeks.

"She's dead, right?" Candy said. "Tell me now. I'll go home, finish off these donuts and chocolate milk and then be history to you guys."

Jacques put his arm around her shoulders. She shrunk down into herself. "No," he said, "it's okay. She'll be fine. They pumped her out, got some fluid and meds in her. There was no damage. Nothing. By tomorrow, she'll be as good as new."

"Sure," Candy said. "You bet." She opened the donuts and stuffed one in her mouth. "And where is the SOB?" she mumbled. "Tell me that, Glynne. I know what happened. Don't ask me how, I just know."

"He's gone," I said. "He won't be back. Everything's going to be okay."

"Okay, maybe," Candy said, "but not the same, not ever again."

I turned onto our road. The tall pines were still there, the cabins, the sign that said: PRIVATE. DO NOT ENTER. OWNER WILL SHOOT. VISITORS!!! NO PARKING BEYOND THIS POINT!!! There was perfectly ordinary smoke rising out of the chimneys and three cats sunning themselves on Leon's woodpile. I pulled into the parking lot and stopped.

Jacques and Candy looked at me. "Yeah," I said. "Yeah. That's right. Never the same again. There's no way to change that." I pulled into Shireen's parking space by the little juniper. I wanted to apologize for the unforgivable, to tell them that I was finished with my part in that. I kept my mouth shut. I knew better about making vows.

"Okay," Candy said. "Okey dokey. Never the same again." She paused for what seemed like half a lifetime. "So what now?" She didn't look at us.

My foot jittered on the brake. Jacques opened the passenger door. "You two work it out," he said. He climbed down, sauntered over to the hoop, faked a shot and went into his cabin.

"Looks like some things are already not the same," Candy said. "What got into him?"

"You know how those short guys are once they feel tall," I said. She laughed. We watched Deacon stride out of his office and into the shower house. He'd do the daily inspection, maybe post a new sign: NO SMOKING, this means NO SMOKING!!! or LA-DIES!! Do NOT leave your leg razors on the soap ledge!!

"So, Glynne," Candy said, "here's how I see it for now. I got six of these donuts left and you got the coffee."

"And maybe," I said, "when it's time, you'll go with me to the health department for the test?"

"Jeez, woman, what do you think? Come on, let's go eat breakfast."

ABOUT MARY SOJOURNER

Mary Sojourner is the author of *29: a Novel; Delicate: Stories of Light and Desire; Bonelight: Ruin and Grace in the New Southwest;* and memoirs, *Solace: Rituals of Loss and Desire* and *She Bets Her Life*. She is a frequent book reviewer for her local NPR station and the author of many essays, columns, and op–eds for *High Country News, Writers on the Range,* and other publications. A graduate of the University of Rochester, Sojourner teaches writing in private circles, one–on–one, at colleges and universities, writing conferences, and book festivals. She believes in both the limitations and possibilities of healing through writing—the most powerful tool she has found for doing what is necessary to mend. She lives in Flagstaff, Arizona.

TORREY HOUSE PRESS
VOICES FOR THE LAND

The economy is a wholly owned subsidiary of the environment, not the other way around.

SENATOR GAYLORD NELSON,
founder of Earth Day

Torrey House Press is an independent nonprofit publisher promoting environmental conservation through literature. We believe that culture is changed through conversation and that lively, contemporary literature is the cutting edge of social change. We strive to identify exceptional writers, nurture their work, and engage the widest possible audience; to publish diverse voices with transformative stories that illuminate important facets of our ever-changing planet; to develop literary resources for the conservation movement, educating and entertaining readers, inspiring action.

Visit **www.torreyhouse.org**
for reading group discussion guides,
author interviews, and more.